"This is one of the most astounding cases this Court has ever witnessed," said the judge.

It was that, and more. Sarah Breel was the most difficult client Perry Mason had ever had. She didn't seem to care how her case came out, even when Mason told her she might be convicted of first-degree murder.

"That automatically means a death sentence?" she asked.

"Unless the jury recommends life imprisonment," said Mason.

"All right," Sarah Breel said with a smile that was almost maternal. "Do your best. If the jury decides I'm guilty of murder, why then I'll hang. Now, Mr. Mason, I'm feeling a little drowsy and I think I'll take a nap."

And with that, she closed her eyes and fell sound asleep!

THE CASE OF THE SHOPLIFTER'S SHOE
was originally published by
William Morrow and Company, Inc.

ERLE STANLEY

GARDNER

THE CASE OF THE
SHOPLIFTER'S SHOE

A POCKET BOOK EDITION published by
Simon & Schuster of Canada, Ltd. • Richmond Hill, Ontario, Canada
Registered User of the Trademark

THE CASE OF THE SHOPLIFTER'S SHOE

William Morrow edition published 1938

POCKET BOOK edition published October, 1945
16th printing . . . . August, 1973

This POCKET BOOK edition includes every word contained in the original,
higher-priced edition. It is printed from brand-new plates made from
completely reset, clear, easy-to-read type. POCKET BOOK editions are
published by Pocket Books, a division of Simon & Schuster of Canada, Ltd.,
225 Yonge Street North, Richmond Hill, Ontario.
Trademarks registered in Canada and other countries.

Cast of Characters

1

As the first big drops of rain splashed to the sidewalk, Perry Mason cupped his hand under Della Street's elbow and said, "We can make it to the department store—if we run." She nodded, held up her skirt with her left hand, and ran lightly, her weight forward on the balls of her feet, her stride long and easy, with lots of knee action. Perry Mason, long-legged as he was, did not have to hold back on her account.

The first forerunners of the shower had caught them on a side street where there were no protecting awnings. By the time they reached the corner, the eaves were sluicing rain. The portico of the department store was twenty yards from the corner. They sprinted for it, while raindrops, pelting like liquid bullets, hit the sidewalk so hard they seemed to rebound before exploding into mushrooms of water. Mason guided Della Street straight through the revolving door. "Come on," he said, "this rain's good for half an hour, and there's a restaurant on the top floor where we can tea and talk."

Her laughing eyes regarded him from under long lashes in sidelong appraisal. "I didn't think I'd ever get *you* into a department store tea room, Chief."

Mason regarded the drops of water on the brim of his straw hat. "It's Fate, Della," he laughed. "And remember, I'm not going to squire you around while you shop. We get in the elevator and go to the top floor. I pay no attention when the attendant says, 'Second Floor . . . Women's fur coats and lingerie, third floor, diamonds, pearl necklaces and gold earrings, fourth floor, wrist watches, pendants, and . . .'"

"How about the fifth floor?" she interrupted. "Flow-

7

ers, candies and books. You *might* stop there. Can't you give a working girl a break?"

"Not a chance," he told her. "Straight up to the sixth floor—tea, biscuits, baked ham and pie."

They crowded into the elevator. The cage moved slowly upward, stopping at each floor while the girl called out the various departments in a tired monotone. "We forgot children's toys on the fifth," Della Street pointed out.

Mason's eyes were wistful. "Some day, Della," he said, "when I've won a big case, I'm going to get a railroad track with stations, tunnels, block signals and side tracks. I'll lay out an elaborate electric railway through my private office, out into the law library, and . . ." He broke off as she tittered. "Matter?"

"I was just thinking of Jackson in the law library," she said, "looking up some legal point in beetle-browed concentration, and your electric railroad train rattling and swaying through the door, heading for the library table."

He chuckled, guided her to a table in the tea room, looked out at the sheeted rain which lashed against the windows. "Jackson," he said, "would hardly appreciate the humor of the situation. I doubt if he ever had any boyhood."

"Perhaps," she ventured, "he was a child in another incarnation." She picked up the menu. "Well, Mr. Mason, since you're buying the lunch, I'm going to make it my heavy meal."

"I thought you were going on a diet," he said, with mock concern.

"I am," she admitted, "I'm a hundred and twelve. I want to get back to a hundred and nine."

"Dry whole wheat toast," he suggested, "and tea without sugar, would . . ."

"That'll be fine for tonight," she retorted, "but as a working girl, I know when I'm getting the breaks. I'll have cream of tomato soup, avocado and grapefruit salad, a filet mignon, artichokes, shoestring potatoes, and plum pudding with brandy sauce."

Mason threw up his hands. "There go my profits on the last murder case. I'll have one slice of melba toast, cut very thin, and a small glass of water." But, when he glanced up to see the waitress hovering at his elbow, he said firmly, "Two cream of tomato soups, two avocado and grapefruit salads, two filet mignons, medium rare, two hot artichokes, two shoestring potatoes, and two plum puddings with brandy sauce."

"Chief!" Della Street exclaimed. "I was only kidding!"

"You should never kid at mealtime," he told her sternly.

"But I can't eat all that."

"This," he said, "is poetic justice for lying to your employer." Then, to the waitress, "Go ahead and start bringing it on. Don't listen to any protests."

The waitress smiled and departed. Della Street said, "Now I suppose I'll have to live on bread and water for a week to keep from putting on weight. . . . Don't you like to watch people in a place like this, Chief?"

He nodded, his steady, tolerant eyes moving from table to table, appraising the occupants in swift scrutiny.

"Tell me, Chief," she said, "you've seen human nature in the raw. You've seen people torn and twisted by emotions which have ripped aside all of the hypocrisy and pretense of everyday life. . . . Doesn't it make you frightfully cynical?"

"Quite the contrary," he said. "People have their strong points and their weak points. The true philosopher sees them as they are, and is never disappointed, because he doesn't expect too much. The cynic is one who starts out with a false pattern and becomes disappointed because people don't conform to that pattern. Most of the little chiseling practices come from trying to cope with our economic conventions. When it comes right down to fundamentals, people are fairly dependable. The neighbor who would cheat you out of a pound of sugar, would risk her life to save you from drowning."

Della Street thought that over, then said, "There's a lot of difference in people. Look at that aggressive woman over there at the left, bullying the poor waitress . . .

and contrast her with that white-haired woman who's standing over there by the window—the one who has such a benign, motherly look. She's so placid, so homey, so . . ."

Mason said, "As it happens, Della, the woman's a shoplifter."

"What!" she exclaimed.

"And," Mason went on, "the man who's standing over by the cashier's desk, apparently trying to cash a check, is a store detective who's followed her in here."

"How do you know she's a shoplifter, Chief?"

"Notice the way she keeps her left arm rigidly at her side. She's holding something under that long tweed coat. I happen to know the store detective. I was in court once when he was testifying on a case. . . . Notice the way the woman's turned her head. I believe she knows she's being followed."

"Will she sit down and start eating?" Della asked, her eyes wide with interest.

"Probably not. She must have quite a bit of stuff concealed under her coat. It would be difficult to eat without . . . There she goes into the restroom."

"Now what?" Della Street asked.

"If she's wise she's being followed," Mason said, "she'll probably ditch the stuff in the restroom. . . . There's the store detective going over to talk with the colored maid. They'll try to handle the thing very quietly."

"I can't imagine her being a shoplifter," Della Street protested. "That white hair, the high forehead, the calm, steady eyes, and the sensitive mouth . . . it just isn't possible."

Mason said thoughtfully, "My experience has taught me that when a person with an honest face has stolen goods in his possession, the face is usually a mask, carefully cultivated as a stock in trade."

Their waitress brought them steaming, fragrant soup. The maid appeared in the door of the restroom and nodded briefly to the store detective. A moment later, the white-haired woman emerged and walked directly to an adjoining table, which had been set for two, with bread, butter, water glasses, knives and forks in place. She calmly seated herself.

Mason heard an exclamation at his elbow. "Oh, *there* you are, Aunt Sarah. I lost you." The lawyer looked up, to see a tallish young woman who moved with quick decision. As he glimpsed her moist gray eyes, his courtroom experience told him there was fear in her voice. The white-haired woman's voice, on the other hand, showed no fear, only calm poise. "I lost you somewhere in the crowd, Ginny, so I decided I'd come up and have a cup of tea. At my age, I've found it never pays to worry. I knew you were perfectly capable of taking care of yourself, calling a cab and going home."

"But *I* didn't know about *you,*" the girl said, seating herself with a nervous laugh, high-pitched with apprehension. "I wasn't certain you were all right, Aunt Sarah."

"I'm always all right, Ginny. Never worry about me. Always remember that no matter what happens, I'll take care of myself, and . . ."

The store detective interposed his bulk between Mason's eyes and the face of the white-haired woman. "I'm very sorry, Madam," he said, "but I'm going to have to ask you to step into the office."

Mason heard a quick gasp of consternation from the girl, but the woman's voice remained calmly placid. "I have no intention of stepping into the office, young man. I'm about to eat lunch. If anyone in the office wishes to see me, he can come here."

"I'm trying," the detective said with dignity, "to avoid making a scene."

Mason pushed back his soup, to watch with frank interest, as the detective stepped behind the woman's chair. She calmly broke off a piece of bread, buttered it, unhurriedly glanced up over her shoulder and said, "Don't try to avoid making a scene on my account, young man. Go right ahead."

"You're making it difficult for me," he said.

"Indeed!" she muttered.

"Aunt Sarah," the girl pleaded, "don't you think . . ."

"I don't think I'm going to budge until I've had my lunch," Aunt Sarah interrupted. "They say the cream of tomato soup here is very nice. I believe I'll try some and . . ."

"I'm sorry," the detective interposed, "but unless you accompany me, Madam, it will be necessary for me to make a public arrest."

"Arrest?" she inquired, pausing with the buttered fragment of bread half way to her lips. "What are you talking about?"

"I'm placing you under arrest for shoplifting," the man said.

The woman conveyed the bread to her mouth, chewed it calmly, nodding to herself as though mentally digesting the possibilities of the situation. "How *very* amusing," she said, picking up her water glass.

The irritation in the detective's voice made it distinctly audible to persons sitting within a radius of three tables. "I've been following you," he charged, "watching you put things under your coat." And, as the woman made as though to open her coat, he added quickly, "Of course I know you haven't them now. You left them in the restroom." He turned and nodded to the maid, who vanished through the curtained doorway.

"I don't think," the woman said reminiscently, as though trying to recall an eventful past, "that I've *ever* been arrested for shoplifting. . . . No, I'm quite certain I haven't."

"Aunty!" the girl exclaimed. "The man's not joking, he's serious. . . . He's . . ." The maid emerged from the restroom, carrying an armful of clothing. There were silk stockings draped over her arm, bits of silk lingerie, a silk blouse, a scarf and a pair of lounging pajamas.

The girl opened her purse, pulled out a checkbook. "My aunt," she explained rapidly, "is rather eccentric. She does her shopping at times in an unusual manner. I'm afraid perhaps she's a little absent-minded. If you'll kindly tell me the exact amount and will be so good as to have the purchases wrapped, I'll . . ."

"I'll do nothing of the sort," the detective interrupted.

"You can't get away with that stuff, and you know it. That's an old gag, pulled by every shoplifter in the country. When you get caught red-handed with the goods, you're '*shopping*.' We have another name for it. We call it *stealing!*"

Other diners, attracted by the scene, were staring. The girl's face flushed with mortification. But the white-haired woman seemed concerned only with the menu. "I think," she said, "I'll have some of the chicken croquettes."

"Madam," the detective exclaimed, placing a hand on her shoulder, "you're under arrest!"

"Indeed!" she said, looking at him over the top of her glasses. "You're an employee of this store, young man?"

"I am. I'm a detective. I'm a duly authorized deputy . . ."

"Then, if you're an employee," she said, "I'm going to ask you to kindly get me a waitress. After all, I want lunch, not dinner."

His hand tightened on her shoulder. "You're under arrest!" he repeated. "Are you going to come down to the office quietly, or will I have to carry you?"

"Aunty! Please go," the girl pleaded. "We can straighten this up somehow. We . . ."

"I haven't the slightest intention of going."

The detective braced himself. Mason's chair scraped back, as the lawyer got to his feet, to tower above the chunky detective. His hand clapped down on the man's shoulder with explosive force. "Just . . . a . . . minute," he said. The detective whirled, his face dark with rage.

"You *may* be a detective," Mason told him, "but you know very little about law. In the first place, that's not the proper way to make an arrest. In the second place, you evidently haven't a warrant, nor has any crime been committed in your presence. In the third place, if you knew any law, you'd realize that you can't make a charge of shoplifting stick until a person attempts to remove the goods from the premises. Anyone can pick up goods in a department store and carry 'em all over the place, and you can't do a thing about it until that person walks out to the sidewalk."

"Who the hell are you?" the detective asked. "An accomplice?"

"I'm a lawyer. The name's Perry Mason," the lawyer told him, "in case that means anything to you."

It was instantly apparent from the expression on the man's face that it meant a great deal to him. "What's more," Mason went on, "you're laying your store wide open to a damage suit. Try using force on this woman and you'll be a very much sadder and perhaps a wiser individual."

The young woman again indicated her checkbook. "I'm quite willing to pay for anything Aunt Sarah has taken," she said.

The detective was undecided. His eyes showed surly rage. "I've a notion to drag you both down to the office," he said.

Mason's voice was quiet. "Put a hand on that woman, and I'll advise her to sue the store for twenty thousand dollars' damages. Put a hand on me, my burly friend, and I'll break your damn neck."

An excited assistant manager, who had evidently been summoned by the telephone, bustled into the room. "What's happening here, Hawkins?" he asked.

The detective indicated the woman. "I caught this moll red-handed," he said, "shoplifting. I've been following her around for half an hour. Look at the pile of stuff she had under her clothes. She must have had a hunch I was on the job, because she ditched the take in the restroom."

"Evidently," Mason said, "your detective is somewhat green at the game."

"And who the devil are you?" the manager demanded.

Mason presented his card. The manager glanced at the card, then his head jerked back and up, as though pulled with a string. "Come down to the office, Hawkins," he said, "I'm afraid you've made a mistake."

"I tell you there hasn't been any mistake," Hawkins said. "I've been following her . . ."

"I said *come down to the office.*"

Once more the girl indicated her open checkbook. "I've repeatedly tried to tell this man," she said, "that my aunt has merely been shopping. If you'll be so good as to give me the total amount of her purchases, I'll gladly make out a check."

The manager glanced from the placid face of the unperturbed woman to the girl, then to the urbane lawyer. He took a deep breath, accepted defeat, and bowed as he said, "I'll have these purchases wrapped. Shall we deliver them, Madam, or would you prefer to take them with you?"

"Just wrap them and bring them here," the white-haired woman said, "and if you're the manager, will you kindly tell one of the waitresses to give this table some attention. . . . Ah, there you are, my dear. I think we'll have two cream of tomato soups, and I want chicken croquettes. What would *you* like, Ginny?"

The young woman, her cheeks crimson, shook her head and said, "I can't eat a thing, Aunt Sarah."

"Nonsense, Ginny! You mustn't let yourself be disturbed by little things. The man was clearly in error. He's admitted his fault." She raised her eyes to Perry Mason. "And I believe, young man, I'm somewhat obligated to you. I'll take one of your cards, if you don't mind."

Mason smiled, glanced at Della Street as he passed over one of his cards. "I wonder," he said, "if you wouldn't care to join us at our table. We could make a foursome. And," he added, lowering his voice, and glancing at the young woman, "you might feel less conspicuous."

"We'll be glad to," the white-haired woman said, pushing back her chair. "Permit me to introduce myself. I'm Mrs. Sarah Breel. This is Miss Virginia Trent, my niece. You're Perry Mason, the lawyer. I've read of you, Mr. Mason. I'm very glad to meet you."

"Miss Della Street, my secretary," Mason introduced.

Della extended her hand. "So glad to meet you," she said.

Mason seated the women, apparently entirely oblivious

of the curious eyes at surrounding tables. "Go right ahead with your soup," Mrs. Breel said. "Don't let it get cold. We'll catch up with you on the rest of the lunch."

"I can't eat a thing," Virginia Trent said.

"Nonsense, Ginny. Go ahead and relax."

"Really," Mason urged, "you'll find the cream of tomato soup very delicious. It'll make you forget—the rain."

She glanced at Mason's steaming cup of soup, met Della Street's friendly eyes, and said dubiously, "Food should never be eaten when one's upset."

"Don't be upset, then," the aunt said.

"Two more cream of tomato soups," Mason told the waitress. "Rush them up right away, please. And I believe there's one order of chicken croquettes and . . ."

"Make it two orders," Mrs. Breel said. "Ginny likes chicken croquettes. And two pots of tea, my dear, with lemon. And make the tea rather strong."

She settled back in the chair with a sigh of complete satisfaction. "I always like to eat here," she said, "they have such wonderful cooking. And, so far, the service has been excellent. This is the only time I've had occasion to make any complaint."

Mason's eyes twinkled to those of Della Street, then back to Mrs. Breel. "It is," he said, "a shame that you were annoyed."

"Oh, *I* wasn't annoyed in the least," Mrs. Breel remarked casually. "My niece, unfortunately, is sensitive about what people think. Perhaps super-sensitive. Personally, I don't give a hoot. I live my life the way I want, and . . . Ah, here comes the man with the things. Just put the packages on that chair, young man."

"How much does it amount to?" Virginia asked.

"Thirty-seven dollars and eighty-three cents, with the tax," the assistant manager said with dignity.

Virginia wrote out a check. As she entered the figures on the stub and performed the subtraction, Mason's eyes, actuated by a curiosity which was stronger than the conventions, glanced swiftly at the figures. He saw that after the check had been paid there was a balance of but twenty-two dollars and fifteen cents in the account.

Virginia Trent handed the manager the check.

"If you'll kindly step down to the office," he said, "and fill out a credit card."

"That won't be necessary," Mrs. Breel interposed. "We'll be right here, eating lunch for the next half hour. The bank is in the next block. You can send over and have the check cashed. . . . I hope you've wrapped the bundle securely, young man. It's raining outside."

The manager said suavely, "I believe you'll find the wrapping is quite satisfactory." He glanced at Perry Mason. "I notice," he said with dignity, "that you have consolidated your party, Mr. Mason. May I inquire if there's any intention on your part to file a suit against the store?"

Mrs. Breel answered the question. "No," she said magnanimously, "I'm quite willing to let bygones be bygones. I think you were frightfully rude. . . . Here comes the waitress with my soup. If you'll kindly step back so she can serve me. . . . Thank you."

The manager bowed affably. There was the hint of a twinkle in his eyes. "If you find any of these things not entirely satisfactory, Mrs. Breel," he said, "remember we'll be glad to exchange them. Perhaps your shopping was somewhat hurried, and you didn't get just the exact sizes required. . . ."

"Oh, but I did," Mrs. Breel interrupted. "I was *very* careful to get just the sizes I wanted. I'm not exactly a young woman, but I'm not absent-minded. I'm quite certain the merchandise will be satisfactory. I picked the very best that was on display."

The manager bowed and withdrew. Craning necks followed his progress across the lunch room, then heads came together as the hiss of sibilant whispers filled the room.

Mrs. Breel, apparently utterly oblivious of the interest she had aroused, smacked her lips over the soup and said to her niece, "There, dear, just taste that and see how nice it is. I told you they had wonderful cooking here."

Virginia Trent showed no enthusiasm over her food,

but Mrs. Breel ate her way through the menu with placid enjoyment. No one made any further mention of the shoplifting episode. There were no explanations offered on the one hand, nor, on the other, did Mason ask for any. He threw himself into the part of acting the perfect host, and Della Street, trained by years of experience to read his moods, followed his lead. Gradually, the air of restraint which had settled about the table disappeared. Mrs. Breel's perfect poise, Mason's urbane hospitality and Della Street's sympathetic understanding conspired to make Virginia Trent lose her consciousness of the gaping interest displayed by the curious diners at adjoining tables.

Mason lingered over his demi-tasse, evidently reluctant to terminate the meeting. Finally, however, he summoned the waitress, announcing that a one-thirty appointment necessitated his departure. In the leave-taking, Virginia Trent showed once more a consciousness of the peculiar circumstances which had drawn them together, but none of this was apparent in her aunt's demeanor.

Back on the street, where patches of blue sky showed between drifting clouds, Mason turned to Della Street. "That," he announced, "was a break!"

"How did you size them up, Chief?"

"I couldn't," Mason admitted. "And, consequently, enjoyed myself immensely."

"Do you suppose she's a professional shoplifter?"

"I doubt it. The girl's embarrassment was too natural."

"Then why did she do it, Chief—I mean the aunt?"

Mason said, "Now you've got me, Della. She's hardly the criminal type. Back of her somewhere is an interesting background of philosophy. . . . We'll chalk it up as one of life's adventures, an isolated chapter which we can't understand without knowing what has gone before, yet interesting, nevertheless. It's like picking up a magazine, getting interested in a serial installment, and reading about characters doing things which don't make sense because we don't know what's gone before, yet getting interested in the people we're reading about.

That's the way it is in this case: We don't know what's gone before and we don't know what's to follow.

"A while ago you asked me if learning to know people didn't make me cynical and I told you it didn't. The real handicap about knowing people too well is that it takes all the thrill out of life. People become hopelessly drab and monotonous as they become more obvious. Nothing is new. The people one meets become a procession of mediocrities hurrying down life's pathway on petty errands. But every so often life makes amends by tossing out an experience which can't be classified. So let's chalk this up as one of life's interesting interludes and let it go at that.

2

But Perry Mason was wrong in supposing that he was not to know of that which followed. He had disposed of his appointment and was studying a recent case dealing with the admissibility of evidence obtained through wire tapping, when Della Street opened the door from her secretarial office and said, "Miss Trent is in the outer office, asking if she can see you without an appointment."

"Virginia?" Mason asked. She nodded. "Didn't say what she wanted, Della?"

"No."

"And she's alone?"

"Yes."

"All right," Mason said, "bring her in and let's get it over with."

He cleared a space on his desk by the simple expedient of pushing back the law books. He was lighting a cigarette when Della Street escorted Virginia Trent into the office. At his first meeting, he had devoted his attention to the aunt. Now he studied the niece thoughtfully as she walked across to seat herself in the big, black leather chair near the lefthand corner of his desk. She was, he saw, a tall, thin girl, with a mouth which showed too much determination and too little lipstick, large, moist gray eyes, clothes which were cut along severe lines, and the slender, slightly nervous hands of one who is very sensitive. "Was there," Mason asked, "something I could do for you?" and his voice indicated that he had quite definitely ceased to be the genial host and had become the busy lawyer.

She nodded and said, "It's about my Aunt Sarah."

"Yes?" Mason asked.

"You saw what happened at lunch. Aunt Sarah didn't fool me, and I'm quite certain she didn't fool you. She was shoplifting."

"Why shoplifting?" Mason asked.

"I'm sure I haven't the faintest idea."

"Did she need the things?"

"No."

"Doesn't she have enough money to buy what she wants?"

"Of course she does."

Mason settled back in his chair. His eyes showed interest. "Go ahead," he said, "I'm listening—but strip it down to essentials."

Virginia Trent's gloved hands smoothed the pleats of her gray skirt. She raised her eyes and said, "I'll have to begin at the beginning and tell you the whole thing. My aunt," she went on, "is a widow. Her husband died years ago. My uncle, George Trent, never married. He's a gem expert, buying and selling stones on commission, cutting and polishing, and redesigning. He has an office and a shop in a loft building at nine thirteen South Marsh Street. He keeps from two to four gem cutters and polishers constantly employed. . . . Tell me, Mr. Mason, are you a student of psychology?"

"Practical psychology," the lawyer said. "I don't go much on theory."

"You have to interpret facts in terms of theory in order to understand them," she said didactically.

Mason grinned. "It's been my experience that you have to interpret theories in terms of facts in order to understand theories. However, go ahead. What were you going to say?"

"It's about Uncle George," she said. "His father died when he was just a boy. George had to take on the support of the family. He did it wonderfully well, but he never had any boyhood. He never had a chance to play and never . . ."

"What does that have to do with your aunt?" Mason asked.

"I'm coming to it," she said. "What I was trying to explain is that Uncle George has an innate repression, a subconscious rebellion against environment which . . ."

"Which does what?" Mason asked, as she hesitated.

"Makes him get drunk," she said.

"All right, go ahead," the lawyer told her. "Never mind the verbal embellishments. He gets drunk. So what?"

"He gets drunk," she said, "periodically. That's why I know it's a subconscious rebellion against a routine environment which . . ." She checked herself as she saw the lawyer's upraised hand, and hurried on to say, "Anyway, what I'm getting at is that he'll be perfectly steady for several months at a time. Then something will happen and he'll go on one of his benders. Poor Uncle George, he's so methodical in everything that he's even methodical about that. When he feels one of these spells coming on, he carefully locks up everything in the office vault, to which my aunt has the combination. Then he takes the ignition keys out of his car, puts them in a stamped envelope, addresses them to himself, puts the keys in the mail and then goes ahead and gets drunk. While he's drinking, he gambles. Three days to a week later, he'll show up, completely broke, his eyes bloodshot, usually he's unshaven, and his clothes are a sight."

"Then what does your aunt do?" Mason asked, with interest.

"Aunt Sarah takes it right in her stride," she said. "There's never a word of remonstrance. She bundles him off to a Turkish bath, takes his clothes, has them cleaned and pressed, sends another suit to the Turkish bath, and, when he's thoroughly sobered and quite respectable, lets him go back to his office. In the meantime, Aunt Sarah has the combination to the vault. She gets out the stones the men are to work on, and sees that they keep busy."

"Rather a nice arrangement all around, I'd say," Mason observed. "They make a nice team."

"Yes," she said, "but you don't realize what all of this is doing to Aunt Sarah. The strain on her nervous system must be terrific. All the more so, because she never gives any external evidences of it."

"Bosh!" Mason said. "Your Aunt Sarah is a woman who's looked the world in the face and isn't afraid of it. She knows her way around, and doesn't quarrel with life. I venture to say she doesn't have a nerve in her body."

"She gives one that impression," Virginia Trent said austerely, "but I feel quite certain, Mr. Mason, that if we are to account for this peculiar shoplifting complex, we will find that it's due to a reflex subconscious disturbance."

"Perhaps," Mason said. "How long's this shoplifting been going on?"

"Today was the first intimation I've had."

"And what explanation did your aunt make?" Mason asked, his voice showing his interest.

"That's just it. She didn't make any. She managed to avoid me almost as soon as we left the department store. I don't know where she's gone. I'm afraid she's still emotionally upset. I'm afraid her psychic balance has been affected by . . ."

"In other words, you mean you're afraid she's shoplifting again, is that it?"

"Yes."

"And you think she's been arrested, and want me to find out. Is that what you're leading up to?"

"No," she said, "not exactly."

"Well," Mason told her, "let's make it exact. Just what *do* you want?"

She shifted her eyes uneasily, then took a deep breath and said, "Very well, Mr. Mason, specifically, I'm afraid that Aunt Sarah has stolen the Bedford diamonds."

The lawyer leaned forward. "Tell me about the Bedford diamonds."

"They're some diamonds belonging to a Mrs. Bedford. They were left with Uncle George to be completely redesigned, placed in more modern settings and brought up to date. There was some recutting to be done. I don't know all of the details of the order."

"Am I to gather that your Uncle George is on one of his sprees?" Mason asked.

"Yes. He didn't come home Saturday night. We knew what that meant. Of course, there was no mail delivery on Sunday, but Aunt Sarah went up to the office and got things all ready for Monday morning."

"Opened the vault?" Mason asked.

"I believe so, yes. Then, this morning, she went up to the office early, got in touch with the foreman, and they planned out the day's work. Sure enough, the keys to Uncle George's car were in the first mail delivery. But there was nothing to indicate where the car was. It wasn't until shortly before noon the traffic department rang up to tell us it was parked in a thirty-minute zone. . . . You see, it had been left there Saturday night after the parking restrictions had been removed, and then, of course, Sunday didn't count. But this morning, the traffic tickets started piling up on the car."

"So you went and moved the car?" Mason asked.

"Yes. Aunty and I went together. We picked up the parking tickets, and moved the car into a garage. Aunt Sarah had some shopping she wanted to do, and I wanted to get a pair of shoes. We went into the department store, and I was getting my shoes and thought Aunt Sarah was standing right behind me. Then suddenly I missed her. . . . You know what happened after that."

"And you found her up in the tea room?" Mason asked.

"Yes, I'd been looking all over the store for her. I found her up there just before . . . well, you know."

"All right," Mason said, "tell me some more about the Bedford diamonds."

"The Bedford diamonds," she said, "came to us through Austin Cullens."

"Who's he?"

"He's an old-time friend of the family. He's known George and Sarah for years. He does a great deal of traveling, is quite a gem collector, and knows lots of interesting people. Uncle George does work quite well and very cheaply, and Mr. Cullens is frequently able to get him some very lucrative business. You see, Mr. Cullens spends a lot of time on shipboard, gets to talk with people about gems, knows a good many gem collectors, and, all in all, is a very valuable business connection for Uncle George."

"When did the Bedford diamonds come in?" Mason asked.

"Saturday. Mr. Cullens brought them in. Mrs. Bedford was to come in later on in the week."

"When did you first realize they were gone?"

"About half an hour ago. I decided to come to you at once."

"Go ahead," Mason told her.

"After I missed Aunt Sarah, I became completely exasperated. I went back to Uncle George's office, thinking she might be there. The foreman showed me a note Uncle George had left, giving directions about working out sketches and designs for the Bedford diamonds. But . . . well, the Bedford diamonds weren't there."

"The vault was open?"

"Yes. Aunt Sarah had opened it this morning."

"How about the men in the shop? Can you trust them?"

"I think so, yes."

"And what makes you think your Aunt Sarah has the diamonds?"

"Well . . . well, you saw what happened this noon. And when a person once gets a complex . . . well,

I don't know whether you've studied much about kleptomania, Mr. Mason, but it's most devastating. Klep-
tomaniacs simply cannot resist the impulse to take things
which don't belong to them. . . . Well, anyway, Aunt
Sarah was up at the office on Sunday, getting things lined
up for this morning. She came back to the house yesterday afternoon, and said she'd been seized with a very
peculiar dizzy spell while she was at the office; that her
mind had gone completely blank for a period of what
must have been half an hour; that she didn't have the
faintest recollection of what she was doing. She thought
it must have been her heart. I wanted her to call a doctor. She wouldn't do it. She said that when she regained
consciousness she had the most peculiar feeling of having done something she shouldn't. She felt as though
she'd killed someone, or something of that sort."

"Did you get a doctor?" Mason asked.

"No, she went to her room and slept for a couple of
hours, and then said she felt better. At dinner, she
seemed to be very much her normal self."

"Well," Mason said, "I don't know just what you want
me to do. As I see it, you'd better find your aunt and
take some steps to locate your Uncle George. His haunts
should be fairly well defined. A man who goes on these
periodical drinking sprees usually . . ."

"But," she said, "Mrs. Bedford wants her stones back."

"Since when?" Mason asked.

"She rang up at noon, while I was out, and said that
she'd changed her mind; that she didn't want anything
done to her stones; that she had a prospective buyer
who was interested in antique jewelry, and she was going
to offer the stones and settings to this buyer."

"Did you talk with Mrs. Bedford?" Mason asked.

"No. The shop foreman did."

"What did he tell her?"

"Told her Uncle George was out at the time, but he'd
have him call as soon as he came in."

"Well," Mason said, "you might get in touch with police headquarters and find out if your aunt has suffered
any relapses. That spell may well have been her heart.

She may have had another and been taken to the emergency hospital. Or . . ." He broke off as the door from the outer office opened, and the girl from the information desk tiptoed quietly into the room, to stand just within the doorway. "What is it?" Mason asked.

"A Mr. Cullens is in the outer office," she said. "He seems to be very much excited and says he must see Miss Trent immediately."

Virginia Trent gave an exclamation of dismay. "You'll have to hide me somewhere," she said to Mason, and then to the girl, "Tell him I'm not here. Tell him I've left. Tell him . . ."

"Tell him nothing of the sort," Mason interrupted. "Let's get this thing straight. How did he know you were here, Miss Trent?"

"I left word at the office that if Aunty came in she was to call me here. I guess Mr. Cullens went to the office and the foreman told him."

"And Cullens was the one who brought your uncle the Bedford business?" She nodded. "You've got to see him sooner or later," Mason told her. "You'd better make it sooner. After all, he's entitled to some sort of a break. I presume he vouched for your uncle to Mrs. Bedford."

"Yes," she said dubiously, "I guess he must have."

Mason nodded to the girl who stood in the doorway. "Tell Mr. Cullens he can come in," he instructed.

Virginia Trent's hands became nervous on her lap. She said uneasily, "Oh, I *can't* face him! I don't know what to say. I just can't think of the proper thing to tell him."

"What's wrong with telling him the truth?" Mason asked.

"But I don't know the truth," she said.

"Well, why not tell him that?"

"Because . . . oh, I don't know. I just can't bear to . . ."

The door from the outer office was pushed open by a beefy individual in the late forties, who ignored Mason entirely, to stride across to where Virginia Trent was seated in the big leather chair. "What the devil's all the run-around, Virgie?" he asked.

She avoided his eyes. "I don't know what you're talking about."

"Where's your aunt?"

"I don't know. She's uptown somewhere. I think she's shopping."

Cullens turned briefly to Mason, surveying the lawyer with swift appraisal. Then his incisive eyes swung back to Virginia Trent. A huge diamond on his left hand glittered in a coruscating arc as his hand grasped her shoulder. "Come on, Virgie," he said, "out with it. What the devil's the idea of running up to see a lawyer?"

She said in a thin, small voice, "I wanted to talk with him about Aunt Sarah."

"And what about Sarah?"

"She's been shoplifting."

Cullens drew back and laughed. It was a deep-chested, jovial, booming laugh which seemed somehow to clarify the atmosphere. He turned, then, to Perry Mason, extended his hand and said, "You're Mason. I'm Cullens. I'm glad to know you. Sorry to butt in this way, but it's important." He turned back to Virginia Trent. "Now, Virgie, come down to earth and give me the low-down. What's happened to Mrs. Bedford's diamonds?"

"I don't know."

"Well, who does?"

"Aunty, I guess."

"All right, where is she?"

"I tell you, she's been shoplifting."

"More power to her," Cullens said. "She'd make a grand shoplifter. I suppose George is on one of his bats?"

She nodded. Cullens said, "Mrs. Bedford telephoned me. She said she wanted her diamonds back. She'd tried to reach George on the telephone, and didn't like the way she'd been talked to. She thought someone was giving her a run-around, so she called me. I knew right away what had happened. But I also knew that George would mail in the keys to his car and that your aunt could get into the vault and carry on the business. Now then, Ione Bedford has a customer who's in the market for her stones. Naturally, she doesn't want to lose the sale. She wants the stones and needs them now."

Virginia Trent's mouth became a firm, straight line. She raised her eyes defiantly and said, "I tell you, Aunt Sarah has been shoplifting. You laugh if you want to, but that happens to be the truth. If you want to know, you can ask Mr. Mason. While she's had one of her spells, she's taken Mrs. Bedford's diamonds and hidden them."

A perplexed frown appeared on Cullens' forehead. "You're not kidding me?" he asked, and then turned to Mason. At what he saw in the lawyer's eyes, he said slowly, "Well, I'll be damned!" He drew up a chair, selected a cigar from his waistcoat pocket, clipped off the end with a thin, gold knife and said to Virginia, "Tell me about it."

"There's nothing to tell," she said. "Aunt Sarah has been laboring under a terrific emotional strain. Also, I think she's suffering from a fixation. However, we don't need to go into that now. There are periods during which she has a complete lapse of memory. During those times she becomes a kleptomaniac, taking anything she can get her hands on. She was caught in a department store this noon, and I had to check out nearly every penny in my bank to keep her from going to jail."

Cullens lit his cigar, studied the flaming match for a moment in thoughtful contemplation, then shook it out, and said, "When was the first time, Virgie?"

"This noon."

"Were those the first symptoms?"

"Well, she went up to the office yesterday and had a dizzy spell and couldn't remember anything which had happened for about half an hour. When she came to, she had a peculiar feeling of guilt, as though she'd murdered someone. I think that was when she took the Bedford gems and concealed them somewhere. She . . ."

Cullens' diamond glittered as he raised his hand to take the cigar from his mouth. "Oh, bosh!" he said, "forget it. She's no shoplifter. She's trying to cover up for your uncle."

"How do you mean?"

"When she went to the office yesterday," Cullens said, "she found the Bedford diamonds were gone. Just between you and me, that's the thing which has always worried her—that some day when your uncle starts on one of these benders he'll forget that he has some stones in his pocket. Your aunt pulled this shoplifting stunt to fool you, and to fool me if it became necessary. She's out looking for George right now."

"I don't think Aunty would do that," Virginia Trent said.

Cullens said shortly, "You don't really think she'd turn shoplifter, do you?"

"Well . . . well, I have the evidence of my own eyes."

Cullens said, "All right. Let's not argue about it. Let's tell Ione Bedford what she's up against."

"Oh, we mustn't tell *her!* No matter what happens, we must keep her from finding out . . ."

Cullens ignored her, to turn to the lawyer. "I'm sorry," he said, "to have to handle things this way, Mr. Mason, but I think I'd better stay right here for the moment. This thing is important. It means quite a good deal to me. Those stones were worth twenty-five to thirty thousand dollars. My car's down in front, a green convertible with the top down. Mrs. Bedford is waiting in the car. I wonder if it would be possible for you to have one of your girls . . ."

Mason turned to Della Street. "Go on down, Della," he said. "Find Mrs. Bedford and bring her up."

Virginia Trent said very firmly, "I don't approve of this in the least. I don't think Aunt Sarah would want it handled this way."

"Well, *I* want it handled this way," Cullens said, "and after all, I'm the one chiefly concerned. Remember, I'm the one who brought the stones in to your Uncle George in the first place." He turned to Perry Mason. "If it's a fair question, Mr. Mason, where do *you* stand in this?"

"I don't stand," Mason told him, grinning. "I'm sitting on the sidelines. It happens that I was present when Mrs. Breel staged what was apparently her first public demonstration of shoplifting. It also happens that it was a most edifying experience."

Cullens grinned. "It would be. What happened?"

"Well," Mason said reminiscently, "she carried it off remarkably well. And after that, she and her niece were good enough to join me at lunch. I hardly expected to hear any more of the matter, until Miss Trent came in to consult me. I haven't, as yet, found out exactly what it is she wants me to do, but I felt you were entitled to an explanation. As nearly as I can tell, you're getting it."

Cullens turned to Virginia Trent. There was a flash of dislike in his eyes. "I suppose you wanted to duck out and leave me holding the sack, didn't you?"

"Most certainly *not!*"

He laughed unpleasantly. "And it was Mason who insisted you should see me, wasn't it?" She said nothing. "What did you want Mason to do?" he asked.

"I wanted him to locate Aunt Sarah for me, and to . . . well, to figure some way of stalling things along until we could find out where we stand."

"We can find out where we stand without stalling things along," Cullens said.

"That's what you think," she told him. "You're saving your own bacon at the expense of Uncle George's reputation. Mrs. Bedford will claim he's stolen the stones and . . . and it'll be an awful mess."

Cullens said, "You don't know Ione Bedford. She's a good scout. She can take it. What we're interested in is finding those stones."

"Well, I don't know just how *you* think *you're* going to go about it," Virginia Trent said.

"Neither do I," Cullens said affably—"yet."

Della Street's rapid heels sounded in the corridor. She unlatched the door of Mason's private office, and escorted a woman in the thirties through the doorway. "This," she announced, "is Mrs. Bedford."

"Come on in, Ione," Cullens said, without getting up. "Have a chair and make yourself at home. This is Perry Mason, the lawyer. Your diamonds have gone bye-bye."

For a moment, Mrs. Bedford stood in the doorway, surveying the occupants of the room with dark, languid eyes. Slightly heavier than Della Street, she possessed an attractive figure, which showed to advantage through a rust-colored frilled blouse and gray tailored suit. Her hat matched her blouse, as did her slippers, whose high heels served to emphasize her short foot with its high instep. She crossed over toward a chair, paused for a moment as she saw Mason's open cigarette case, raised her eyebrows in a gesture of silent interrogation, and, at his nod, helped herself to a cigarette. She leaned forward for his light, then went over to the chair and said, "Well, now *that's* something. Tell me about it, Aussie."

"I can't tell you much until I get the details," Cullens said. "I'm getting them now—or trying to. George Trent is just what I told you, one of the best gem men in the country. His work is dependable and reasonable. He's thoroughly honest. He has one vice, and only one vice. He's a periodical drunkard. When he gets drunk, he gambles, but he does even that methodically. He puts all of his gems in the vault, leaves himself a limited amount of money in his pocket, mails in his car keys, and then goes out and gets drunk and gambles. When he loses his money, so he can't buy any more liquor, he sobers up, comes home and goes back to work. This time, he seems to have inadvertently taken your stones with him. I gave them to him Saturday afternoon. He started his drunk Saturday night. That, my dear, is the bad news in a nutshell."

She inhaled a deep drag from the cigarette, exhaled the smoke in twin streams through appreciative, distended nostrils. "Why the lawyer?" she asked, jerking her head toward Perry Mason.

Cullens laughed. "Virginia Trent, over here—George's niece—thinks that her Aunt Sarah has become suddenly seized with kleptomania. She thinks the aunt took the stones while her mind was a blank and did something with them."

"What's the matter?" Ione Bedford asked the niece in a rich, throaty voice. "Been reading Grimm's fairy tales, dearie?" Virginia Trent drew herself up indignantly. Her mouth tightened into a formless gash.

"Not fairy tales," Cullens answered easily, "psychology —fixations, complexes and all that stuff. The girl studies, if you know what I mean—Freud, sex, crime . . ."

"It happens," Virginia Trent said acidly, "that my aunt has surrendered in public and in the presence of witnesses to these impulses of kleptomania. She was caught shoplifting less than four hours ago."

Ione Bedford raised inquiring eyebrows in the direction of Austin Cullens. Mason noted that it was evidently an habitual gesture with her, noticed also that they were good-looking eyebrows, and that the mannerism served to direct attention to eyes which were undoubtedly beautiful. Nor did Ione Bedford give any indication that she failed to realize the beauty of her eyes, or the graceful lines of the trim leg which her short skirt disclosed to advantage.

Cullens said, "That's just a stall, Ione. If you saw Sarah Breel for just ten seconds, you'd realize that it's a stall. When the foreman started checking over the work orders this morning, he found your gems were missing. Sarah knew at once George had them. So she started the old cover-up—bless her soul! It's meant well, but it isn't going to get us any place."

A huge emerald on Mrs. Bedford's hand showed to advantage as she flicked ashes from the end of her cigarette with a graceful little finger. "Just what," she asked, *is* going to get us any place?"

Cullens said, "I'm going to get out and start looking for George Trent. He's in a gambling house somewhere, beautifully plastered. Your stones are wrapped up in tissue paper and carried in a chamois-skin belt next to his skin, and he's completely forgotten that he has them. *But,* if he gets drunk enough and desperate enough, he may hock them with some gambler." Cullens turned to Mason and said, "How about it, Mr. Mason, can we claim embezzlement and get them back if he does?"

"Probably not without a lawsuit," Mason said. "It will depend somewhat on circumstances, somewhat on the manner in which the stones were given to him, and by whom."

"I gave him the stones," Cullen said, "but we don't want any lawsuits, do we, Ione?"

She shook her head and flashed Mason a smile. "No one makes any money out of lawsuits," she said, "except lawyers."

Mason matched her grin, "And *they* don't make half enough," he told her.

Cullens ignored the byplay. "Okay, Ione, what do we do?"

She studied the tip of her cigarette meditatively. "Suppose he's hocked them," she said musingly. "How much do you s'pose he'd have been able to raise on them, Aussie?"

"Not over three or four thousand at the most," Cullens said. "Being drunk, wanting the money for gambling, and with the strong possibility of a kick-back, it's a cinch no gambler would take a chance for more than a fifth of their clear market value."

She turned to Perry Mason. "How much would a lawsuit cost?" she asked.

Mason grinned. "Is three or four thousand, at the most, the answer you're waiting for?" he asked.

"Yes," she said, and once more the emerald flashed as her hand made a gesture of dismissal. "That settles it, Aussie. Find Trent. If he has the stones, get them back. If he hasn't, find out where he's hocked them, and pay off the loan. That's cheaper than a lawsuit—and faster."

She turned to Virginia Trent and said, "I understand exactly how you feel. Poor child! I suppose you were afraid of me. You needn't have been. After all, it's not *your* fault."

Virginia Trent said, "I'm not a child. I'm adult. What's more, I still feel there's something back of my aunt's conduct, that there's some emotional upset which . . ."

Cullens got to his feet. "Well, come on, everybody," he interrupted, "we have work to do, and there's no use taking up more of Mr. Mason's time."

He shepherded them toward the exit door. Virginia Trent, once more, started to talk about psychology as she stepped out into the corridor. Ione Bedford flashed Cullens a roguish glance, then said to Virginia Trent, "And what do you know about suppressed emotions, dearie?"

Virginia Trent drew herself up in rigid dignity. "I wasn't discussing suppressed emotions," she said with calm finality.

Mason, watching Della Street hold the door, ready to close it behind the departing visitors, could have sworn that the rapid flicker of Ione Bedford's right eyelid as she smiled a farewell at him was not accidental.

When the door had clicked shut, Mason grinned at Della and said, "And only this noon I was talking about people being mediocrities, marching inanely through life."

"A combination of characters like that," Della Street said, "should be able to scare up *something*."

"Not a mystery, I'm afraid," Mason rejoined. "They're all so beautifully normal. Aside from Virginia Trent, there isn't anyone who has so much as a nerve."

"Where do you suppose the aunt is?" Della Street asked.

Mason's eyes narrowed. "Having seen her in action," he said, "I'm inclined to agree with Cullens' explanation. I think she's trying an elaborate cover-up for her brother. But, just as a concession to the vagaries of a whimsical fate which has catapulted us into the situation, Della, we're going to find out. Call up police headquarters. See if she's been arrested or is in an emergency hospital anywhere. Check on automobile accidents and ambulance calls."

3

■

At approximately seven-thirty Mason was called to the telephone from the cocktail lounge of his apartment hotel. He recognized the rich, throaty voice of Mrs. Bedford, even before she gave him her name. "Have you," she asked, "heard anything from the aunt in the case— Breel, I believe her name was?"

"Not yet," Mason said. "Her disappearance, however, is apparently voluntary. I've had my office telephone the various police stations, emergency hospitals, and check the ambulance calls."

"And she hasn't been arrested for shoplifting?" Mrs. Bedford inquired, in an amused drawl.

"If she has," Mason told her, "the police haven't heard of it."

She laughed. "Well, I think my gems are safe. I thought I'd ring up so you could reassure that poor little starved wallflower."

"You've recovered them?" Mason asked.

"Well, not exactly recovered them, but Aussie telephoned he's found where George Trent had pawned them. It's a second-rate gambling joint on East Third street, known as The Golden Platter. They have a café downstairs, and a little bit of everything upstairs. Aussie said George had the stones with him, all right, and hocked them for six thousand. I told Aussie three was my limit. Aussie said he thought three thousand was all the money Trent actually got on them; that the other three thousand was an attempt at a shake-down. He said he could bring some pressure to bear on the man who ran the place, and get the stones for three thousand. I told him to go ahead. We'll adjust the three thousand with Trent when he sobers up. . . . I thought you'd like to know."

Mason said, "Thanks. I do. Cullens hasn't found Trent?"

"No. He figures Trent can take care of himself. Aussie's on his way to get the stones. I expect to hear from him within an hour."

"How," Mason asked, "did you get this number?"

She laughed, and there was something purring in the quality of her laughter, a sensual, feline something which was quite definitely calculated to rouse the male to conquest. "You forget, Mr. Mason, that you're famous," she said. "And," she went on, "having forgotten that, you are apparently oblivious of the additional fact that you're interesting. Good night, Mr. Mason," and he heard the sound of a definite click at the other end of the line as the wire went dead.

Mason hung up the receiver, casually and mechanically noted the time on his wrist watch, and returned to his cocktail. Thinking the matter over, he called Della Street and instructed her to telephone Virginia Trent that the gems were located and would soon be recovered. Thereafter, Mason dined in the apartment hotel, and, as a matter of preference, dined alone. Finishing his coffee and cigarette, a bellboy approached him. "Telephone, Mr. Mason," he said.

"Let it go," Mason told him. "Get the number and I'll call back."

"Beg your pardon, sir, but it's Sergeant Tremont at headquarters. He says it's important."

Mason ground out his cigarette, pushed back his coffee cup, laid down his napkin and a tip, and followed the boy to the telephone, where he heard Sergeant Tremont's voice, crisp, businesslike, and coldly efficient, coming over the wire. "Mason, your office rang up all the hospitals this afternoon, looking for a Mrs. Sarah Breel. You were trying to trace ambulance calls and automobile accidents."

"That's right," Mason said, his eyes wary and watchful, but his voice jovial. "What about it, Sergeant?"

Sergeant Tremont said, "Mrs. Breel was knocked down half an hour ago by a motorist out on St. Rupert Boulevard. She's receiving emergency treatment at the ambulance receiving station right at present. She's unconscious, fractured skull, broken leg and possible internal injuries. . . . Now then, Mason, what we're particularly interested in, is what led you to believe she was going to be hurt."

Mason laughed, and tried to keep the laugh from sounding forced. "Naturally, Sergeant, I couldn't look ahead and anticipate that she was going to be knocked down by an automobile."

"No?" Sergeant Tremont asked, his voice containing more than a faint note of skepticism. "Just in case you had, you couldn't have been any more solicitous."

Mason said, "Forget it. I was interested in getting information, that's all."

"Well, you have it now," Sergeant Tremont told him. "What are you going to do about it?"

"I happen to know her niece," Mason said, "a Miss Virginia Trent. I'm going to advise her."

"Well, we've tried to advise her and can't locate her." Sergeant Tremont told him. "There are a couple of angles on this. I think you'd better run down to headquarters and talk things over."

There was a hint in the officer's voice that the invitation might become more insistent if the occasion seemed to require, so Mason said casually, "Well, that's not a bad idea. I'd like to investigate the circumstances and see if there's anything I can do. Who hit her, Sergeant?"

"A man by the name of Diggers. He seems to be all broken up about it."

"Are you holding him?"

"Temporarily. We're going to let him go in a few minutes. Evidently she ran out in front of the automobile."

"I'm just finishing dinner," Mason told him. "I'll get in my car and run down."

"Better make it snappy," Sergeant Tremont told him.

"We want to ask you some questions about some diamonds."

"Diamonds?" Mason echoed.

"Uh-huh," Tremont said, and hung up.

Mason had his car brought out of the garage, and, while he was waiting for it, telephoned Della Street again. "Any luck with Virginia Trent?" he asked.

"Not a bit, Chief. I've been calling her at ten minute intervals. She doesn't answer."

"All right, let it go," Mason told her. "Mrs. Breel was knocked down by an automobile out on St. Rupert Boulevard. Apparently she has a fractured skull, a broken leg, and possible internal injuries. The police are trying to locate Miss Trent. Sergeant Tremont has given me what amounts to an official summons to appear at headquarters and answer questions about some diamonds. There are a couple of angles about the thing I don't like. Ring up the Drake Detective Agency. Get Paul Drake personally on the job. Tell him to grab a cab and go down to headquarters. He'll find my car parked somewhere in the block. It'll be unlocked. Tell him to climb in and wait. Also, tell him to get a couple of good men and hold them in readiness."

Della Street said, "Okay, Chief. I'll get busy right away. What's all the shooting about?"

"I don't know," Mason told her, "something in Sergeant Tremont's voice which I didn't like."

She chuckled and said, "I never heard anything in an officer's voice yet that you *did* like, Chief."

"Baggage!" he charged, and hung up the receiver as the doorman brought him his car.

Mason drove slowly to police headquarters, his eyes, narrowed to thoughtful slits, staring out from beneath level eyebrows. He realized he had neglected to obtain any address where he could communicate with Ione Bedford, and the realization was disquieting. For reasons of his own, Mason felt that it would be very much to his advantage to know just what had transpired at The Golden Platter before talking with the police.

He parked his car near the ambulance receiving station and had walked less than twenty steps when Sergeant Tremont stepped out of the shadows to take his arm in a cordial but firm grasp. "Who is this woman, Mason?" he asked. "A client of yours?"

"Not exactly," Mason said.

"A friend?"

"Hardly that. I had lunch with her today, as it happens."

"Where?"

"Oh, in a department store tea room."

"How does it happen you're eating in department store tea rooms?"

Mason paused to light a cigarette. "Since it seems to be a matter of professional interest," he said, "I don't mind telling you that the food was excellent. Moreover, the selection was somewhat forced upon me. You'll remember that it started raining pitchforks about noon."

"In which event," Sergeant Tremont said, "you evidently didn't invite the lady to lunch, but met her *at* lunch."

Mason grinned. "That," he said, "is the result of having a deductive mind."

"It still isn't answering my question," Tremont said.

"You've already answered it," Mason told him.

Tremont faced him abruptly. "How about the diamonds, Mason?"

"What diamonds?"

"You know what diamonds I mean."

Mason shook his head slowly and said, "Diamonds are a little out of my line, Sergeant. I specialize in murders and retainers. The retainers, thank Heaven, are usually cash. The murders the inevitable by-products of the hatreds and rivalries engendered by a competitive civilization. You know, Sergeant, I've always been fascinated by the knowledge that there's never a period of more than forty-five days in the city without a homicide. Imagine waiting, say on the forty-fourth day, in police headquarters, knowing that within a matter of minutes someone somewhere is going to be murdered, or else there'll be a new record hung up. It's uncanny . . ."

"It's also an attempt on your part to spar for time and get a little information out of me," Tremont interrupted. "It's not going to work. I want to know about those diamonds."

"Diamonds?" Mason echoed.

"Yes. Diamonds. You know, Mason, women wear them in rings and things. They're polished gem stones which reflect the light. They're hard. They cut glass. Sometimes they call them ice, sometimes rocks. If that description doesn't serve to give you a rough idea of what they are, there's a dictionary in headquarters which you can consult."

"Oh, the diamonds," Mason said. "Come to think of it, I believe she *did* mention that she had some diamonds, or was to get some diamonds, or something of the sort—I can't remember just what. Her brother, you know, is a dealer in stones."

"Yes," Tremont told him, "we know all about her. The minute your office became so insistent trying to find out what had happened to her, we decided it might be a good plan to look her up. So many of the people you take an interest in get mixed up in murder cases sooner or later."

"Thanks for the tip," Mason said. "I'll bear it in mind when I'm inclined to ask for information in the future."

"Don't mention it. It's a pleasure. You *still* haven't answered the question about the diamonds."

"I'm sure I couldn't tell you a thing, Sergeant," Mason said, frowning as though trying to recall something to his mind. "She mentioned her brother's being in the diamond business. It seems to me he's out of town, or away, or something, and she's running the business in his absence. I'm sorry I can't tell you just what *was* said."

"Well, we'll come to that again later," Sergeant Tremont said. "In the meantime, we go in through this door, Mason." He led the way into an anteroom where a wiry individual in the early fifties jumped to his feet as the door opened, then, as he saw the expression on Sergeant Tremont's face, sank slowly back into the chair. Sergeant Tremont said, without turning his head, "That's

Harry Diggers, the man who was driving the car. This is Perry Mason, the lawyer, Diggers."

Mason nodded reassuringly. Diggers came forward to shake hands. Sergeant Tremont said to a property clerk behind a grilled window, "Let me have that Breel bag."

The clerk passed out a voluminous black bag. The handles consisted of two imitation jade rings, some six inches in diameter. By pulling the rings apart, the contents of the bag were easily visible.

"That looks very much like it might be hers," Mason said. "Is that some knitting she's working on?"

The sergeant nodded, pulled out the start of a knitted blue sweater, a pair of knitting needles wound around with yarn, and a ball of dark blue yarn. Underneath that, he retrieved half a dozen pairs of silk stockings and said to Mason, "Notice the price marks, and the stock tags. We've checked back on those stockings. They weren't sold. Someone picked 'em up off the counter."

"Indeed?" Mason said.

"Would you know anything about that?" Sergeant Tremont asked. Mason shook his head. "All right, you haven't seen anything yet," Tremont told him. He dug deeper in the bag and pulled out some packages done up in soft, white tissue. He unwrapped these, one at a time.

Mason stared down at the five large diamonds in antique settings. "Gosh!" he exclaimed. "I don't know much about stones, but those look like a lot of money."

"They are," Tremont said. "Any idea where they came from?"

Mason shook ashes from the end of his cigarette, then faced the officer. "At the time I met her," he said, "there seemed to have been a slight misunderstanding. One of the department store detectives thought she'd been shoplifting. Her niece thought she had been shopping. Since the things she had selected had never been removed from the store, I was inclined to join with the niece in insisting that the matter should be interpreted in a charitable light."

"Then what?" Sergeant Tremont asked.

"Then," Mason said, "we sat down and had lunch. Rather an enjoyable affair all around. I found her quite a character. Later on, the niece called on me. Something was said about some diamonds which had been left with Mr. George Trent. I think, Sergeant, if you'll get hold of Miss Trent, you'll find these diamonds will be readily identified as stones which were left with Mr. Trent in the due course of his business."

"Then how did they get in this handbag?"

"I'm sure I couldn't answer that question."

"This other stuff," the sergeant said, tapping the pile of silk stockings with the back of his fingers, "was stolen. Therefore, what does it make the diamonds?"

Mason's laugh was genial. "Applying the same reasoning, Sergeant," he said, "what does it make the knitting?"

"Don't try to crack wise, Mason. The knitting is something a woman would naturally carry in her bag."

"Remember," Mason pointed out, "that her brother is a gem expert. He buys and sells on commission and does original designing, repair work, and recuts and polishes gems. While he's away, she's in charge of the business."

"Where's he now?"

"Apparently," Mason said, "he's on a toot."

"Well," Tremont said, "it's going to be mighty fortunate for her if it turns out these diamonds are ones which were legitimately left in her possession. Just how did you enter in on it, Mason?"

"I didn't particularly," the lawyer said. "I was more entered against than entering. Having invited her and her niece to have lunch with me, the niece showed up later on in the afternoon with the report that her aunt was missing and would I please try to locate her. Then some people who had some entirely different business with the niece followed her to my office and insisted on having their business conference there."

The sergeant nodded to the property clerk. "The shoes, Bill," he said. The property clerk passed up a pair of gray kid shoes, with medium high heels and pointed toes. Sergeant Tremont picked up the left one and said,

"Now these were her shoes, Mason. Take a look at this left one." Mason examined the thick, reddish-brown stains which adhered to the leather of the shoe, and which had turned the sole a rusty brown. "How'd the blood get on that shoe?" the officer asked.

Mason shook his head. "You can search me, Sergeant. I'm telling you, the last I saw of the woman was when I paid her lunch check at the department store. That must have been about one-fifteen or perhaps one-seventeen, to be exact. I had a one-thirty appointment at my office, and had to get back for it."

"That still doesn't explain the blood on the shoe."

"Well," Mason said, "she was in an automobile accident, wasn't she?' Her leg was broken."

"The bone was broken," Sergeant Tremont said, "but the skin wasn't. Moreover, you'll notice the blood on the sole of this shoe. . . . Now then, Mason, your client wouldn't by any chance have stuck up someone and lifted these sparklers, would she?"

Mason decided it was time to show his impatience. "How the devil do I know?" he asked. "In the first place, she isn't a client of mine. In the second place, I know nothing whatever about her, and in the third place, I was only trying to accommodate a string-bean girl with pop eyes and a lantern jaw, who has very definite ideas about the conventions."

Sergeant Tremont grinned. "Well," he said, "that's that. We were hoping you could help us."

"Well, I can't," Mason told him shortly, snapping the stub of his cigarette into a cuspidor.

The man at the table said, "Have you any idea when I can go, Sergeant?"

"Pretty quick," Tremont told him, without shifting his eyes from Mason.

Mason turned to Diggers. "Just how did the accident happen?" he asked.

Sergeant Tremont said, "This man is a lawyer, Diggers. You've already made your report. You don't have to tell anyone anything."

"I most certainly have nothing to conceal," Diggers

said. "I was driving my car along St. Rupert Boulevard. I was in a thirty-mile zone, and don't believe I was going more than twenty-five or twenty-six miles an hour. In any event, I was keeping right along with the stream of slow traffic. I was well over on the right, in the right-hand lane. Traffic on the outside whizzing past anywhere from five to twenty miles an hour faster than I was. There was a big blue sedan parked at the curb. That car started out from the curb all of a sudden, and I swerved to the right to keep on the inside because I was going pretty slow. This was just after I'd passed Ninety-First Street. I guess I was about the middle of the block. Well, just as soon as I swung in toward the curb, this woman jumped out right in front of my headlights—just about where the blue sedan had been. When she saw me, she got rattled and flung up her hands. I slammed on the brakes, gave her the horn, and swerved the car. The running-board on the right-hand side struck her leg and broke it below the knee. She fell down and hit her head. This bag was lying on the pavement right near where she fell. I was going to load her in my car and bring her to the emergency hospital, but some people who had stopped told me they'd already telephoned for an ambulance, and I'd better let the ambulance move her . . . let them take the responsibility."

"You were driving alone?" Mason asked.

"Yes."

"How long before you hit this woman did you first see her?"

"Just a second or two. She jumped out from the curb, ran right in front of my headlights, and then seemed incapable of doing anything. She just stood there. A lot of people stopped, and I made them inventory the contents of the bag. You see the fact that there was a gun lying on the . . ."

"A gun!" Mason exclaimed.

Sergeant Tremont took Diggers by the arm. "Come with me, Diggers," he said. "I don't think there's any necessity for holding you any longer. And I'd just as soon you didn't answer any more questions."

Mason made for the door. "I'm going to see Mrs. Breel, Sergeant."

The sergeant shook his head. "Oh, no, you're not," he announced.

"The devil I'm not!"

Sergeant Tremont grinned affably. "In the first place, Mason," he said, "she's in the care of a doctor who has prohibited visitors. In the second place, she's under a police guard. In the third place, you've been very emphatic about stating that she wasn't a client of yours, but merely a casual friend. Under the circumstances, you don't see her."

Mason thought for a moment, then reached for his hat. "Under the circumstances, Sergeant," he admitted with a wry grin, "you win."

4

Paul Drake, head of the Drake Detective Agency, was tall, thin in stature, and perpetually pessimistic in outlook. His face was florid, his eyes regarded the world from behind a glassy film. But, by some quirk of the facial muscles, the corners of his lips turned up, giving him the appearance of continually smiling at life, whereas his actual outlook was exactly the opposite. Slumped down in the seat of Perry Mason's automobile, his head drooping, a pendulous cigarette hanging from his lips, he straightened slightly as he saw the lawyer walk around the car and open the door on the driver's side. "What is it this time, Perry?" he asked. "Have they finally pinched you as an accessory?"

"Not yet," Mason told him cheerfully, "but we're doing some investigating, Paul."

"What sort of investigating?"

"I don't know," Mason said, and then added after an appreciable pause, "yet."

"When will you know?"

"I'll know," Mason said, "as soon as I can get to a telephone book and find out where a man by the name of Austin Cullens lives."

"What does that have to do with it?"

"If he lives on St. Rupert Boulevard between Ninety-First and Ninety-Second Streets," Mason said, "it's going to have a hell of a lot to do with it."

He swung his car in a U-turn, drove rapidly to the corner drug store, where he said to the detective, "Alibi yourself out of any tickets for double parking, Paul. I want to take a look at a telephone directory." He ran into the store and looked up Austin Cullens. The address was 9158 St. Rupert Boulevard. Mason stepped into the telephone booth, dropped a coin, dialed Della Street's number. "Sorry to keep bothering you, Della," he said, when he heard her voice on the line. "Hope I'm not interrupting a heavy date."

"When I have a heavy date," she said, "I can't even hear the telephone. What is it this time?"

"I don't know," he told her. "There's something here I can't figure. Do we have Mrs. Bedford's address?"

"I don't think so," she said.

"That's too bad—better get it," Mason told her. "Then get in touch with her and put her under cover. Get her where the police can't find her."

"Shall I let her know what I'm doing, Chief?" Della Street asked, her voice losing its tone of informal banter and becoming crisply businesslike.

"Not unless you absolutely have to, Della. Make any kind of a stall. Tell her I've asked you to come and get her and keep her available for important developments. Or, just try the old personality stuff. Tell her you understand she's a stranger in the city and how would she like to go out to dinner. In short, tell her anything. But put her where the police can't find her, and don't let her know that's what you're doing."

"Okay, Chief, where will I reach you?"

"Keep in touch with the Drake Detective Agency," Mason said. "Leave word with whoever's in charge of the office. Tell them Drake or I may telephone later for the information, and not to let it out to anyone else. Of course, if you can't locate her, you'll just have to . . ."

"Leave it to me, Chief," Della Street said competently, "I'll locate her. What's happened?"

"I don't know yet," Mason said. "I'm on my way to find out. Remember, keep in touch with Drake's office."

"Okay, Chief," she said, "I'm starting right now," and hung up the telephone.

Back in the automobile, Mason slid in behind the steering wheel and jerked the car into motion. Paul Drake, sliding half around in the seat so that his back was propped across the corner formed by the door and the seat cushion, said, "So what?"

"So we go places," Mason told him.

"What do we do when we get there?"

Mason said, "We go up on a porch and ring a doorbell."

"You're such a help," Drake murmured, squirming himself into a position where he was entirely comfortable, with his head resting on the back of the cushion. "Let me know when you get there." He closed his eyes and apparently dropped into prompt sleep.

Mason raced the traffic for the breaks at the intersection signals, swung into St. Rupert Boulevard and gave the car plenty of speed. He glided into the curb directly opposite a house on the right-hand side which sat back somewhat from the street, surrounded by a well-kept lawn. It was a pretentious, two-and-a-half storied residence, with wide veranda and a driveway leading back to a three-car garage with chauffeur's quarters over the garage.

"Who lives here, Perry?" Drake asked.

"Austin Cullens," Mason said. "Come on, Paul," and ran across the sidewalk and up to the porch. He found a doorbell and rang it. He could hear the bell jangling in the interior of the house, but there was no sound of motion back of the somber, unlighted windows.

The tall detective said casually, "The door's ajar, Perry. Does that mean anything?"

"I think it does," Mason said. "We're going in."

Drake slipped a flashlight from his pocket and said, "I suppose you know, some people shoot burglars."

"Uh-huh," Mason said. "Let's find the light switch, Paul."

The beam from Drake's flashlight spotted a light switch. Mason reached for it, then stopped and said, "Wait a minute. This switch is already on." He clicked it twice, to no avail.

"Looks like a fuse," Drake said.

"All right," Mason told him, "keep going. Throw your flashlight down on the floor. Let's look for . . . there it is."

Drake examined the red spot on the floor and said, "Now, wait a minute, Perry. Before we go any farther you'd better tell me exactly what you're looking for. If this is . . ."

Mason jerked the flashlight out of the detective's hand and said, "If this is what I think it is, Paul, we haven't any time to waste in argument." He swung the beam of the flashlight in a circle. Drake said, "Here's another track coming out of this door."

Mason pushed open the door, and Drake said, "Oh— Oh!" as the beam of the flashlight rested on the sprawled, lifeless figure of Austin Cullens.

"Try those lights," Mason said.

Drake fumbled for the light switch, and clicked it ineffectively. "Listen, Perry," he said, "let's not leave any finger-prints around here. Let's notify the police and . . ."

"In a house of this size," Mason interrupted, "there'll be several circuits. One fuse blown out won't kill all the lights. Of course, the main switch may have been pulled, but it's more apt to be a fuse. Try some of the other rooms, Paul, until you get one where the lights are on."

Drake said, "Perry, I don't like this. Every time we touch anything we leave finger-prints."

"Don't touch things, then," Mason said shortly.

"Let me have the flashlight," Drake said.

"You'll just have to fumble around, Paul," Mason told him. "Remember, you're looking for a telephone with which to notify the police."

"And what are *you* doing?" Drake said.

"I'm also looking for a telephone," Mason told him.

"Now listen, Perry," the detective said, "when I find a telephone, I'm going to call the cops, see?"

"I know," Mason said impatiently, "that's why I'm giving you an out. You'll tell a straightforward story. As soon as you found the body, you started looking for a telephone. As soon as you found the telephone, you called the cops. Now get started."

Drake stepped out into the hallway. Mason swung the beam of the flashlight about the room and to the body of the man on the floor. He had evidently been shot, the bullet entering the left side just above the heart. The man's vest and shirt were open. His undershirt had been pulled up to disclose a chamois-skin belt, in which the flaps of several of the pockets had been raised. Apparently the belt was empty. A viscid red pool had formed beside the body. There were various red smears about the edge of this pool, as though someone bending over the body had stepped in the blood two or three times.

The room was a living room, with a large fireplace at one end, bookcases on either side, lounging chairs, a huge mahogany table, and an all-wave radio set in the corner. The floors were hardwood, waxed to a smooth sheen, with some half dozen Oriental rugs artistically placed. A top coat, scarf, hat and gloves, presumably belonging to Cullens, had been thrown hastily over the back of a chair. Mason, taking care to touch nothing, moved closer to the body, bent over, and suddenly heard a man's voice saying, "Car number sixteen, proceed at once to the intersection of Washington and Maple Streets to investigate an automobile accident. Car number thirty-two, call your station. Car fourteen, go to thirty-eight nineteen Walpole Street to see a woman about a prowler." Thereafter, the radio became silent.

Mason heard Drake's footsteps in the corridor, saw that some light was filtering in through the half-open doorway. A moment later, Drake came back and said, "Okay, Perry, I notified Homicide."

"Did you tell them I was here?" Mason asked.

"No, just told them about the body, and . . ."

He broke off as a voice from the corner of the room said, with startling clarity, "Calling car twenty-two. Proceed at once to ninety-one fifty-eight St. Rupert Boulevard. A private detective named Drake has just telephoned that the body of a murdered man is in the house. Probably the body is that of Austin Cullens. Proceed at once to the house. Hold for questioning anyone found on the premises. The homicide squad is on its way."

The message was repeated. Drake asked, "Did you turn that radio on to police calls, Perry?"

Mason shook his head and said, "You didn't need to tell them the name of the dead man, Paul."

"They asked me about it," Drake said, "asked me how I came to be here, and I told them I'd come to call on an Austin Cullens, accompanied by his lawyer."

"Give them my name?" Mason asked.

"No. I just said, 'his lawyer.'"

"That helps," Mason observed sarcastically. "You didn't need to tell them your life's history, you know. Why didn't you just say there was a corpse out here, and let it go at that."

"The man at the other end of the line didn't want it that way."

"You can always hang up a receiver," Mason pointed out.

"Yeah," Drake told him, "*you* can, but I *don't*. My license comes up for renewal next month."

"Oh, well," Mason said, "they'd have got the dope sooner or later anyway. I'm just not keen about having that information go out over the police radio. You can't tell who's listening in. How about the lights, Paul?"

"They're just off in this corner of the house. The circuit which supplies the dining room, pantry, kitchen, and stairway is okay."

"Did you leave them all on?"

"Uh-huh."

"Where was the telephone?"

"The one I found was in the dining room. I think it's an extension. There's probably one in here."

Mason swung the beam of the flashlight, and Drake said, "That's a telephone over there in the corner."

Mason said, "Uh-huh, I didn't see it. All right, Paul, call your office. A man by the name of Harry Diggers had an accident out here in front of the house an hour or so ago. He hit a Sarah Breel. He claims she stepped out from the sidewalk right in front of his car. Police held him for a while and then let him go. I want a complete statement from him, and I'd like it before the police pick him up again. Your men can get his address from the records. There's a gambling club down on East Third Street over a café known as The Golden Platter. Have a couple of men find out all they can about that. A gem broker by the name of George Trent is out somewhere on a drunk. Get men on the job to find him. Get the best description you can from people who know him. Pick up a photograph if it's at all possible. Burgle his office if you have to. He has a stringbean niece, name of Virginia. She lives at his house. It's listed in the telephone directory. Get a photograph and a description of George, and put enough men to work to find him. He'll be hanging around a place where he can get liquor and gambling in combination."

"How about women?" Drake asked.

"Perhaps women too, I don't know. Never mind that. Get busy. You'll have to hurry before the officers come."

Drake, moving with a swiftly silent efficiency which belied the gangling appearance of his arms and legs, melted back into the corridor, and a few moments later, Mason heard the muffled sound of his voice over the telephone. From the street came the sound of tires as a car slid to an abrupt stop. Mason, trying to give Drake more time at the telephone, walked out to meet the radio officers half way up the cement walk leading to the porch.

"Your name Drake?" one of the men asked.

Mason shook his head, said, "No. My name's Mason. I found the body."

"Thought your name was Drake."

"No," Mason said, "it isn't. Here, have a card." He fumbled around in a card case, gaining valuable seconds.

"What's the dope?" one of the men asked.

"I'm sure I don't know," Mason said. "I was calling on Austin Cullens, who lives here. I wanted to see him in connection with a certain business matter, about which I'd been consulted earlier in the day. I found the lights off and the door ajar. I stepped inside and found him . . ."

"The lights are on now," one of the officers interrupted, indicating the lighted windows on the right-hand corner of the house.

"That's another circuit," Mason explained. "Apparently one fuse was blown. The room where the body lies has a fuse blown out. However, it's only taken one of the circuits. I notice the radio is still on."

"Who turned on the lights in the other part of the house?" the officer asked.

"That was done," Mason said, "in order to locate a telephone."

"Okay, we'll go take a look. I thought the report came in that your name was Drake."

Mason decided it was impossible to stall any longer. "Mr. Drake," he said, "accompanied me at the time."

"Where is he now?"

"Inside."

"Why the hell didn't you say so?"

"Why," Mason said, with an expression of hurt innocence, "you didn't ask me. I came out to explain to you what you'd find."

"What's Drake doing?"

"Waiting inside."

One of the officers took Mason's arm. The other ran ahead up the sidewalk and into the house. Drake came sauntering down the corridor to meet them, a cigarette dangling from his lips. "Hello, boys," he said. "I see you got my call all right. I've notified Homicide."

"Okay," one of the officers said, "where do you fit into the picture?" Drake showed them his card and his license as a private detective. "You haven't touched anything, have you?"

"Nothing except the telephone," Drake said.

"And why the telephone?"

"I had to call Homicide, some way, didn't I?"

Mason said, "Drake was careful to avoid using the telephone in the room where the body was found. We haven't touched anything in there. The man was shot once. It looks as though robbery was the motive."

A siren screamed in the distance. One of the men said, "Okay, Jim, here comes Homicide. Let's give it a quick look before they get here. . . . Hell, it's dark in the corridor."

"That's what I told you," Mason said. "One of the fuses is blown."

"How did you see the stiff?"

"With a flashlight."

"Where's the flashlight?"

Mason took it from his pocket.

"You usually carry a flashlight with you?" the officer asked suspiciously.

"Drake does," Mason said. "It's his flashlight."

One of the officers produced a flashlight from his own pocket, played the beam around the room, brought it to rest on the corpse and said, "Dead all right."

The sirens screamed at the corner. A car skidded to a stop. Pounding feet came up the cement walk and across the porch. Sergeant Holcomb, of the homicide squad, stared at Mason. "So you're in on *this,* are you?"

"I'm in on nothing except the house," Mason told him.

"What was your lead?"

"I wanted to see Mr. Cullens on a matter of business."

"What business?"

"Something about which he'd consulted me."

"Was he a client of yours?"

"Not exactly."

"All right, then, what was the business?"

Mason said, "I was looking for a man named George

Trent, a gem expert. I had reason to believe Cullens knew something."

"What made you think so?"

"Call it a hunch if you want to," Mason said.

"I don't want to," Holcomb told him, "and it doesn't sound logical."

"All right, then," Mason said, letting anger creep into his voice, "it wasn't a hunch, and it isn't logical. So what?"

Holcomb said to one of the officers, "Take these two guys into a separate room. Don't talk with them and don't let them talk with you. Don't let them do any telephoning. Don't let them touch anything. And, above all, don't let them do any rubber-necking around. . . . Okay, boys, go through the house. We'll take the room in here. . . . Make sure the men are posted at the back . . . Okay, let's go."

Mason and the detective were escorted into the dining room by an officer who indicated seats with silent hostility, and continued to watch over them in sullen silence while Mason heard steps on the stairs, the pound of feet in the upper corridors, heard additional cars roar down the boulevard to come to a stop in front of the house, and men pell-mell up the cement walk to the front door.

It was twenty minutes later when Sergeant Holcomb descended on the pair for questioning, and at the end of fifteen minutes' questioning he knew no more than when he had started. "All right," he said, "you birds can go. But there's something about this I don't like."

"I don't know of anything else we could have done to cooperate," Mason said. "Drake notified the police the minute we arrived and found the body."

"Where were you just before you came here?" Holcomb asked.

"Immediately before I arrived here," Mason said, "it happened that I was in a drug store telephoning."

"To whom?"

"To my secretary, if you want to know."

"About what?"

"Trying to find out the address of a certain client."

"This address?"

"No, it was another client."

"Who?"

"It has nothing to do with this case," Mason said, "and, as it happens, I didn't get the address."

"Then how'd you happen to come here?"

"I wanted to see Cullens."

"And you decided you wanted to see him right after you found out you couldn't get that other address?"

Mason said, "As a matter of fact, I looked up Cullens' address in the telephone book in the drug store."

Holcomb said, "Okay, you birds can go. . . . And remember, Drake, your license is coming up one of these days."

Mason said, "I resent that as an attempt at intimidation. Drake has been entirely courteous throughout this entire matter. Both of us have answered every question you've asked."

"Yeah, I know," Holcomb said, "but somehow I have a feeling I haven't asked the right questions."

"Then go ahead and ask the right questions," Mason told him.

"How the hell can I when I don't know what they are?"

"Well," Mason said irritably, "how the hell can I answer them when you don't ask them?"

Holcomb jerked his thumb to the door. "On your way," he said, "and don't just happen to stumble on any more corpses before morning. There *is* such a thing as a private detective being altogether too damned efficient, if you get what I mean, Drake."

Drake started to say something, but Mason interrupted. "Is it your pleasure," he asked, "that in the future Drake refrain from notifying the homicide department of any corpses he may stumble on?"

Holcomb's face darkened. "You know what I mean," he said. "Get started."

The officers ushered them past a corridor, which, by this time, was well filled with newspaper photographers, a representative from the coroner's office, and half a dozen plainclothes officers. Half way to the car, Drake said vindictively, "Damn him! He'll try to give me a black eye with the Board of Prison Directors when my license renewal comes up."

Mason laughed. "He's just being nasty on general principles," he said. "He can't block your license except for cause, and he can't get any cause. Try to be respectful to a man like that, and he keeps pushing you around. Stand up to him and tell him where he gets off at."

"Just the same," Drake said, "let's not find any more corpses."

"Okay," Mason agreed.

"Where to now?"

"Where we can telephone your office and find out what's in the wind. If nothing startling has developed, we go down to The Golden Platter and try to get some information before the police frighten those birds to cover."

Drake said, "That's the thing I don't like about your business, Perry. You're always trying to beat the police to something."

"That's the way I protect my clients," Mason said.

"And some day it's gonna cost me my license."

"On what grounds?"

"On the ground that I'm withholding information from the police."

"Just what information do you have that the police should know about?" Mason asked.

"Nothing. But I have a hunch *you* have."

"All right," Mason said grimly. "Try not to be a mind reader, then. In other words, Paul, as your attorney, my best advice to you is to not only act dumb, but be dumb and follow directions."

Drake said, "Okay, Perry, I'm dumb."

_____

5

Mason drove around the block, looking for a parking space. "Tell me, Paul," he said, "just what you've found out about them."

"Understand, Perry," Drake apologized, "the information's a little sketchy. After all, my men only had a few minutes. . . ."

"Sure, never mind all that stuff," Mason said. "Give me what you have."

"Well, in the beginning, it started out to be a legitimate restaurant. They called it The Golden Plate then. They changed the name to The Golden Platter about the time they opened up the gambling joint upstairs."

"Just the two of them?"

"That's right, Bill Golding and Eva Tannis. Lately they've been passing as husband and wife, but apparently they aren't married."

"Any gambling experience before?" Mason asked.

"Lots of it. Golding ran a place in San Francisco, and then was floorman at a big casino in Mexico. Then he came back here, apparently broke, but always intending to open up a gambling place as soon as he got the funds."

"How about the girl?"

"Eva Tannis was a come-on girl in the San Francisco place where Golding worked. You know, she gives the boys lucky hunches and a few drinks. Makes them feel like gay young blades. Pulls a little sex stuff and imbues the boys with the idea that faint heart never won fair lady. Then they feel their oats, and start plunging on the gambling table."

"And it's all fixed beforehand?" Mason asked, turning the corner to the right and preparing to edge into a parking place.

"No, that end of it's on the up-and-up. All the gambling house wants is to get the play."

"What if the boys win?" Mason asked.

"Then she's already in strong with them. She keeps them playing until the house wins it back. In case the sucker quits while he's still winner, she goes out with him, keeps in touch with him, makes a date for a couple of nights later, and steers him back to the joint. By that time, he's cold and imbued with the idea that he has to buck the game in order to get anywhere. Then it's all over."

Mason, looking the neighborhood over, said, "Doesn't look like much of a soup-and-fish trade, Paul."

"It isn't," the detective told him. "It's a joint. They're trying to make a stake for a bigger place."

"Okay," Mason said, looking at the numbers, "let's go."

They detoured past a bedraggled blonde who held down the cashier's desk, and Drake indicated a door which opened on a stairway. There was no protest as they climbed up a flight of dark stairs to a feebly illuminated corridor. The front end of the corridor was apparently fitted up as the office of a rooming house. There was a little counter, a register, a call bell on the table, and a sign saying, "Ring for the Manager." Drake smacked his hands down smartly on the bell button and said to the lawyer, "We'd better flash a roll and act a little bit hilarious."

The lawyer pulled a wallet from his pocket, leaned against the counter, and started counting money with the grave dignity of a drunk man trying to act sober. A door opened and a man said, "What do you boys want?"

Mason looked up at him and grinned. Drake motioned vaguely down the corridor and said, "Action. Wha'd'yuh s'pose?"

"I don't exactly place you," the man said dubiously.

Mason lunged against Drake, pushing the bills back into his wallet. "C'mon, Paul. The guy don't want us. Let's go back the other place."

Drake said, "Not'n your life. This joint owes me a hun'erd forty bucks. I'm gonna col'ect."

The man behind the counter said, "Okay, boys, go on in. Second door to the left."

They walked down what was apparently the corridor of an ordinary rooming house, turned the knob of the second door on the left. Mason heard the sound of an electric buzzer, then a bolt shot back and a man opened the door.

What had, at one time, apparently been a series of rooms, had been joined into a large room. There was some pretense of g.ving it a veneer of elegance. The painted board floors were covered with brightly colored rugs. There were cheap oil paintings on the walls, but they were illuminated after the manner of masterpieces, with little individual electric lights shielded in chromium cylinders. There were two roulette tables, a crap table, two games of 21, and a wheel of fortune. A bar at the far end of the room was elaborately fitted with mirrors and subdued lights. There were probably thirty or forty men in the place, Mason judged, and perhaps fifteen women, of whom seven or eight were wearing backless evening gowns. Nearly all of the men were in business suits. Mason noticed but two dinner jackets. "Let's not waste any time," Mason said to Drake. "We've got this far, let's go the rest of the way."

"Okay," Drake said.

The two men walked over to the bar. Mason slapped a five-dollar bill on the counter and said, "A couple of Old Fashioneds, and tell Bill Golding we want to talk with him."

"Who does?" the bartender asked.

"We do."

"Who are you?"

Mason sl d one of his business cards across the moist mahogany bar. "Take that to him," he said, "but don't forget the Old Fashioneds."

The bartender nodded, summoned a floorman and spoke to him in an undertone, his eyes on Mason and Drake. He handed the card to the floorman, who looked at it, scowled, and vanished through a door. The bartender mixed up the Old Fashioneds and was just serving them when the floorman returned and nodded at the bartender, then stationed himself by the door.

"Okay," the bartender said, "Golding will see you." He made change out of the five dollars. Mason said to Paul Drake, "Cover this end, Paul. Keep your eyes open." He left his liquor and walked across the room. The floorman opened the door. Mason pushed his way through heavy green hangings and into an office. A man stared coldly at him from behind a desk. A woman, some years younger, her contours displayed by a clinging blue evening gown, stood near the corner of the desk. Her hair was glossy black and filled with highlights. Her full red lips held no smile. Her brilliant black eyes blazed with emotions she strove to suppress. Full-throated, well-nourished, she seemed seductively full of life, in striking contrast to the man who sat behind the desk, his waxy skin stretched so tightly across his prominent cheekbones that there hardly seemed enough left to cover the teeth, which showed in that ghastly grin seen on starving people. Against the pallor of his skin, just below where it crossed his cheekbones, were twin patches of brilliant coloring. His eyes were as dark as those of the woman, but where hers sparkled with vitality, his glittered feverishly.

"Sit down," the man said in a husky voice.

Mason sat down on a leather davenport and crossed his long legs in front of him. In the seconds of silence which followed, it became apparent that the man was not going to introduce the woman, equally apparent that she did not intend to depart. Mason took his cigarette case from his pocket, glanced at the woman and asked, "Mind if I smoke?"

"On the contrary," she said, "I'll have one with you."

She moved over to Mason's side, the muscles of her well-developed figure sliding smoothly under the blue satin of her evening gown.

"Don't get up," she said.

Mason struck a match, and she steadied his hand in hers as she held the flame to the cigarette.

Bill Golding, behind the desk, husked, "Okay, what do you want?"

"Where are the stones you got from George Trent?" Mason asked.

The man behind the desk moved uneasily. The red patches of color on his cheeks intensified. "So," he said, "you're going to sing *that* song, are you?"

"Take it easy, Bill," the woman remarked, seating herself beside Mason, her bare arm propped on the back of the davenport, her body so close that Mason could detect the faint scent of perfume behind her ears.

Golding said, "I didn't get any stones from George Trent."

"A couple of hours ago—perhaps three hours ago," Mason went on, "Austin Cullens was up here."

"I don't know any Austin Cullens."

"He's a big man," Mason said, "around six feet, somewhere in the forties, curly chestnut hair, a big diamond ring and a diamond scarf pin."

"Haven't seen him."

"He'd have been up here, asking questions about George Trent and talking about redeeming gems Trent had left with you."

"He hasn't been here. No man like that has been in here."

"I think he has," Mason said calmly.

"I'm lying, is that it?"

Mason grinned mirthlessly. "Let's say you're mistaken," he said.

"Well, I'm not lying and I'm not mistaken. The way you came in is the way out. You'd better start while you can still go under your own power."

Mason said, "Nice radio you have there on your desk."

"*I* like it," Golding said.

"Why not turn that switch," Mason said, "and listen to some music?"

"I'm not demonstrating radios, thank you."

"The reason I asked," Mason went on, in a conversational voice, "is because I notice that it's turned over to the short wave dial and the hand points to police calls.

Perhaps you heard the announcement that Cullens had been murdered."

"I don't know what you're talking about," Golding said.

Mason maintained his calmly conversational tone. "Cullens stopped to telephone while he was on his way up here. Perhaps that will change the situation some."

"You're nuts!" Golding said.

"Of course," Mason went on, "I can appreciate *your* position. Running a place of this kind, you're not anxious to attract any publicity. With the police investigating the murder, you'd prefer to be dealt out."

"Go on," Golding said with a sneer, "you're singing a solo. Don't think I'm going to make it a duet."

"Of course," Mason remarked, "if you wanted to be friendly, we could talk things over. If you didn't, I could telephone my friend, Sergeant Holcomb, on Homicide, and give him a tip. He's accused me of holding out lately. This would square things a lot."

"Go ahead," Golding said. "See if I care. Telephone the whole damn force if you want to."

"No," Mason said casually, "Holcomb would be enough. He'd come up here and start asking questions— not only of you two, but of some of the customers in the front room. Perhaps they saw Cullens go in or come out."

The man behind the desk stared straight ahead, with steady, expressionless eyes.

Mason laughed and said, "That hurt, didn't it?"

Golding moistened his thin lips with the tip of his tongue. His eyes shifted uneasily to glance questioningly at the woman who sat at Mason's side.

She said, in her full-toned, throaty voice, "All right, sweetheart, he's got us."

"He's bluffing," Golding said.

"He may be bluffing," she retorted, "but he's bluffing with the high hand "

Mason, without taking his eyes from Golding, said over his shoulder, "Thanks."

"Don't thank me," she told him. "Thank your luck.

You'd better go out and play roulette. You're getting the breaks tonight."

Golding said, "All right, Mason, he came here. He said he wanted to see me. He came in and pulled that stuff about me having picked up some stones from George Trent. I told him he was nuts, that George Trent hadn't been in here for two months. We argued for a while, and then he got up and went out."

"That was all?" Mason asked.

"That was all."

"That doesn't coincide with the facts the way I have them," Mason said.

"All right," Golding told him, "suppose you tell your story."

"Cullens," Mason said, "found out that you had some stones that you'd picked up from Trent. He told you they didn't belong to Trent. You had an argument about whether you could hold them if Trent didn't have title to them. You had about six thousand tied up in them. Cullens offered to pay off half the indebtedness and take over the stones. You didn't like that. So Cullens showed you you were in a spot because Trent didn't own the stones. You didn't want any lawsuits. You took the money and gave Cullens the stones. Cullens went out and someone bumped him off."

"Where'd you get that pipe dream?" Golding asked.

"A little bird told me."

Golding said, "They have open seasons on birds sometimes."

"Do you make the game laws?"

"I might," Golding said menacingly.

"Bill!" the woman exclaimed. "Shut up!"

Mason puffed at his cigarette. "Someone declared an open season on Cullens," he said.

Golding started to say something. The woman screamed at him, "You shut up, Bill Golding. You talk too damn much!"

"Or not enough," Mason said.

"Well, all he's going to," the woman insisted. "You've got our story—all of it."

"That story," Mason said, "doesn't hold together."

"Try and pull it apart," Golding invited.

Mason said, "You were tipped off Cullens was killed. You decided it'd be fine if he hadn't been here. You tipped off your employees. You didn't figure you'd get such prompt action. When I came up and offered to have the homicide squad go through the customers in the place, you knew you were licked. So you decided to admit he'd been here, but swear that was all. You figure no one alive can contradict you."

"That's your story," Golding said. "I've told mine and I'm sticking to it. You start pushing me around and I'll make things hot for *you*."

Mason laughed sarcastically and waved his hand in the general direction of the gambling room. "The way you're organized," he said, "you couldn't make anything hot for anybody."

The woman at Mason's side leaned closer. "Why don't you boys get along?" she asked.

"I'm willing to get along," Mason said, "but I want the low-down."

"All right, you've got it."

"Were *you* here when Cullens was here?" Mason inquired, turning toward her.

"No."

"Who was?"

"I don't know. Was anyone else here, Billy?" she asked the man behind the desk.

His grin was triumphant. "No one," he said, "just Cullens on that side of the desk and me on this."

Mason got to his feet. "Okay," he said casually, "if that's the way you feel about it. Remember that you were the last person to see Cullens alive. If Cullens tried to get hard with you and make a squawk which would get you in trouble, there's some chance you might have followed him and bumped him off."

Golding's face became distorted with rage. "If I bumped him off," he said, "I did it with a six-shooter."

"Meaning what?" Mason asked.

"Meaning there'd be five more . . ." The woman started for the desk, her eyes blazing.

Bill Golding's face suddenly became an expressionless mask. The woman said thickly, "That's all of it. It won't do you any good to stick around. The party's over."

Mason said, "Rather nice hooch you serve out there, Golding."

"It wouldn't have been so good if I'd known who they were getting it for," Golding snapped.

Mason said, "That line isn't going to get you anywhere."

The lawyer marched through the door, picked up Drake in the casino and went down the stairs, and out through the restaurant. "Now what?" Drake asked.

Mason said, "Cullens was here—they're not talking. Call your office, Paul. Shoot two or three men down here. Sew this place up tight. I want Golding and the woman tailed when they leave, and I want the names of some of the customers who were up there, to use as witnesses."

Drake said, "Hell, Perry, we can't go busting into a place like that and ask the people who . . ."

"Watch the customers as they come out," Mason said. "Follow them to their automobiles and get the license numbers."

"They won't talk," the detective objected. "Once they get home, they'll swear they never even heard of the joint."

"Be your age, Paul," the lawyer said impatiently. "Pick the prosperous guys who are with the flashy wrens about half their ages. Those birds will do anything to avoid publicity. You get them staked out and I'll do the questioning. Let them tell *me* they never heard of the joint, and I'll read 'em a riot act."

Drake said, "Yes, I guess we *could* do that."

"Well, get started," Mason told him. "And, while you're about it, tell your outfit to look up an Ione Bedford, who's a friend of Austin Cullens. Get all the dope on her. Have one of your men tell Harry Diggers he's representing an insurance company and get a written

statement out of Diggers. Get an inventory of the stuff
that was in that handbag Mrs. Breel was carrying."

"Okay," Drake said, "I'll get started. I can get some
operatives who know Bill Golding and Eva Tannis. That'll
release me so I can go back to the office and direct things
from there."

"I'll watch the place while you telephone," Mason told
him. "Make it snappy."

Drake nodded and walked to the corner, where he telephoned his office from a cigar store. When he returned,
Mason said, "Okay, Paul, I'm on my way. Keep this
place sewed up."

Drake nodded, fumbled in his pocket for a cigarette
and said, "It's sewed, Perry."

6

Mason unlocked his car, started to get in, then stopped to
stare in frowning concentration at the sidewalk. Abruptly
he slammed the car door shut, and walked into an all-
night restaurant where he found a telephone. He thumbed
through the telephone directory, called a number and
said, "I want to talk with Dr. Charles Gifford—tell him
Perry Mason's calling on a matter of the greatest importance."

He heard steps receding from the telephone. A moment
later. Dr. Gifford's voice said, "Okay, Mason, what is it?"

Mason said, "A woman by the name of Sarah Breel,
down at the ambulance receiving station at headquarters,
broken leg, possible fracture of the skull, and internal injuries. She's unconscious. The cops are laying for her. You
know how they are. They don't give a damn about the
patient. All they want is information. They'll start ham-
mering questions at her as soon as she flickers an eyelid.
Officially, I don't appear as attorney, so I can't enter into

the picture. No one's hired a private physician for her. I'm hiring you. You don't need to tell anyone who's paying the bill. Move in with a couple of special nurses. Move her, if she can be moved, to a private room in the best hospital in town. If she can't be moved, see that she has the best accommodations money can buy. Keep nurses with her every minute of the time. Keep in touch with the nurses. The minute she becomes conscious, I want you on the job."

"Any particular instructions?" Dr. Gifford asked, in a crisply professional voice.

"I don't think I need to give any, do I?" Mason asked.

Dr. Gifford said, still in that swiftly efficient voice. "Without having seen her, Mason, I would say that she's suffering from a nerve shock; that as soon as she regains consciousness, it will be imperative to keep her quiet. That she can't be questioned for several days without seriously jeopardizing her chances of recovery. I'd want her kept absolutely quiet, with *no* visitors."

Mason said, "I think you're a hell of a good doctor. . . . If possible, get red-headed nurses."

"Why the red-headed nurses?" Dr. Gifford asked.

"Oh, nothing," Mason said, "only in case the dicks should start getting rough it's always nice to have a red-headed nurse on the job. You can't bully a red-head."

"I know a couple who'll do fine," Dr. Gifford told him. "One of them's a red-head, the other's a brunette. They're competent professionally, and you can't bully them. You know, Mason, people who are suffering from severe concussions have to be kept *very* quiet."

Mason said, "You're what I'd call a damn good doctor," and hung up.

He telephoned the Drake Detective Agency and asked for messages. The man at the telephone said, "Your secretary telephoned, Mr. Mason, and said she'd located the party you desired and was carrying out your instructions."

Mason thanked him, hung up and drove directly to the loft building at 913 South Marsh Street, where George Trent had his office and shop. Mason rang for the janitor, whose surliness changed into smiling co-operation as Mason slipped a folded bill into the man's palm.

"Trent?" he said. "Oh, yes. He has an office on the fifth floor. The niece went up about five minutes ago."

"Virginia?" Mason asked.

"I think that's her name. She's a tall, thin girl."

"I want to see her," Mason said. "Let's go."

The janitor took him up in the elevator, stepped out into the corridor to indicate a lighted doorway. "That's the office," he said, "down there on the left."

Mason thanked him and pounded his way down the corridor. He knocked on the door, and Virginia Trent said, "Who is it, please?"

"Mason," he told her.

"Oh, just a minute, Mr. Mason."

She threw back a bar and opened the door. Mason entered a room fitted up as an office, a small desk at one side of the room, filing cases, a stenographer's desk and chair on the other. A door opened from the side of the room, another from the back. Virginia Trent was wearing a light tweed overcoat with deep side pockets. Her hands were encased in light weight tan kid gloves. A brown hat was pulled down low, to slant slightly over her right ear, balancing a bird wing of bright colors.

"What are you doing here?" she asked.

Mason watched her as she closed the door and slipped the bar into place. "Just dropped in to have a chat with you," he said.

"What about?"

Mason looked around for a chair. She indicated the chair at the desk. Mason looked across to where her large dark brown purse reposed on the stenographer's desk. "Been typing?" he asked.

"I just got here."

"Where've you been?" Mason asked casually. "I've been trying to get you."

"I went to a picture show," she told him, "I wanted to get my mind off Aunt Sarah. You know, when you continually brood over anything, you lose your mental perspective. I think it's better to go to a picture show and give your mind a rest. Don't *you* ever do that when you're working on a case, Mr. Mason?"

"No," he said grinning, "I don't dare to take the time for fear someone might steal a march on me. Was it a good show?"

"Pretty fair. . . . Mr. Mason, I want to ask you something."

"Go ahead," Mason told her.

"What's a lie detector?" she asked.

Mason studied her and failed to find any expression in her eyes. "Why the question?" he asked.

"I wanted to know, that's all."

"Any particular reason?"

"Well," she said, "I'm interested from a psychological standpoint, that's all."

Mason said, "It's really not much more than an instrument for taking blood pressure, the theory being that when a witness gets ready to lie, he sort of mentally braces himself, and that shows in a change of blood pressure, which, in turn, shows on a needle. Telling the truth is easy and effortless. Telling a lie involves mental effort."

"Are they of any real value?" she asked.

"Yes," Mason said, "their value, however, depends on the skill of the man who does the questioning. In other words, the machine registers what you might call a psychic change in the individual. The skill of the questioner accentuates those psychic changes and makes them significant."

She looked at him steadily and said, "Mr. Mason, do you know something? I believe I could beat the lie detector."

"Why should you?" he asked.

"Just as a psychological experiment," she said. "I'd like to try."

"What," Mason asked, "would you like to lie about?"

"Oh, anything."

"For instance, about what you were doing here?"

Her eyes widened. "Why," she said, "I came up here to write a few personal letters. The typewriter was here and I thought I'd tap out a couple of letters to my friends."

"How long have you been here?"

"I don't know, five minutes or ten minutes."

"But you hadn't started writing when I knocked?"

"No."

"What were you doing?"

She laughed and said, "What is this, Mr. Mason, some sort of a third-degree?"

"Were you," he asked, "thinking about beating the lie detector?"

"Don't be silly, Mr. Mason. I just asked you that because I'm interested in the psychological significance. . . . You said *you* wanted to see *me,* Mr. Mason. What did you want to see me about?"

"I wanted to tell you about your aunt," he said, watching her narrowly.

"About Aunt Sarah?" He nodded.

"Oh, dear," she said, "I knew it. I had the most awful premonition all the time I was in the show. I felt certain that it had happened."

"That what had happened?" Mason asked.

"That she'd been arrested, of course."

"For what?"

"For shoplifting," she said, "or . . . or about the diamonds."

Mason said, "I'd like to find out something about the Bedford diamonds. Can you give me a description of them?"

"Yes," she said, "Uncle George had some notes. . . . But tell me about Aunt Sarah. What happened? Is she arrested?"

"She was hit by an automobile," Mason said.

"An automobile!" the girl exclaimed.

Mason nodded. "Out on St. Rupert Boulevard," he said, "near Ninety-First Street. Does that mean anything to you?"

"Way out there?" the girl asked. "Why, what would Aunt Sarah be doing out there?"

"That's where Cullens lives, isn't it?" Mason asked.

She knitted her forehead in thought. "Yes, I guess it is.

Wait a minute, I have his address here in the files, Mr. Mason, and . . ."

"You don't need to look at it," Mason told her. "Cullens lives out there. That is, he *did* live out there."

"Has he moved?" she asked.

"No," Mason said, "he was killed."

"Killed!"

"Yes, shot in the left side with a revolver."

"What are you leading up to, Mr. Mason? Please tell me."

Mason said, "Your aunt stepped out on the street right in front of an automobile. The automobile hit her and broke her leg and fractured her skull. There are possible internal injuries. There was blood on her left shoe. That blood didn't come from any injuries she'd received. Moreover, there was blood on the sole of the shoe, indicating that she'd . . ." He broke off as the girl swung half around and toppled into a chair, her face white, her lips a pale pink. "Take it easy," Mason cautioned. She tried to smile. "Any whiskey in this place?" the lawyer asked.

She indicated the desk. Mason jerked open the upper right-hand drawer, and found a bottle half filled with whiskey. He unscrewed the stopper and handed it to Virginia Trent. She drank awkwardly from the bottle, trying to suck the liquid from the container, and spilling some down the front of her dress as she removed the bottle from her lips, making a wry grimace.

Mason said, "You'll have to learn to drink out of a bottle. Let some air into it. Like this."

She watched him and smiled wanly. "You do it very expertly," she said. "Go on, Mr. Mason, I can take it. Tell me the rest of it."

"There isn't any rest of it," Mason said. "Your aunt is unconscious. They found a gun, a bunch of diamonds, some silk stockings which had been stolen from another department store, and some knitting in your aunt's bag."

"Will Aunty—will she . . . recover?"

"I think so," Mason said. "I have the best doctor in the city on the job. I've taken it on myself to order special nurses." Her eyes thanked him.

"Now then," Mason said, "there were five diamonds in your aunt's handbag. They were wrapped in tissue paper. They looked to me as though they might be the Bedford diamonds."

"There were five in that collection," she said. "Where . . . where did Aunt Sarah . . ."

"That," Mason said, "is an open question. Cullens had a chamois-skin belt next to his skin. Someone had ripped that belt open and probably taken the contents."

"But where would Cullens have got Mrs. Bedford's stones?" she asked.

"Probably," Mason said, "from a gambling joint known as The Golden Platter. He telephoned Mrs. Bedford that your uncle had pawned the stones there for six thousand dollars; that he was going to bring pressure to bear and try to redeem them for three. In the meantime, the gamblers didn't like the idea of having pressure brought to bear."

"But," Virginia said, "Aunty could never have taken those stones from Mr. Cullens. He might have given them to her, but . . ."

"If she didn't get them from Cullens," Mason said, "she probably got them from the safe."

"Well, she *might* have done that," Virginia Trent said. "I never thought of looking in that bag of hers. It's a regular suitcase. She carries all kinds of stuff in it."

"She didn't have it with her in the department store, did she?" Mason asked.

"No, not this noon. She left it in the automobile."

"She'd hardly have done that if it had five big diamonds in it, would she?"

"Well, you can't tell. . . . After all, if Aunty had intended to do any shoplifting, it might have been the safest place for them."

"Yes," Mason said slowly, "I can see that. . . . It's a thought. What's behind that door, Virginia, the shop?"

She nodded.

Mason opened the door, looked into the dark interior. "You seem to have quite a lot of space here," he said.

"Yes," she admitted, "it's more than Uncle George really has use for, but he needs more room than he could get in an office building."

"Where's the light switch?" Mason asked.

"There isn't any," she said. "You turn on each light as you want it by pulling on the drop-cord which hangs from the light. That keeps the men from wasting electricity. . . . Here, I have a flashlight if you want to find the drop-cord."

She opened her brown leather handbag and took out a nickel-plated flashlight some six inches long by half an inch in diameter.

"That's a cute little gadget," Mason said. "Carry it all the time?"

"Yes," she said. "It . . . it comes in handy."

Mason switched on the flashlight, and, by its aid, located the drop-cord on the first light. He was moving over toward it when the beam from the flashlight, sliding over a pile of packing cases in a corner, caught a patch of color. Mason paused to center the beam on the discolored wood.

"What's this?" he asked.

"What?"

"This big pile of packing cases," Mason said. "The top one has a . . . Never mind, I'll take a look myself."

Holding the flashlight in his left hand, Mason walked over to the corner and examined the reddish-brown stain which had seeped out to stain the boards. The lawyer sniffed the air, then stood a small box on end and climbed up on it.

The box swayed under the lawyer's weight. Before he could step down, it buckled under him with a crashing sound. Mason flung out his hand to catch his balance, and caught the edge of the large packing case on top of the pile. A moment later, the entire pile of cases tottered precariously.

"Look out!" Virginia Trent screamed from the doorway.

Mason flung himself to one side. The big packing box slid down the pile, lit with a crash on one corner, and spilled out the inert body of a man, which slumped to the floor, where it lay, indistinct in the half-light, a grotesque sprawl of death.

Virginia Trent stared, then started to scream, shrill, hysterical screams which cut through the silence of the building.

Mason moved toward her. "Shut up!" he said. "Help me find that drop-cord."

He had dropped the flashlight in his fall, and now groped, with outstretched hands, searching for the cord which controlled the light. Virginia Trent backed away from him, as though, in some manner, associating him with that which lay on the floor. Her eyes were wide and staring. Her mouth formed a great dark circle as she continued to scream.

Mason heard feet in the corridor, heard someone pounding at the door.

"Shut up, you little fool!" Mason said, jumping toward her. "Can't you see . . ."

She ran screaming back into the outer office. The pound of fists on the door became louder. Virginia Trent backed into a corner. Someone knocked out the glass panel in the door, reached in through the jagged break in the glass and turned the knob.

Mason stood facing the door as Sergeant Holcomb twisted back the knob. "What the hell's coming off here?" he asked.

Mason jerked his head toward the shop. "I don't know. There's something out there you'd better look at, Sergeant."

Virginia Trent continued to scream. Sergeant Holcomb said, "What's eating her?"

"Having hysterics," Mason said.

Virginia Trent pointed toward the shop, tried to control herself, and couldn't. Mason moved toward her and said, "There, there, kid, take it easy."

She recoiled from him in horror, flung her arms around Sergeant Holcomb and clung to him, trembling and shaking.

"What the hell have you been trying to do?" Holcomb demanded of Mason.

Mason said, "Be your age, Sergeant. The kid's upset. There's a body in the other room."

"A body!"

Mason nodded.

"Whose?"

Mason said, "I wouldn't know. It was stuffed in a packing case on the very top of a pile. I saw a stain which looked suspicious. I climbed up on a box and started to investigate. The box gave way. I grabbed at the packing case, and the whole pile toppled over. The body fell out. It's half dark in there. She started to have hysterics and I tried to quiet her down."

Holcomb said, "Let's take a look."

Virginia Trent clung to him in a frenzy of fear. Holcomb fought against the thin arms which clamped so rigidly around his neck. "Take it easy," he said. "Snap out of it. . . . Hell, you're drunk!"

"No, she isn't drunk," Mason said. "There's some whiskey in the desk. She fainted when I told her about her aunt, and I gave her some whiskey."

"When was that?"

"Just a minute ago."

"The janitor says you just came," Holcomb grudgingly admitted. "Which drawer's the whiskey in?"

"The upper right."

Holcomb opened the drawer, took out the bottle of whiskey, then stopped, peered farther in the drawer, reached in and pulled out a gun. "What's this?" he asked.

Mason, inspecting it, said, "I'd say it was a thirty-eight caliber revolver."

Holcomb said, "Here, help me hold this girl's arm while we pour some hooch down her. She won't let go of me."

The girl screamed with fear as Mason approached her.

"Seems to think you're responsible for her troubles," Holcomb said.

"Shut up!" Mason told him. "She's nuts. Here, Virginia, drink some of this. . . . Can't you see, she's having crazy hysterics." She turned her head from side to side, fighting against the proffered whiskey. Mason said, "It's the only way. Hold her on that side, Sergeant. It's a good thing she has gloves on and can't scratch." Between them, they forced a generous draught of whiskey down her throat. She choked, sputtered, and started to cough. "Anyway," Mason said, "that'll make her quit screaming. Come on, Virginia, buck up. You've got to take it."

The janitor stood in the doorway. "What's the matter?" he asked.

Holcomb said, "Take charge of this girl," and half pushed Virginia Trent over to his arms. She clung to the janitor as she had clung to Sergeant Holcomb. Holcomb and Mason entered the shop and groped for the drop-cord, found it and switched an overhead incandescent into blazing brilliance.

Mason said, "I presume that's George Trent. He's evidently been dead for a while."

Holcomb called to the janitor, "Hey, you! Come in here and take a look at this fellow and see if you can identify him."

As the janitor moved toward the door, Virginia Trent released her hold, dropped into the stenographer's chair at the typewriter desk, put her head on her arms and sobbed violently.

The janitor stared, open-mouthed. "That's George Trent," he said simply.

Holcomb moved toward the telephone, reached over the girl's shaking shoulders to pick up the instrument, dialed headquarters and said, "Homicide. . . . This is Holcomb. We have another one out here at nine thirteen South Marsh Street. This time it's George Trent. Come on out."

He hung up the telephone and said to Mason, "Show me where he was."

Mason indicated the pile of packing boxes. "I heard them fall just as I was getting out of the elevator," Holcomb admitted. "How did you know he was there?"

"I didn't," Mason said. "I happened to notice that peculiar reddish-brown stain which had seeped through the crack in the bottom of the packing case. I climbed on a box. The box collapsed. I grabbed at the packing case, and the whole pile came down."

"Where was he?"

"Jammed in that big packing case."

"Where was it?"

"Up on the very top of the pile."

Sergeant Holcomb inspected the packing case and said, "He was evidently shoved in there right after he'd been shot."

"And then put up at the top of the pile," Mason said.

Holcomb nodded. "That was because they didn't have a cover for the packing case, and they didn't want him discovered."

Mason said, "It's a cinch he'd be discovered there sooner or later."

"Later," Holcomb said, "not sooner. The man who killed him was sparring for time."

He stood staring moodily down at the body for several seconds, and then said musingly, "At that, it's a hell of a place to leave a body."

"Are you," Mason asked, "telling me?"

There was silence for several seconds, a silence which was broken only by the sobbing of Virginia Trent. Then Mason said, "Take a look under his shirt, Sergeant. See if there's a chamois-skin belt with some stones in it."

Sergeant Holcomb said acidly, "I'll make my investigation after the coroner arrives. If you want any further information, Mason, you can get it by reading the newspapers."

"You mean you don't want me to stick around?" Mason asked.

Holcomb considered for a moment, then said, "No. The janitor tells me you went in just a minute before I did. I heard the packing cases upset as I got out of the elevator, then heard the girl start to scream. I guess this is once I can give you a clean bill of health, and something seems to tell me I can get a lot more information out of this young woman if you're not hanging around giving her advice."

"She's hysterical," Mason said.

"She'll get over it."

"It'd be a shame to question her now. You'll make a nervous wreck of her."

"What was she doing here?" Sergeant Holcomb wanted to know.

"She works here off and on. It's her job."

"Yeah. What was she working on here this time of night? . . . When you come right down to it, Mason, how did *you* know she was going to be here?"

"I didn't," Mason said. "I just dropped in. She'd been at a picture show, and came up here to write some letters."

"What letters?"

"I don't know. Some letters she wanted to write on a typewriter."

Sergeant Holcomb jerked his thumb in the direction of the corridor door. "Okay, Mason," he said, "that's all. She talks English. I won't need an interpreter."

7

Mason rang Paul Drake's office. "Any messages for me?" he asked.

"Yes, Mr. Mason. Your secretary said to call her at the Green Room of the Maxine Hotel. She said it was important."

"Anything else?" Mason asked.

"Drake just came in. He wants to talk with you."

Mason heard the click of the connection and then Paul Drake's voice on the line. "What's the commotion down at Homicide, Perry?"

Mason said, "I dug up another body for them."

"You did!"

"Uh-huh."

"That's a break," Drake told him.

"What is?"

"That I wasn't with you. Who's the body, Perry?"

"George Trent."

Mason heard Drake's whistle of surprise. "Where was it?" the detective asked.

"In a packing case in his workshop. What had you been able to find out about him, Paul? Anything?"

"Just a description. I have men out looking for him. I'll call them in."

"Did you have a good description?"

"Yes. Fifty-two years old, six feet tall, two hundred and ten pounds, brown hair, brown eyes. . . . Tell me, Perry, are you certain it's George Trent?"

"Reasonably so," Mason said. "The niece had hysterics. The janitor identified him. The body had been jammed into a packing case. I wanted to look around some, but Holcomb kicked me out. He wanted to work on the girl while she was still hysterical. What else, Paul?"

"I have a couple of likely prospects my men picked up coming out of The Golden Platter. I'm breaking license numbers down into names and addresses."

"Get anything on Ione Bedford?" Mason asked.

Drake said, "She's at the Green Room of the Maxine Hotel with Della right now, Perry."

"Okay," Mason said, "Take advantage of her being there to have a man frisk her apartment. See what he can dig up."

"Right," Drake said. "They've moved Sarah Breel— came to the conclusion her skull wasn't fractured after all."

"Where did they move her?" Mason asked.

"The Dearborn Memorial Hospital."

"Was she conscious?" Mason asked.

"I gathered not, but aside from possible internal injuries, hey've figured it down to a broken leg and a concussion. How about Trent, Perry? What killed him?"

"Apparently a bullet," Mason said. "Incidentally, there was a thirty-eight caliber revolver in the upper right-hand drawer of the desk in Trent's office. That may or may not be significant. There was also a bottle of whiskey in the drawer. I'd been feeding whiskey to the niece and told Holcomb about the bottle. He pulled out the drawer a little farther than I had and got a glimpse of the gun."

"I'll get men on the job and see what I can find out," Drake said. "Della wants you to call her."

"I'm calling," Mason told him.

He hung up the telephone, dialed the Maxine Hotel, asked for the Green Room and had Della Street paged. A few moments later her voice, a bit higher-pitched than usual, said, "How long does this keep up, Chief?"

"What keep up?" he asked.

"You know," she told him, and giggled.

"You mean following instructions with Ione Bedford?"

"That's right."

"I don't know," Mason said, "perhaps not much longer. Why?"

"The girl has ideas," Della Street said.

"Such as what?" Mason asked.

"Such as what we're doing now."

"And what are you doing now?"

"Putting drinks on the expense account," she told him.

"Stay with it," Mason told her. "The expense account can stand it." Della Street hiccoughed into the telephone. Mason couldn't tell whether she was joking or if the hiccough were genuine.

"Pardon me," she said with dignity. "Somethin' I ate . . . Maybe the expense account can stand it, but I can't."

"Hold everything," Mason told her; "I'm coming up."

"You've heard about the music, haven't you, Chief?"

"What about the music?"

"Goes round 'n round," Della Street said, and hung up.

Mason drove to the Maxine, entered the Green Room, and found Della Street, Ione Bedford and three men sitting at a table. Mason tried to make the meeting appear casual. "Well, well, well," he said, "what have we here? . . . And, Mrs. Bedford. This is indeed a pleasure."

Ione Bedford grinned up at him. "Are you," she asked, "telling me?"

"Sit down, Chief," Della Street said. "We can always crowd in one more chair."

"It's your secretary's birthday," Mrs. Bedford explained.

A waiter brought up a chair. Mason sat down at the table. The men nodded to him without enthusiasm. No one performed any introductions. Della Street fidgeted about in her seat, looking around for the waiter. "Well," she said, "I've just about reached my capacity. I'd better pay my check and get out." She opened her purse, fumbled in the interior, opened a coin purse, and her face showed consternation. "Good gosh!" she said. "I came away without my billfold, just my coin purse."

Mason started to reach for his pocket, but checked himself as Della Street kicked his shins under the table. Dance music started. One of the men said, "You'll excuse me, I'm dancing this one with a girl from San Francisco." Della Street caught the waiter's eye. Mason heard the scraping of chairs in a general exodus. Della Street grinned delightedly and pulled a roll of bills from her purse.

Mrs. Bedford said, "Now, was *that* nice."

"I had to get rid of them some way," Della said. "The boss wants to talk business."

"Who were they?" Mason asked.

"Just table lizards," Della Street said. "They come over and dance, and drink and go away, and come back. It's a racket, you know, circulating around and looking 'em over, but not getting stuck for anything." She returned the bills to her purse.

"You could have been more tactful about it," Ione Bedford said to Della Street. "One of the men hadn't had a chance to ask for my telephone number yet." She giggled.

Mason said, "That's what comes of letting you two girls get on the loose. Come on, Della, we're going places."

The waiter moved over to the table. "Something?" he asked.

"Yes," Della Street said, "my check." She fumbled around in her purse. "I just can't find those bills," she said. "I guess I came away without them."

The waiter gravely slid the check over in front of Perry Mason. Mason grinned, pulled his billfold from his pocket, left a twenty-dollar bill on top of the check, looked at the amount of the check again and said to the waiter, "The change will just about make up your tip."

The waiter bowed thanks. Ione Bedford said, "Where're we going?"

"Down to the police station," Mason said.

"The police station!"

"Uh-huh. There are some diamonds down there I want you to identify."

"My diamonds?"

"I think so. . . . Just a minute, I have to put in a phone call first."

"Well, I can use a little powder," Mrs. Bedford told him, "and by the time we get our coats and our noses powdered, you should be finished with your telephoning. Come on, Della, and give me moral support."

Mason called Drake's office. "Now listen, Paul," he said, "this is important. Ione Bedford, Della Street and I are going down to police headquarters. I'm going to try to get a look at those diamonds. Then I'm going to make a few comments and turn Mrs. Bedford loose. I want to know where she goes and what she does after she leaves headquarters. I want you to have men there who know me and know Della. They'll see us go in and that will put the finger on Mrs. Bedford. She may go out alone."

"Okay," Drake said, "I'll have the men on the job."

Mason hung up, loitered around the checking counter until the girls emerged from the restroom. He helped them on with their coats, tipped the attendant, and led the way toward his car. "What makes you think they're my diamonds?" Mrs. Bedford asked.

"I don't," Mason said. "I just want you to look at them."

"Where were they discovered, and how do they happen to be at police headquarters?"

"Mrs. Breel," Mason said, "was hit by a motorist. She was taken to the emergency hospital. Among other things which were found in her bag, were these diamonds, done up in paper."

"But they couldn't have been my diamonds," Mrs.

Bedford said, "because Aussie was getting those diamonds from The Golden Platter."

"Did he," Mason asked casually, "telephone you to say he *had* the diamonds?"

"Not after that first time. He said he'd located them, that they'd been hocked for six thousand, and he could get them for three. I told him to pay the three thousand."

Mason said, "You'll pardon me, Mrs. Bedford, if I seem to hold out on you, but there's one angle of this case that I'd prefer not to comment on until after you've seen the diamonds."

She nudged him playfully and said, "Go on, Big Boy, be mysterious. I like it."

Della Street said, "You *should* know, Chief, that you mustn't be so serious on my birthday. The trouble with you is you're cold sober."

Mason glanced surreptitiously at his wrist watch. "Well," he said, "it's not an incurable disease."

Della Street surveyed him with exaggerated gravity. "Yes," she said, "in your case it is. You're working. You might hoist a drink or two, but it would run off your back like water off a duck's stomach." Ione Bedford laughed gleefully. Della Street turned on her reproachfully. "I didn't say that accidentally," she said. "I said it on purpose. It was a wisecrack."

"I know it, dearie. That's why I laughed."

Della Street said, "No, one woman doesn't laugh that way at another woman's wisecracks—not when there's a man in the party. She laughs courteously and politely. You didn't laugh politely. You thought I was trying to say that his drinks ran off his back. . . . Oh, skip it. It isn't important. Who wants to waste drinks on a duck's back?"

Ione Bedford said to Mason, "Your secretary is younger than I thought she was."

"Indeed," Mason said.

Della Street laughed. "What she's getting at is that I'm too inexperienced in holding my birthdays down to have seen many of them."

Ione Bedford said, "After all, my dear, you've only had five or six highballs."

Della Street let her eyes get large and round, as she looked up at Perry Mason. "Imagine," she said, "being so calloused that one can use the word *'only'* in connection with five or six highballs."

Mason said, "Well, it sounds as though it had been a perfectly gorgeous birthday."

"Don't use the past tense," Ione told him. "Her birthday isn't over until midnight. And now that you've put in an appearance, we're filled with new ideas for celebrating. . . . That reminds me, I have to put in a call myself. I'll only be a minute."

She made a dive for the telephone booth, and was careful to pull the door tightly shut. Mason said to Della Street, "Have any idea whom she's calling, Della?"

"No."

"What's the idea of the party?" Mason asked.

She grinned and said, "The woman was plying me with drinks, and trying to get me to talk. I didn't know how long it'd be before you showed up, so I pretended I was feeling the effects."

"How much of it," Mason asked, "is pretense?"

She gave the matter the benefit of frowning consideration, said, "About fifty percent of it is genuine, Chief," then hiccoughed and said, "Well, perhaps you'd better make it seventy-five percent," and laughed.

Ione Bedford emerged from the telephone booth, sailed up to Mason, linked her arm through his and said, "Okay, let's go places. Can we get a drink at police headquarters?"

"That," he told her, "remains to be seen." He led the way to his car and drove to police headquarters, while the two girls, in high spirits, made hilarious comment on the cars they passed, the electric signs, and such other matters as came to their attention. At police headquarters, the property clerk regarded Mason with frowning suspicion. Mason indicated Ione Bedford. "Mrs. Bedford," he said, "left some diamonds with Austin Cullens to give to George Trent. There's some possibility that the diamonds found in Mrs. Breel's handbag may be the Bedford diamonds."

"So what?" the man behind the cage asked.

"I wanted to see if Mrs. Bedford could identify them," Mason said.

The man said, "Just a minute," picked up a telephone which had a device clamped on the mouthpiece making his conversation inaudible. He talked for some two or three minutes, then turned from the phone to Mason. "What'd you say her name was?"

"Mrs. Bedford, Ione Bedford."

The man returned the telephone to his lips, there followed additional conversation, then he nodded, hung up the telephone, and moved over to the vault. He brought out Mrs. Breel's bag, took the tissue-covered jewelry from the bottom, placed the pieces on the counter, and unwrapped the tissue. Mrs. Bedford, her hilarity completely dissipated, watched the paper coverings being removed with eyes which were narrowed in scrutiny. "No," she said slowly, as the diamonds came to view, "those aren't mine."

"You're certain?" Mason asked.

She nodded, then turned to face him. "I never saw them before in my life," she said. "They're somewhat similar to my pieces, but they're not mine."

"That's all," Mason told her. "Thanks."

The property clerk carefully rewrapped each of the diamonds. "How did it happen Mrs. Breel was carrying those stones around in her handbag?" Mrs. Bedford asked. "They're worth money."

"That," Mason told her, "is something we don't know. Mrs. Breel stepped out from the curb, apparently right in front of an automobile. It was out on St. Rupert Boulevard between Ninety-First and Ninety-Second Streets and . . ."

"What was she doing out there?" Ione Bedford interrupted, her voice suddenly hard.

"I don't know," Mason said. "No one knows. Of course, with the finding of Cullens' body, the police think . . ."

"With the finding of *what?*"

Mason looked at her in surprise. "Why, don't you know?" he said.

"Know what?" she inquired, seeming to bite the ends off the words as she uttered them.

Mason said, "Oh, I'm *so* sorry. I thought you knew."

"Go on, out with it."

"Austin Cullens was shot sometime this evening. The police found his body lying on the living room floor of his house."

Ione Bedford stood rigidly motionless. Della Street said to Perry Mason, "Why, Chief, why didn't you tell me?"

"I thought I had told you." She shook her head. "Things have been so frightfully mixed up tonight," Mason apologized, "that I haven't been certain . . . I'm very sorry if this comes as a shock to you, Mrs. Bedford. You'd known him a long time, I believe?"

She suddenly turned to Della Street. There was cold suspicion in her eyes. "All right. You two go ahead and celebrate Della Street's birthday. I'm finished."

"Is there," Mason said, "some place I can take you? Remember, I have a car."

"No," she said, striding toward the door.

As the door slammed shut, Della Street said reproachfully, "After all, Chief, that was cruel. She may have cared for him a lot."

"That," Mason said, "was exactly what I wanted to find out."

8

Mason, freshly shaved and seeming as bouyant as a new tennis ball, deftly scaled his hat over the curved brass hook on the rack, walked over to his desk, picked up the file of important correspondence which Della Street had place on his blotter, and deposited it on the far corner of the desk. Della Street opened the door of her office, grinned a greeting and said, "Hi, Chief. What's new?"

"How are the birthdays?" he asked.

"Well," she said, "I've recovered all right, but don't give me any more."

He laughed. "After all, it was just a fake birthday, Della. You really aren't a year older, you know."

"Well," she observed dubiously, "I *feel* a year older."

"Whose suggestion was the birthday?" he asked.

"The Green Room seemed to be the only thing Mrs. Bedford was interested in," Della said, "and naturally, I had to have some excuse to put on the party."

"Some party," Mason told her. "How about the sheiks?"

"What sheiks?"

"The group that flapped around the table, dancing and . . ."

"Oh," she said, "you mean the table lizards. I won't hear from them."

"How about it?" he asked, amused. "Did they all ask for Ione Bedford's telephone number and none for yours?"

"Don't be silly," she told him.

"And you mean to say you refused to give them your number?"

She smiled reminiscently. "I told them," she said, "that my name was Virginia Trent, and gave them her number. It should be a good break for the girl."

Mason laughed. "Paul Drake," she went on, "wants to see you as soon as you come in."

"Give him a ring," Mason told her. "What's in the papers? Anything?"

"Oh, a lot of stuff," she said, "and Drake seems to be bursting with information. I'll give him a buzz."

She entered her office, and Mason picked up the newspapers, to skim through them. A few moments later, Della Street crossed the office to stand by the exit door which opened into the corridor. When she heard Paul Drake's steps outside, she opened the door, and, making a mock salute, stood at attention. "Hello, Della," the detective said. " 'Lo, Perry."

Mason indicated a chair. "What's new, Paul?"

The detective sat down in the big leather chair, and turned around, draping his legs over one of its arms. "Lots of things," he said, lighting a cigarette.

"Well," Mason told him, "begin in the middle and work both ways."

"On the gambling business," Drake told him, "I have a couple of live ones spotted, a contractor about fifty-five who was there with a girl who couldn't have been over thirty and looked twenty. Then there was a bank executive with a fluffy little blonde. Either of those two should be just what we want."

"How about Ione Bedford?" Mason asked. "Did you follow her?"

"I'll say."

"Where?"

"When she left the property room in the jail," Drake said, opening a notebook and consulting it, "she was in a hurry to go places. She ran over to the corner to flag a cab, didn't have any luck, and walked down the street a couple of blocks to the Spring Hotel. There's a taxi stand there. She had the taxi driver crowding signal lights and cutting corners until she came to the Milpas Apartments on Canyon Drive. She went into apartment three fourteen, which is rented by a Pete Chennery. Apparently she's Mrs. Chennery."

"Why, her apartment's at the Bixel Arms on Madison Avenue," Della Street said, "under her own name. The name isn't listed in the telephone book because the phone was connected too late to be put in, but it's under her name, and you can get it by calling Information."

Drake nodded. "How do you figure she's Mrs. Pete Chennery at the Milpas Apartments?" Mason asked.

"The boys did a little snooping around," Drake told him.

"Where is she now?"

"At last reports, still at the Milpas."

"Did your men go through her apartment at the Bixel Arms?"

"We got in," Drake said, "but were crowded for time. You met her out at the Green Room, took her down to headquarters, and she didn't stay long. When she left, we figured she might be headed for her apartment, so I flashed the men on the job the signal to get out. They made a pretty good job of it, though. No letters, no correspondence, no checkbook. Nothing personal, except what you'd expect—tooth brushes, cosmetics, clothes, and a couple of hundred engraved visiting cards, together with the copper plate."

"How about Chennery, was he home when she got there?"

"Apparently not. The apartment was dark."

Mason said, "I'd like to know more about Chennery, Paul. I want a description. I'd particularly like to find out if there's any chance Chennery was also known as Austin Cullens."

"I'm sending some more men out there," Drake said. "I'm going to pick up everything we can without making her suspicious. You don't want her to know she's being tagged, do you?"

"No," Mason said. "She mustn't . . ."

His desk phone rang and Della Street picked up the receiver, listened a minute, turned to Mason and said, "Dr. Gifford."

Mason took the telephone. Dr. Gifford, speaking with close-clipped, professional rapidity, said, "Try and get this all at once, Mason. I won't have an opportunity to repeat. Mrs. Breel is fully conscious. Actually she was conscious but sleeping most of the night. She had a concussion. No fracture, no internal injuries, the fracture in the right leg has been reduced, the leg's in a cast, she's been placed under arrest, with an officer on guard at the door of the room, no one is allowed to visit her. She refuses to make any statement except in the presence of her attorney, says you're her lawyer, Sergeant Holcomb is on his way over here. It might be a good plan for you to come down. She's in six twenty."

"You're at the hospital now?" Mason asked.

"Yes."

"What's she under arrest for?"

"Charged with the murder of Austin Cullens."

"She hasn't made any statement, not even to the nurses?"

"Not a cheep," Dr. Gifford said. "I'm sneaking this call through to you. Keep it dark. Good-by."

Mason dropped the receiver into place, strode across the office and grabbed his hat. "Sarah Breel's recovered consciousness," he said. "So far, she isn't talking. They've charged her with first-degree murder."

Drake said, "That means just one thing, Perry."

"What?" Mason asked.

"That the ballistics department has tested the bullet which killed Cullens with the bullets found from the gun in Mrs. Breel's bag and find they're the same."

"I'm not so sure that gun actually was *in* her bag," Mason said.

"Diggers says there was a gun at the scene of the accident," Drake said. "He evidently thought the bag might contain something valuable, because he made the ambulance men inventory the contents."

"Anyone see that accident?" Mason asked.

"You mean see her step out in front of the car?"

"Yes."

"Apparently not," Drake said. "There were people along just a few minutes afterwards. Mrs. Breel was lying unconscious on the ground."

Mason said, "Check on Diggers. Find out everything you can about him. I'm on my way."

"Can I help, Chief?" Della Street asked.

"No," he told her. "They'll have a shorthand reporter. I'll stand more of a chance of crashing the gate alone."

He clamped his hat on his head, shot through the door and sprinted for the elevator. He caught a cruising cab and said, "Dearborn Memorial Hospital, and what I mean, make it snappy." In the taxicab, Mason turned over in his mind the various bits of information which had been given him. Undoubtedly, the revolver found in

Mrs. Breel's handbag had been the determining factor in influencing the district attorney's office to advise her arrest. Had that weapon not discharged the bullet which had caused Cullens' death, the circumstantial evidence of the stained shoe would not have been sufficient. On the other hand, given the shoe, the gun with which the murder had been committed, and the indisputable evidence which placed Mrs. Breel at the scene of the crime at approximately the time of the murder, the district attorney had a case which, unexplained, would go far toward trapping Mrs. Breel in a net of circumstantial evidence. At the Dearborn Memorial Hospital, Mason took an elevator to the sixth floor, and found Mrs. Breel's room without difficulty. An officer was on guard in the corridor. From within the room, Mason could hear the sound of excited voices. Mason started to push open the door. The officer interposed a stalwart arm. "No, you don't, buddy," he said.

Mason said with dignity, "I wish to see Mrs. Breel. She has asked for me."

"I don't care who she's asked for," the officer said. "You get in here on a pass, or you stay out."

"Who's in there?" Mason asked.

"The doctor, a deputy D.A., a court reporter, Sergeant Holcomb, and a few others."

"Well, I'm Mrs. Breel's lawyer."

"That's nice."

"I want in."

"You said you did."

Mason sized the officer up. "Tell Sergeant Holcomb I'm here."

The officer said, "Nope. I ain't paid for telling anybody anything. I'm here to guard the door."

Abruptly Mason raised his knuckles and knocked on the door. The officer frowned and jerked Mason's arm down. "Now, who told you you could do that?" he asked.

Mason's voice was conciliatory. "Forget it. You're here to keep anyone from coming in without a pass. That doesn't mean I can't knock . . ."

A man opened the door, glowered at Mason and said, "What?"

Mason raised his voice. "I'm Perry Mason, Mrs. Breel's lawyer. I want to see my client."

Mason heard Mrs. Breel say, "Come in, Mr. Mason," and, at the same time, the man in the doorway and the uniformed officer on guard converged on him, pushing him back into the corridor. The man who had opened the door pulled it shut behind him and said to the guard, "We told you there were to be no visitors."

The guard said, "The guy knocked on his own. I wouldn't let him in."

"Well, don't let him knock," the man said, and turned back toward the door.

The uniformed guard held Mason back in the corridor. The lawyer waited until the detective had opened the door, and then, raising his voice so that it was distinctly audible within the room, said, "Mrs. Breel won't answer any questions unless you let me in."

The door swung shut. The officer glowered at Mason belligerently and said, "You're hard to get along with."

Mason grinned, offered him a cigarette. "Oh, no, I'm not."

The officer hesitated a moment, then took the cigarette, scratched a match and jerked his head down the corridor. "On your way," he said.

Mason smiled. "I'm waiting right here."

"You just think you are."

"You," Mason told him, "are guarding the room. You're not guarding the corridor."

"You don't have any business here."

"I'm going to have."

There was a moment of silence, while the officer contemplated the situation in frowning belligerence. Once more, there was the sound of angry voices raised behind the door. A few moments later, Sergeant Holcomb suddenly pushed the door open and said, "All right, Mason, come in."

Mason entered the room. A court reporter was seated at a small table, a shorthand notebook spread out in front of him, a fountain pen held poised over the page. Larry Sampson, a deputy district attorney, was standing by the foot of the bed with his hands jammed down in his coat pockets. Over by the window, Dr. Gifford stood professionally aloof. Beside him stood a red-headed nurse with large brown eyes, a peaches-and-cream complexion, and a mouth which was a hard, straight line of determination. Lying on the hospital bed, the back of which had been raised a few inches, so as to prop up her bandaged head, Sarah Breel surveyed them with calm, untroubled eyes. A rope attached to the broken leg ran from underneath the covers, up over a pulley, and terminated in a weight which dangled over the foot of the bed.

Dr. Gifford said, "Gentlemen, I want to repeat, all of this argument is getting us nowhere. My patient has sustained a severe nervous shock. I am not going to permit her health to be jeopardized by any sustained questioning, or any browbeating."

"Oh, forget it!" Sergeant Holcomb said irritably. "No one's trying to browbeat her."

"The minute I see any indication of it," Dr. Gifford said, "the interview will be terminated."

Sarah Breel smiled at Perry Mason. It was rather a lop-sided smile, what with the bandages about her head and a swelling on one side of her face. "Good morning, Mr. Mason," she said, "I want you as my lawyer."

Mason nodded. "I understand," she went on, "that I'm accused of murder. I've refused to make any statement until my lawyer was present."

Sergeant Holcomb said, "You understand, Mrs. Breel, that your failure to deny the charges against you . . ."

"Let me handle it, Sergeant," Larry Sampson interrupted. "I may explain once more to Mrs. Breel, and for the benefit of Mr. Mason, that the object of this interview is not to try to trap Mrs. Breel into making any admissions. The circumstantial evidence, standing by itself, is sufficiently black against her to more than justify the charge of first-degree murder. Now then, if she's innocent and can explain the evidence in the case, we'll withdraw the charge. This is an opportunity we're giving her to avoid newspaper publicity and the stigma of a public trial."

"Bunk!" Mason said. "That's the old line of hooey, Mrs. Breel. Having once filed a first-degree murder charge against you, it'll take a miracle to make them quit. All this business about giving you a chance to explain is simply an excuse to get you talking, so they can catch discrepancies in your story and trap you into an admission."

Sampson flushed. Sergeant Holcomb said, "You start cracking wise, and you'll go out of here on your ear."

Mason said, "I have a right to see my client. It's my duty to advise her. I'm advising her."

"Advising her not to answer questions?" Sampson asked.

"Not at all," Mason said. "I was merely correcting the inaccuracies in your statement. My client can do anything she wants to. I consider it my duty, however, to advise her that she doesn't have to answer any questions, and if she is at all nervous or emotionally upset, she can postpone this interview until after she has talked with me."

"You mean until after you've told her what to say," Sergeant Holcomb sneered.

"I meant exactly what I said," Mason told him.

"Well," Mrs. Breel interrupted. "There's no use arguing about it. I'm going to make a full and complete statement. I just wanted my attorney here when I did it."

"That's better," Sampson told her. "You're a woman of understanding. You can appreciate the damaging effect of letting this circumstantial evidence stand uncontradicted."

"I'm sure I don't know what you're talking about when you refer to circumstantial evidence," Mrs. Breel said.

Sampson said, "Mrs. Breel, I'm going to be frank with you, perhaps brutally frank. I'm doing it for your own good. When you were struck by that automobile last night, there was a thirty-eight caliber revolver in your bag. The police have discharged a test bullet from that revolver. They have made micro-photographs of that bullet. They have also recovered the fatal bullet which killed Austin Cullens. They have made micro-photographs of that bullet. The two bullets, compared side by side under a powerful microscope, and as shown in the micro-photographs, are not only identical bullets, but moreover, they were both discharged from the same gun. In other words, Mrs. Breel, the gun which you had in your possession in your handbag last night fired the bullet which killed Austin Cullens."

Mrs. Breel regarded him sternly. "Young man," she said, "are you *sure* that a gun was found in my bag?"

"Absolutely," Larry Sampson said. "The bag was lying on the pavement near you when . . ."

"But that doesn't indicate that it was *my* bag," Mrs. Breel said. "I was unconscious at the time. You can't hold me responsible for a bag which was found near me. I don't know who put it there."

Mason grinned and flashed a wink at Dr. Gifford. Sergeant Holcomb said disgustedly to the doctor, "And this is the woman you said shouldn't answer questions because her thoughts might not be coherent."

Larry Sampson hesitated a moment, then opened a leather handbag which was on the floor near the corner. "Mrs. Breel," he said, "I am going to show you a handbag. I'm going to ask you to say whether this is your handbag."

Dramatically, he jerked out the handbag with the two imitation jade rings, and whirled to hold it out in front of him. Mrs. Breel surveyed the bag with an appraisal which was almost disinterested. "I think," she said, "that I *did* have a bag like that once, but I can't be certain. However, young man, I most certainly can't say that that is my bag. . . . You see, I had it some time ago."

Sampson looked nonplused. Abruptly, he reached into the bag and pulled out the partially knitted garment. "Try and deny the ownership of this," he said. "This is yours, isn't it?"

She looked at it with a perfectly blank countenance. "Is it?" she asked.

"You know it is."

She shook her head and said, "No, I don't know it is."

Sampson said, "Now, look here, Mrs. Breel, this isn't a game. This is a serious matter. You're charged with the crime of first-degree murder, which is the most serious crime known to our law. The questions which I am asking, and the answers which you are giving, are being taken down in shorthand. They can be used against you at any time. Now then, Mrs. Breel, I am not going to take an unfair advantage of you. I am going to state to you frankly in the presence of your counsel that the circumstantial evidence against you looks very black. I am going to state further, however, that the evidence is largely circumstantial; that perhaps some of that evidence can be explained away. If you co-operate with the authorities, if you make every effort to assist us in uncovering the truth in this matter, it will go a long way toward establishing your innocence. If you make a single false statement, and it can be proven that statement is false, it is going to crucify you so far as this charge is concerned. Mr. Perry Mason, your own lawyer, is present. He will tell you that I am telling you the truth. Now then, if you deny the ownership of this bag, and we can prove that it really is your bag, that statement will absolutely pillory you. Now, Mrs. Breel, I am asking you: *Is that your bag?*"

"I don't know," she said calmly.

"Look at it," Sampson said, "examine it. Take it in your hands. Look it over and then tell us whether it is your bag."

"I tell you I don't know."

"Do you mean you can't tell whether this is your bag or whether this is not your bag?"

"That's right."

"You were carrying a bag last night, weren't you?"

"I don't know."

"Do you mean to say that you don't know whether you

were carrying a bag in your hand when you went to call on Mr. Austin Cullens?"

"That's right—I don't even know that I went to call on Mr. Austin Cullens."

"You don't know *that?*"

"No," she said placidly. "As a matter of fact, I've been trying to cudgel my brains ever since I regained consciousness. I can remember yesterday morning, that is, I guess it was yesterday." She turned to Perry Mason and said, "This is Tuesday, isn't it, Mr. Mason?"

He nodded. "Yes," she said, "it was yesterday morning. I can remember yesterday morning. I can remember everything that happened. I can remember receiving the keys to my brother's car. I can remember going and getting the car. I can remember putting it in the garage. I can remember waiting in the shoe department of a department store. I remember, later on, being accused of shoplifting. I remember having lunch with Mr. Mason. . . . And I can't remember one single thing that happened after I left that store."

"Oh," Sampson said, sneering, "you're going to pull that old stuff, that your mind's a blank, are you?"

Mason said, "That isn't a question, Sampson, that's an argument."

"Well, suppose it *is* an argument?"

Dr. Gifford said, "I think Mr. Mason is right. Within reasonable limits, you may question my patient, but you certainly aren't going to argue with her, or attempt to browbeat her."

"That old alibi has whiskers on it a foot long," Sergeant Holcomb said sneeringly.

Dr. Gifford said, "As a matter of fact, in case you gentlemen are interested, it quite frequently happens that following a concussion, there's a complete lapse of memory covering a period of from hours to sometimes days prior to the shock. Occasionally, with the passing of time, that memory slowly returns."

"How much time, would you say, would have to elapse in this case," Sampson asked sarcastically, "before Mrs. Breel would recover her memory?"

"I don't know," Dr. Gifford said. "It depends upon a variety of factors which are outside of my consideration."

"I'll say it does," Sampson said disgustedly.

Mason said, "Let me ask you, Dr. Gifford, is there anything particularly unusual in this lapse of memory in connection with a concussion history such as we have in the present case?"

"Nothing whatever," Dr. Gifford said.

Sampson pulled the knitting from the bag. "Look here, Mrs. Breel," he said. "Can't you recognize your own knitting?"

She said, "May I see it, please?"

Sampson extended it to her. She looked it over critically and said, "Rather a nice job of knitting. Whoever did this was very expert."

"You knit, don't you?" Sampson asked.

"Yes."

"Do you consider yourself an expert knitter?"

"I am very good," she said.

"Do you recognize that as your knitting?"

"No."

"Would you say that it was not your knitting?"

"No."

"Would you say that if you were knitting a blue garment, of that sort, you would knit it in about that manner?"

"I think any expert knitter would."

"That isn't answering my question. Would you knit in that way?"

"Yes, I think so."

"And you won't say that is your knitting?"

"No. I don't remember ever having seen it before."

Sampson exchanged an exasperated glance with Sergeant Holcomb, then dug down into the bag and said, "All right, Mrs. Breel, I'm going to show you something else and see if *this* refreshes your recollection." He unwrapped the paper from the diamonds. "Did you ever see this jewelry before?"

"I'm sure I couldn't tell you," she said.

"You can't tell us?"

"No. I cannot *remember* ever having seen it before. But, until I completely recover my memory, I wouldn't care to make a positive statement."

"Oh, no, certainly not," Sampson said sarcastically. "You want to give us every assistance in the world, don't you?"

Dr. Gifford said, "May I remind you once more, Mr. Sampson, that this woman has suffered a very severe nerve shock?"

Sampson said sarcastically, "She seems to need a mental guardian, all right. It's too bad about her being such a babe in the woods."

Mason said, "As Mrs. Breel's lawyer, I am going to ask you gentlemen to complete this examination as quickly as is humanly possible. Are there any further questions you wish to ask of Mrs. Breel?"

"Yes," Sergeant Holcomb said. "Mrs. Breel, you went out there to Austin Cullens' house, didn't you?"

"I don't remember."

"You knew where Austin Cullens lived, didn't you?"

"I can't even remember that."

"His name's on the address book at your brother's office, isn't it?"

"I suppose so, yes. . . . Come to think of it, I believe I've mailed a few letters to him at his address . . . out on St. Rupert Boulevard, I believe."

"That's right. Now, you went out there last night, at about what time?"

"I tell you that I don't know that I went out there."

"You entered that house," Sergeant Holcomb said, "and you entered it surreptitiously. You unscrewed one of the electric light globes and placed a copper penny inside the socket so that in case Cullens should come home and press the light switch, the copper coin would short-circuit the wires and burn out every fuse on the circuit, didn't you?"

"I'm sure I don't know what you're talking about," she said.

"You don't remember doing that?"

"Most certainly not. I tell you the last thing I remember was shaking hands with Mr. Mason in the department store."

"Then," Holcomb said triumphantly, "if you can't remember where you were or what you did, you can't positively swear that you didn't take a thirty-eight caliber revolver and shoot Mr. Austin Cullens last night about seven-thirty, can you?"

"Of course not," she said. "I can't tell you what I did, and it follows that I can't tell you what I didn't. I may have assassinated the President. I may have wrecked a train. I may have forged a check. I might have got married. I don't know what I did or what I didn't do."

"Then you won't deny that you killed Austin Cullens, will you?"

"I most certainly have no recollection of having killed Austin Cullens."

"But you won't deny that you did it?"

"I can't remember having done so."

"But you *may* have done so."

"That," she said, "is another matter. I'm certain that I can't tell what might have happened. I only know that I never killed anyone before yesterday afternoon, and I have no reason to believe that yesterday afternoon was any different from any other afternoon in my life."

"You were worried about your brother, weren't you?"

"No more so than I have been on other occasions."

"You knew he'd gone out to get drunk?"

"Yes. I surmised that."

"Let me ask you this," Larry Sampson said. "Do you remember doing any shoplifting?"

She hesitated a moment, then said, "Yes."

"You do?"

"Yes."

"Where? When?"

"Yesterday afternoon, or rather yesterday noon, just before I met Mr. Mason."

"And you did do what is generally known as shoplifting?"

"Yes. You see, my brother had gone on one of his periodical toots. I was worried about him. Sunday I went to the office to check on the contents of the vault. I couldn't find the diamonds which had been given to my brother Saturday morning by Austin Cullens. It occurred to me that my brother must have taken them with him. Cullens knows all about George's periodical sprees. He's absolutely the only one who does—aside from my niece and myself. I was afraid Mr. Cullens might want his stones before George sobered up. I was afraid it might make something of a scandal, so I decided to cover up for George. I thought I could pretend I'd developed a kleptomania. Looking back on it, it seems very foolish now, but at the time it seemed the only thing to do, the only way I could stall things along until I could find George and sober him up."

"So you deliberately planned to get caught stealing . . . ?"

"Not exactly," she said. "Somewhere, I'd read that a person couldn't be charged with shoplifting until they'd removed the things from the store. I planned to get caught while I was still in the store. However, if it hadn't been for Mr. Mason . . ."

Sergeant Holcomb interrupted. "All right, now I'm going to tell you something else. Your brother was found . . ."

Dr. Gifford came charging forward. "No, you don't!" he shouted. "I warned you my patient was to be spared that nerve shock. You agreed to this interview on that understanding. You can't . . ."

"I can do anything I damn please," Holcomb said. "You aren't in charge here. I'm in charge here."

"You may not think I'm in charge here," Dr. Gifford said, "but this woman is under *my* care. I stretched a point in letting you question her at this time. You're not going to inflict any shock on her. That was definitely understood before the interview commenced."

"Well, as it happens," Holcomb said, "I've changed my mind. I may not know a lot about medicine, but I think this woman is in full possession of her faculties right now and . . ."

Dr. Gifford nodded to the red-headed nurse. She produced a package from under her arm. Dr. Gifford said, "Just a moment," and stepped forward. "Let me see your left arm, please, Mrs. Breel," he said.

She extended her left arm. Dr. Gifford made a quick jabbing motion with his right hand. Sergeant Holcomb pushed forward and said suspiciously, "Say, what are you doing?"

Dr. Gifford stood so that his body shielded his hand and Mrs. Breel's arm from Sergeant Holcomb's eyes. Then he stepped away and motioned to the nurse. She handed him a piece of cotton. Dr. Gifford placed the piece of cotton to the neck of an alcohol bottle and swabbed off a place on Mrs. Breel's arm. He turned to the court reporter and said, "You might make a note at this time that I have just given Mrs. Breel a powerful narcotic and sedative, administered hypodermically. While I don't ordinarily consider such treatment indicated in a case of this nature, I consider that it is infinitely preferable for the patient than being subjected to further nerve shock."

Sergeant Holcomb said, "I don't give a damn what you've given her. I'm going to go ahead with this thing. . . ."

"Go right ahead," Dr. Gifford advised. "The patient is now beginning to feel the influence of the narcotic. As a physician, I would say that *any* answer to *any* questions she might make from now on will be completely unreliable."

Mrs. Breel sighed, settled back on the bed, and closed her eyes. There was the faint trace of a smile visible at the corners of her mouth. Sergeant Holcomb yelled, "She's shamming. That's a damn fake. That hypodermic couldn't have taken effect this soon."

"I take it," Dr. Gifford said, "that you consider your knowledge of medicine superior to mine."

Sergeant Holcomb lost his temper. His face darkened as he shouted, "Well, *I* know what *I* think. I think she's shamming. I think this whole thing is a stall. Now then, I'm going to tell her about her brother. Mrs. Breel, you can play possum all you want to, but your brother was found . . ."

Sampson lunged for Holcomb, clapped his hand over Holcomb's lips. "Shut up, you fool. I'm in charge of this."

Holcomb jumped back with his fist doubled, then squared away to face Sampson belligerently. "All right," he said, "you asked for it. You . . ."

"Shut up!" Sampson said. "Can't you see that you'd be playing right into their hands?"

Sergeant Holcomb said, "I'll show you," and swung.

Sampson jumped back. Gifford said, "Gentlemen, I'm going to order hospital attendants to clear this room. This is a disgraceful scene, and it's having a most harmful effect on my patient."

Sampson said, "Don't be a damn fool, Holcomb. Can't you see that if you . . ."

Holcomb, still facing Sampson with his fists doubled, said, "Stand up and fight, you little rat! You can be taken in by all this flim-flam, but *I'm* not being taken in by it." Still holding his fists doubled, and keeping Sampson away from him, he turned around to face the bed. "All right, Mrs. Breel," he said, "let's see how you take this. . . . Your brother's body was found in his office. He'd been shot by a thirty-eight caliber revolver and the body jammed in a packing case."

Mrs. Breel might not have heard him. With her eyes closed, her face utterly without expression, she breathed steadily and deeply, as though sleeping. Sampson said sarcastically, "All right, flat-foot, now you've done it! You've played the one trump card we had at a time when she was under the influence of a narcotic."

"She's no more under the influence of a narcotic than I am," Sergeant Holcomb said, but his voice somehow lacked conviction.

"No?" Sampson said. "Well, you'll never be able to surprise her with that bit of information now. You've put your cards on the table. She'll sleep that hypodermic off and decide how she wants to play *her* cards after she wakes up."

Mason said, "Now that there's a lull in the furious recriminations, I want the court reporter to be quite certain that he has noted the time at which Dr. Gifford gave the patient the hypodermic. I want him to note that, notwithstanding the nervous condition of the patient, the deputy district attorney and the sergeant of the homicide squad engaged in a fist fight, across the foot of the bed . . ."

"There wasn't any fist fight," Sampson said. "Don't be a fool, Mason."

"I considered it a fist fight," Mason observed.

"Well, I didn't," Sampson said. "I didn't even make a pass at Holcomb. I kept out of his way."

"Holcomb certainly made a swing at *you*," Mason said.

"Well, that's neither here nor there," Sampson remarked.

Mason grinned his fighting grin. "It may not be here, but it's either in that shorthand record or I'm going to find out why it isn't."

The court reporter nodded wearily and said, "It's in."

"Thank you," Mason said.

There was a moment of silence. Mrs. Breel, on the bed, gave a peculiar gurgling sound which might have been a snore. Sergeant Holcomb asserted once more, "No hypodermic in the world ever took effect that quick."

"Did you," Mason asked, "note the exact time when Dr. Gifford administered the hypodermic?"

"No," Holcomb said, "but it was less than two minutes ago."

Mason said, "Time passes very rapidly, Sergeant, when you're engaged in fisticuffs with a deputy district attorney in the room of a patient whose physical condition is so grave that the doctor has warned you not to subject her to any undue shock."

Sampson said disgustedly, "Come on, we're not getting anywhere with this. We're just playing into Mason's hands now."

Holcomb said, "Well, there's a lot about this that needs to be explained."

"Not here," Sampson told him.

Sergeant Holcomb stood staring at the woman on the bed, as though the sheer impact of his eyes would stir her to life. Dr. Gifford said, "You gentlemen might just as well do your brawling elsewhere. My patient is now completely oblivious to everything which is taking place."

Holcomb turned to the doctor and said, "You'll hear more about this."

"Yes, there'll be a lot more heard about it," Dr. Gifford said grimly. "If there are any resulting complications, I am going to hold you personally responsible."

Mason said, "I think, Doctor, we can get a court order restraining the officers from asking any further questions until after you have decided that such questions won't jeopardize her health."

"That interval," Dr. Gifford said with dignity, "will, of necessity, be somewhat prolonged because of the mental strain to which she had just been subjected. Gentlemen, I am going to ask you to clear the room." As they hesitated, Dr. Gifford said, "In the event you don't go now, I am going to ask the hospital office to send up sufficient orderlies to see that the room *is* cleared."

Sampson said, "Come on, Holcomb. We can't do anything here."

Holcomb said, "Well, I'm not going to leave Mason behind to tip her off what to say."

Mason started toward the door. In abrupt contrast to the vociferous recriminations which had taken place in that room, he made an elaborate show of tiptoeing so that he would not disturb the sleeper. "I," he said in a hoarse whisper, "see nothing to be gained by trying to disturb the slumbers of a drugged woman."

Dr. Gifford nodded. Despite himself Sampson suppressed a smile. Sergeant Holcomb, seeming about to choke with indignation, started to say something, but Sampson touched him on the shoulder and said, "That's all of it, Sergeant."

9

■

Mason stopped in the telephone booth at the hospital to call Paul Drake. "Listen, Paul," he said, "things are happening fast up at this end. Give me the low-down on Virginia Trent."

"They're keeping her in the custody of a police nurse," Drake said. "They took her to headquarters last night, and gave her the works until she had hysterics good and plenty. Then they had a doctor give her a big sedative and a police nurse took her home. The nurse is standing guard."

"Any formal charge?" Mason asked.

"None at present. They're probably holding her as a material witness if it comes to a show-down, but they're not too certain about her. The uncle was killed with one bullet fired from a thirty-eight caliber revolver found in the upper right-hand drawer of the desk. You were there when Sergeant Holcomb found the gun."

"So what?" Mason said. "She came in there just a few minutes before I did. The body had been there for some time."

"I know, but they're wondering whether she didn't go in there to do something about disposing of the body or trying to get something out of the pockets or . . ."

"All that's absurd," Mason said.

"Well, *I'm* not arguing with *you*," Drake told him philosophically, "I'm telling you what the authorities claim. They've claimed absurdities before and they'll probably do so again. What's happened up there, Perry? You seem to have your fighting clothes on."

"Oh, they tried to get rough with Mrs. Breel," Mason said.

"Did they get anywhere?"

"Nowhere at all," Mason reported, and chuckled at the thought.

"How about Ione Bedford?"

"She's still in the Milpas Apartments."

"Has Pete Chennery come in yet?"

"Not according to latest reports."

"All right, then," Mason said, "we'll take the gambling-house angle. I'm out at the Dearborn Memorial Hospital. You'd better come out and pick me up. I came out in a cab."

Drake said, "I'll be out there in ten minutes."

Mason hung up the telephone, strolled down the linoleum-floored corridor to the big marble steps in front of the hospital, where he enjoyed the sunlight and concentrated over a cigarette until Paul Drake slid his car in close to the curb. Mason ran down the steps, jumped into the car and said, "Let's tackle that banker on the gambling angle, Paul."

"Okay," Drake said, spinning the wheel. "Why is the gambling-house angle so important?"

Mason said, "Because the books don't balance, Paul."

"What do you mean?"

Mason said, "Notice that, according to the reports Cullens gave Ione Bedford over the telephone, George Trent had been up to The Golden Platter on Saturday night and had hocked the stones for six thousand dollars. Cullens was going to get them for three."

"Well?" Drake asked.

"George Trent's body," Mason said, "was found in his office. According to all the reports I get, when he goes out on a drunk he doesn't shave, bathe or change his clothes. He gets pretty disreputable. Now then, he was neatly dressed, and there wasn't any stubble on his face when his body was found. He must have been killed in his own office. *If* he went to the gambling house and pawned those stones for six thousand dollars, he must have returned to his office some time that night and was killed there."

"Well," Drake said, "why couldn't that have happened?"

"It just doesn't fit into the picture. In the first place, he'd mailed in the keys to his car. He'd gone out to get drunk. It's a moot question whether he'd have taken the Bedford diamonds with him. Now then, if he did, it's hard to believe he'd have hocked diamonds which didn't belong to him—at least that early in the game. After he'd been on a bat for two or three days and his sense of perspective had become pickled in alcohol, it might have been different."

"What are you getting at?" Drake asked.

"Simply this: If Trent didn't leave those stones at The Golden Platter in return for six thousand dollars, why did Cullens tell Ione Bedford that he did? If Trent didn't leave the stones there, and Cullens thought he did, and went up and started to get rough with those gamblers, they might have been responsible for what happened to Cullens. Apparently, a copper penny had been inserted in the socket of one of the lights out at Cullens' house so that when anyone came in and turned on the light switch, it'd blow the fuse. That doesn't sound like an amateur to me. Moreover, if those were the Bedford diamonds in Mrs. Breel's bag, and *if* it was Mrs. Breel's bag, there's no definite proof that the diamonds actually came from that chamois-skin belt which Cullens was wearing. Now then, you add to that the fact that Ione Bedford swears they *weren't* her diamonds, and we get into some complicating factors."

"I'll say we do," Drake said. "It's all tangled up like a cat in flypaper, and the more you move it around, the worse it gets."

"Therefore," Mason said, "it's important to go back to first principles. I want to find out whether those stones actually were pawned with The Golden Platter."

"I don't see how the witness we're going to interview now can help you on that," Drake said.

"He can help us to this extent," Mason told him. "Suppose Cullens was playing some kind of a game and simply stringing Ione Bedford along? Suppose he didn't have any actual tip that the stones had been hocked at The Golden Platter . . . ? Or, suppose he didn't go to The Golden Platter, but was standing in cahoots in some way with Bill Golding?"

"I get you," Drake said. "You want to check on everything. Is that right?"

"On everything," Mason told him.

"Well, here we are," Drake observed, driving the car into a parking station. "The bank's across the street."

They crossed the street, to enter the sumptuous marbled interior of the bank, where a uniformed policeman paraded back and forth in slow dignity. Officers sat behind desks, dictating, making notations, holding conferences. Cashiers were busily engaged in accepting deposits and paying out checks. "Who's our man?" Mason said.

"The white-haired bird over here on the left," Drake told him.

Mason said, "He looks absolutely impregnable."

Drake chuckled, "Remember the story about the banker's glass eye, Perry. Come on, let's go."

They approached a breast-high marble railing on which appeared a brass plaque bearing the name, MR. MARQUAD. The white-haired man was listening with cold impassiveness to a man who sat on the opposite side of his desk. The visitor was leaning forward, sitting on the very edge of the chair, giving the impression of wanting to crawl up on the desk in order to get nearer to the banker. Finally, Mr. Marquad shook his head. The man engaged in a barrage of conversation. Again the banker shook his head and, with a gesture of finality, picked up some correspondence on his desk. Mason heard him say, "I'm sorry, but it's absolutely impossible."

As the man still lingered, Marquad said, "That, of course, is my judgment. I'll take it up with our advisory board if you desire. . . . Very well, I'll make a note and submit it to them. You can drop in at ten-thirty tomorrow morning for your answer."

He made a note on a pad, smiled a cold farewell at the departing visitor, and then got up to come to the partition and regard Mason and the detective with an expression of neutral greeting. Mason felt that the face could change instantly into patronizing courtesy or cold negation without seeming in the least inconsistent with that initial expression. Drake flashed a questioning glance at Mason. Mason nodded and said, "I'll handle it, Paul."

Mr. Marquad turned to Mason. Mason said, "I wonder if you read the morning paper, Mr. Marquad?"

"Just what did you have in mind?" Marquad asked. Mason slid his card over the counter. Marquad looked at it, and his face showed a flicker of expression. "Yes, Mr. Mason," he said, "I've heard of you. What did you have reference to particularly?"

"The murder of Austin Cullens," he said.

"Indeed!" Marquad remarked.

"I'm trying to check up on Cullens' activities immediately preceding the murder," Mason said. "There was a photograph and, in addition to the photograph, an excellent description. In case you haven't read about it, Mr. Marquad, I'll call your attention to the clipping." Mason took a newspaper clipping from his pocket, unfolded it and handed it to the banker. Marquad glanced at it and nodded. "Please read the description," Mason insisted.

The banker read the description and then said, "I'm sure I don't know just what you're getting at, Mr. Mason."

"Did you know him?" Mason asked.

"No," the banker said. "I don't remember ever having seen him."

Mason said, "Think back, Mr. Marquad. I think you saw him last night."

"Last night?"

"Yes."

"What makes you think that?"

"My records," Mason said, "show that Mr. Cullens went to The Golden Platter shortly before he was murdered."

The banker stiffened and said, "The Golden Platter? To what do you refer, Mr. Mason?"

Mason said, "A restaurant and gambling joint on East Third Street."

"I don't think we carry their account," Marquad observed haughtily.

Mason slightly squared his shoulders, pushed forward his jaw and said, "I'm not asking you about an account. I'm asking you if you weren't at The Golden Platter last night."

"Me?" the banker said, in indignant surprise. "At a resort of that nature? Surely, Mr. Mason . . ."

Mason glanced a sidelong interrogation at Paul Drake. The detective nodded. Mason said, "All right, Mr. Marquad, if you want it straight from the shoulder, I'll dish it out. You were there with a cute little blonde trick."

Marquad said with dignity, "Mr. Mason, I'm going to ask you to excuse me. This is indeed most insulting. There's an officer on duty over there."

Drake took a notebook from his pocket and said, "You left at eleven forty-five, Mr. Marquad. You drove the jane to her apartment at ninety-three sixty-two Phyllis Avenue. You parked the car and went up with her. She has apartment nine hundred six under the name of Ruby Benjamin. You turned the lights on and pulled the shades down. At two forty-five A.M. you came out and . . ."

The banker looked around him in alarm, lowered his voice and said, "Hush! Please, gentlemen, hush!"

"All right," Mason said, "what's the answer?"

The banker moistened his lips with the tip of a nervous tongue. "What is this," he asked, "blackmail?"

"No," Mason said, "this isn't blackmail. I'm trying to find out whether this man was at The Golden Platter some time around seven or eight o'clock in the evening. I think you would have seen him there. Now, think back and see what you can remember."

"Do you mean to say that you want to call me as a witness to what occurred in that place?" Marquad asked.

Mason said, "If you give me the information I want, that'll probably be all that's necessary. If you don't give me the information I want, I'm going to subpoena you, put you on the witness stand, prove that you were there, and ask you what you saw."

"You can't do that," Marquad said.

Mason pulled a folded paper from his pocket and said, "The hell I can't. I'll subpoena you right now."

Marquad made as though to push the paper back. "No, no, Mr. Mason," he said. "Please, please. Can't you understand? This place is open to the public."

"All right," Mason said, "did you see him there?"

Marquad shifted his eyes and said, "There was a little commotion at the club. I don't remember exactly what time it was. I was having a mild stimulant at the bar. A gentleman who answers this description had been in the inner office. There was the sound of rather loud conversation. After a moment, the bartender picked up something from behind the bar and stepped through the door into the office, but there was no trouble when the gentleman came out."

"Could you hear what was said?"

"No. I could hear the tone in the voices, however."

"Was the meeting friendly or hostile?"

"Decidedly hostile."

"What else did you see?"

"That's all."

"Were you there when we came in?" Mason asked. Marquad nodded. "How long were you there after that?"

"Nearly an hour, I guess. My—er—the young woman who was with me, was alternating between the bar and the gambling table. . . . Now, gentlemen, I certainly trust there won't be any publicity about this."

"Were you drinking?" Mason asked.

"Very sparingly. The bartender can vouch for that, Mr. Mason. I don't think I had over three drinks during the entire evening."

"All right," Mason said. "What's your contact with the place? How did you get in there?"

"What do you mean?"

"You don't ordinarily go around to gambling joints, do you?"

"No."

"Were you paying cash for your drinks?"

"Well—er—I—er, that is, I was, in a sense, the guest of the management. They'd asked me to drop in several times."

"Bill Golding?" Mason asked.

"Yes."

"He banks here?"

"Yes, I . . ."

"How well do you know him?" Mason interrupted.

"I have talked with him frequently."

"You know the woman who lives with him?"

"You mean his wife?"

"We'll let it go at that," Mason said.

"I've met her, yes."

"Now, then, did you have any talk with either of them after Cullens left?"

"No."

"Did you see them?"

"Only when they went out."

Mason's eyes narrowed slightly. "When did they go out?" he asked.

"I don't know just when it was, some time after Cullens left, and before you came in."

"Did you see them come in?"

"Yes."

"How long would you say they were gone?"

"I don't know, Mr. Mason, I'm sure."

"Could it have been as much as half an hour?"

"It could have been, yes. I didn't pay very much attention. . . . I . . . well, I was just as glad they didn't come over and speak to me. That is, the young lady who was with me . . ."

"I understand," Mason said. "Now, you noticed Mr. Drake and me when we came in?"

"Yes."

"Bill Golding and his wife had returned prior to that time. Do you know how long before?"

"It was some little time," Marquad said, "but I can't tell you how long."

"And how long was it after Cullens went out that Golding went out?"

"Well . . . Oh, say from fifteen minutes to half an hour. We were at the bar when Cullens came in, and we were eating dinner when Golding and his wife went out. As I remember it, we had finished dinner when they returned."

"All right," Mason said, "that's all. I just wanted to check up."

"You won't make my statement public in any way, Mr. Mason?"

"Not unless I have to," Mason told him, "and I don't think I'll have to. I'm just checking up, that's all. Come on, Paul."

They walked out of the bank, leaving Marquad standing at the counter, his eyes watching them with ill-concealed anxiety. Mason turned to Drake and said, "Check up on Bill Golding's car, Paul. There was a blue sedan parked at the curb just before Mrs. Breel stepped out into the street. You know, there's just a chance Bill Golding might be driving a blue sedan. I believe Diggers said the left rear fender was damaged."

Drake said, "That should be easy, Perry. I'll get at it right away. Want me to telephone the office?"

"Not now," Mason said. "It'll keep until you get back."

"What's next on the program?"

"Ione Bedford," Mason said.

"You don't want to wait until Pete Chennery shows up?"

"No," Mason said, "we haven't time to wait for anything. I want to get to her before the police do."

"Hold everything," Drake said. "Here we go."

It was Drake's theory that a detective car should be so completely average in appearance that an observer would find nothing sufficiently distinctive about it to attract attention on the one hand, or encourage memory on the other. Mason, sitting back against the cushions of the medium-priced, light-weight car two years old, watched Paul Drake cut through traffic and cheerfully take chances with fenders which had nothing to lose by an occasional lapse of judgment on the part of the driver.

"If," Mason said musingly, "Austin Cullens got the diamonds from Bill Golding, why didn't he notify Ione Bedford? If those were the Bedford diamonds, why did Mrs. Bedford deny they were hers? If they weren't the Bedford diamonds, where did they come from? If Bill Golding had the stones in the first place, why did he deny having them when we talked with him?

"If, on the other hand, Cullens got the stones from some other source and not from The Golden Platter, how did he discover that other source? Approximately two hours before his death, he was evidently firmly imbued with the idea that Bill Golding had the stones, was holding them for six thousand, but could be forced to part with them on the payment of three thousand."

"In other words," Drake said, "it's like making out an income tax statement. Every time you add up the figures, you get the wrong answer."

"I didn't know the income tax department bothered with detective agencies," Mason said, grinning.

"They don't. Detective agencies bother with the income tax department."

Mason lapsed once more into thoughtful silence. Drake swung his car into a parking place at the curb and said, "Well, Perry, get your ambush planted, because we're here."

Mason said, "I'm not going to plant any ambush. I'm going to play it straight from the shoulder."

"Do you think that will get you anywhere?" Drake asked.

"I don't know," Mason told him, "but somehow I figure her as a pretty straight-from-the-shoulder young woman."

"Remember," Drake warned, "that no matter what good points she may have, she's definitely living a double life."

"I know," Mason told him, and slid out from the seat, to stand on the sidewalk. "Is that your man in the roadster across the street, Paul?"

Drake nodded. The man in the roadster touched the

brim of his hat, lit a cigarette, shook out the match and settled back in the seat as though waiting for someone to join him. Drake interpreted the signals to Perry Mason. "The girl's in there. The man hasn't showed up yet."

Mason said, "All right, let's go," and led the way into the foyer of the apartment house. They took the elevator to the third floor. Mason tapped on the apartment door and said in a low voice to Paul Drake, "She doesn't know your voice. If she opens the door, we walk in. If she asks questions, tell her you have a package and a telegram."

Drake nodded. Ione Bedford's voice from behind the door called out, "Who is it, please?"

"Telegram and a package for Mrs. Chennery," Drake said.

She opened the door at once. Mason, stepping slightly to one side, placed the palm of his hand between Drake's shoulder blades and pushed him forward, so that her eyes focused on Drake first. "Well," she said impatiently, "where's the telegram and package? You can't come in . . ."

Mason pushed Drake slightly to the left while he moved to the right, pushing the door farther open. She swung to face the detective, apparently oblivious of the fact that another man was with him, until Mason had pushed the door completely open and was circling past her left arm. She turned to face him then, with an expression of annoyance, and her face froze into a mask of consternation. Mason, moving back, retrieved the edge of the door and swung it shut, calmly walked over to a chair and seated himself.

"What *is* this?" Ione Bedford demanded.

Mason said, "Drake's a detective, Mrs. Bedford."

"Chennery," she corrected.

"All right," he said, grinning, "he's still a detective, Mrs. Chennery."

Drake, watching Perry Mason for a signal, moved cautiously over to the arm of a davenport and sat down, taking care to keep himself between Mrs. Bedford and the door. She stood for a moment, nonplused, then abruptly laughed and said, "You're bluffing. He isn't a detective."

"What makes you think he isn't?" Mason asked, selecting a cigarette from his case.

"He's taken off his hat," she said. "Detectives don't take off their hats."

Mason grinned, and offered her a cigarette. She took it, and leaned forward for Mason's match. Her trembling manifested itself through the tips of her fingers as they guided the lawyer's hand against the match. "You," Mason charged, "have been to too many picture shows."

"No," she said, "I've seen too many detectives."

"Criminal record?" Mason asked.

"No," she said shortly.

"Sit down," Mason told her, "and tell me about it."

"There's nothing to tell."

"I think there is."

"Tell you about what?" she asked defiantly. "If you want to know, I'm really and truly Pete Chennery's wife. We're legally married."

"That," Mason said, "makes it more conventional, even if less romantic."

"Are you," she asked, "going to keep on with that casual wisecracking until you've drawn me out?"

"I think so," Mason said. "I don't know of any better way, do you?"

She settled back in a chair, crossed her knees, and said, "Where do you want me to begin?"

"At the beginning."

"Pete and I," she said, "had a fight."

"Much of a fight?" Mason asked.

"Quite a little squabble," she admitted.

"Over what?"

"Two blondes and a red-head."

"That," Mason told her, "should be grounds for a pretty good-sized battle."

"It was."

"So what happened?"

"I left him."

"And then?"

"Met Aussie," she said.

"With ideas in your head that you'd like to make your husband realize cheating was a game two could play at?"

She shook her head, started to say something, then caught herself, and was silent. "Don't kid me," Mason told her, "because you don't need to."

"How about your friend?" she asked, with a jerk of her head toward Drake.

"Like a dime bank," Mason told her. "Things go in easy, but you have to break him to get them out."

She studied the tips of her fingernails for a moment, then said, "All right, you win."

"What," Mason asked, after a moment, "have I won?"

She said, "Aussie was on a boat I took. I fell for him."

"Hard?" Mason asked.

"So-so," she admitted.

"And then what?"

"What do you want?"

"Everything."

"Well," she said after a moment, "Aussie had a way about him. He'd been places and done things. He had a genial way of taking life as a big adventure. It was all a game to him. I'd taken the cruise with a feeling of tragic frustration in my heart, a sense of tension, a feeling that I'd been wronged, that love was a mess, and marriage a mockery. I . . ."

"I don't want all that," Mason told her. "I've seen you and I've seen Cullens. I've seen the bitter side of married life as a lawyer sees it. You don't need to give me all that."

"What *do* I need to give you?"

"The gems."

"Oh, those," she said.

Mason smoked in silence. Then, after a moment, as she continued to study the tinted tips of her fingers with downcast eyes, Mason said, again, "Those."

She raised her eyes to his. "Well," she said, "I don't know much about those myself."

"Just what?" Mason asked.

"Of course," she said, by way of explanation, "I wasn't overly burdened with money. I had a little savings account. I ripped it wide open when I left Pete, to go out in the world and seek my fortune. I could have gone out and tried to get a job. Pete would have followed me then and begged me to forgive him. In the end, I'd have either had to give up my job and go back, in which event he'd have been the winner, or I'd have had to stay with the job and give up Pete, in which event I'd have been the loser."

"You didn't really intend to give him up, then?" Mason asked.

She said scornfully, "I thought you knew all about domestic tiffs."

Mason grinned and said, "Go ahead."

"So," she said, "I decided to buy myself some sport clothes, take along my best formals and cocktail gowns, go on a cruise, and leave Pete to do the guessing."

"And, of course," Mason said, "you wanted him to know that you were enjoying yourself on the cruise."

She smiled and said, "I sent him a picture postcard from Cartagena."

"Anything else?" Mason asked.

"The steamship company," she said, "put out a folder dealing with the romantic possibilities of the cruise—moonlight on the placid waters of the Caribbean, gay bathing parties under the slanting cocoanut palms, pleasant evenings, beginning with dances in the dance pavilion, and winding up as couples sauntered out into the moonlight to look at the churned wake of the boat, while tropical breezes bathed them in a gentle caress. I simply gave my husband's name as a possible customer, and suggested that they mail him folders.

"So, after having the folders on the one hand, and your postal on the other, he could draw his own conclusions, is that right?" Mason asked.

She nodded. "Go ahead," Mason said.

"Well, naturally, I thought he'd be waiting at the gangplank when I returned. But, a day or two out of port, I realized that I'd been foolish. Pete would never do anything like that. He's proud and haughty, and Southern."

"With quite a temper?" Mason asked.

"Lots of it."

"Jealous?"

"Yes."

"So what?" Mason inquired.

"Well," she said, "I'd gone so far I couldn't surrender. I was going to be pretty short of cash when I landed. Having started out to play the game the way I did, I couldn't possibly go to work, even if I could get a job. That would be a terrific come-down."

"So what did you do?" Mason asked.

"I think Aussie sized up the situation pretty well," she said. "Aussie was a shrewd judge of character. He'd done quite a bit of traveling and . . . well, he knew women."

"Meaning that he knew you?"

"He knew women, yes."

"Go ahead."

"Aussie," she said, "approached me with a proposition. He had some gems which he wanted to sell through a commission man. Aussie was a gem collector. Aussie explained it was like selling second-hand automobiles through classified ads. People sometimes hesitate to buy through a dealer, but if they think they can buy through a private party, they'll show more interest, so auto dealers would arrange with people to stay home Sundays and exhibit second-hand automobiles as private cars and . . ."

"I know," Mason interrupted, "and Aussie's proposition was that you were to pose as the owner of certain gems?"

"Yes."

"What were you to get out of it?"

"A salary and bonus," she said, "and I was to be put up in style in an apartment. I was to be a sophisticated, dashing divorcee, a woman of the world who was young, attractive, and had outgrown the conventions."

"Why the outgrown conventions?" Mason asked.

"So it would give me a reasonable excuse for flashing gems and wanting to dispose of them. Aussie said that people liked to think they were getting stones which had been lavishly bestowed on a careless sweetie who didn't fully realize their value, who found herself temporarily cast off and in need of keeping up appearances."

"Then Cullens really wanted you to be a front through which he could dispose of stones. Is that it?"

"Yes."

"But these old-fashioned stones hardly seemed to fit into that picture," Mason told her, interestedly.

"I think," she said, "that was part of the build-up."

"And what did they look like?"

She faced him then and said, "I don't know. I never saw them. He told me he was taking them up to George Trent to be recut and put in modern settings."

"And you were to sell them after that?"

"Mr. Trent, I believe, was to sell those. But I was to be in the background. If anyone made inquiries, I was to be the owner."

"So Trent could get a better price for them?" Mason asked. She nodded. "But," Mason said, "you rang up Trent on Monday morning, told him that you had a purchaser, that you'd decided not to . . ."

She said, "Aussie told me to do that."

"When?"

"About half an hour before I telephoned. He came over and coached me carefully in what I was to say. Then he stood by my side while I did the actual telephoning."

"You asked for Mr. Trent?"

"Yes."

"What did they tell you?"

"That he was out."

"Then what?"

"I asked with whom I was talking. The man said that he was the foreman in charge of the shop."

"And you told him what you wanted?"

"Yes."

"Cullens knew at the time that Trent wasn't there?"

"Yes," she said, "because he told me that I was to ask for Mr. Trent, that Trent was out on a drunk, that the shop would make excuses to stall me off; that I wasn't to be stalled. I was to insist on a return of the stones."

Mason regarded the smoke which spiraled upward from the tip of his cigarette. "Now, wait a minute," he said, "let's get this straight. You'd never seen these stones you were supposed to own?"

"No."

"Therefore," Mason said, "when you saw those stones in the handbag at police headquarters, you couldn't tell whether they were the ones you were supposed to have owned or not."

"That's right."

"But you said positively that they were not yours."

"I had to say something," she said. "I certainly couldn't say I didn't know my own stones and I figured . . . well, I figured it was a trap."

"You didn't know Cullens was dead at the time?" Mason asked.

Her eyes drifted away from his, then flashed back, as though the wince had been involuntary, and she had willed herself to face him as soon as she realized she had avoided his gaze. "No," she said, and then added after a moment, "of course not. How could I have known?"

Mason said, "You could have stalled along on the gems some way."

"Perhaps I could," she said, "but you put it up to me, cold turkey. I had to think fast and take the course which seemed best."

Mason got to his feet and walked over to the window. He stared moodily down into the street. A convertible with wire wheels drove up slowly. A tall young man got out. Mason shook his head, turned back to face the woman and said, "It doesn't make sense."

"I don't care," she said defiantly, "whether it makes sense of not."

"And then," Mason told her, "when I told you that Cullens was dead—that he'd been murdered—you streaked out of police headquarters and burned up the roads getting out here."

"Yes," she said. "I knew then that there'd be an inquiry, and I didn't want to get caught in it."

"Why?"

"Because of Pete," she said. "Can't you see? I didn't want Pete actually to catch me in an affair. That would have been fatal. On the other hand, I didn't want him to think he could start chasing around and get away with it. If I'd gone out and been a drab little personality, virtuously plodding my way through some routine job which would have barely paid my keep, Pete would have come and got me. He'd have been contrite on the surface, but he'd have had the smug feeling that I was his woman, that no one else wanted me, that I knew it, that if I left him again, it would be to go to work. He'd let me work a while, until I got good and lonely, and then come and pick me up. But, by going away and sailing on a cruise, I kept him guessing. I wanted to keep him guessing, but I certainly didn't want any of that guessing to become a cold certainty."

"You thought an inquiry would make that a cold certainty?"

She said, "I was living as Ione Bedford in an apartment which was paid for with Aussie's money. Frankly, it was a straight business deal. But any explanation I could have made to Pete wouldn't have held water."

"And so," Mason said, "with your desire to avoid getting trapped in the inquiry, you decided to come dashing back here. Is that right?"

"Yes."

Mason hooked his thumbs through the armholes of his vest and started pacing the floor. She watched him with wide, alert eyes, paying no attention whatever to Paul Drake, who slumped down on the davenport, his elbow propped against the upholstery, his palm holding the side of his head. For several seconds, Mason paced back and forth in thoughtful silence. Then he said, "No, it doesn't make sense."

"What doesn't?"

"You coming here."

She laughed nervously and said, "But I came here. It has to make sense."

"No," Mason said, "it doesn't. With the motivation you've outlined, your natural move would have been to go to some hotel, register under an assumed name and then let Pete know where he could find you. The sole object you had in leaving Pete was to make him come to you. You're too clever a woman, and too resourceful a woman, to have surrendered once you had victory practically within your grasp."

"Well," she said shortly, "I'm here."

Mason turned and faced her. "The reason you're here, Ione," he said slowly and steadily, "is because, when I told you Austin Cullens had been murdered, the thought which first flashed through your mind was that Pete had found Austin Cullens was keeping you in an apartment; that with his hot-blooded, Southern temper, his jealous disposition, and his ideas of protecting his home, he'd sought out Austin Cullens and . . ."

"It's a lie!" she screamed. "I tell you, it's a lie!"

The door from the corridor banged open. A tall young man, with black hair and cold, blue eyes, stood on the threshold and said, "What's a lie?"

"Pete!" she screamed.

Drake got to his feet. She ran toward the man who was standing on the threshold. Drake's arm reached out to circle her waist. She struggled with him like a wild cat. The man stepped forward two paces. Drake took one look at his eyes, and tried to free his arm from the girl's waist to block the punch. He was too late. The blow hit him on the side of the chin and staggered him backwards. The arm of the davenport, catching on the back of his legs, sprawled him back at full length, his feet kicking in the air. The girl flung her arms around the man. He brushed her to one side and kicked the door shut. He marched past the davenport, ignoring the struggling form of the detective, and stood facing Mason. "All right," he said with deadly calm, "now we'll hear from *you.*"

Mason, his thumbs still hooked in the armholes of his vest said calmly, "I think I'll hear from you instead, Chennery."

The woman said, "That's Perry Mason, the lawyer, Pete."

Chennery didn't take his eyes from Mason's. "What the hell's he doing here?" he asked her over his shoulder.

Drake, rolling from the davenport, got his feet under him and said to Chennery, "All right, let's try that again."

Chennery didn't even turn his head. He said to Mason, "Go ahead, start talking."

Mason looked past him to Drake and said, "You might frisk him, Paul, and see if, by any chance, he has a thirty-eight caliber revolver in his hip pocket."

"Pete! Don't let them!" the woman said. "You don't understand. They're two jumps ahead of you. They've . . . they know things you don't . . . they . . . they're going to frame you to save . . ."

Chennery said coolly, "Why the thirty-eight caliber revolver?"

Mason said, "Austin Cullens was shot with a thirty-eight caliber revolver."

"Who the hell's Austin Cullens?" Chennery asked.

His wife turned to look at Perry Mason with pleading anguish in her eyes. Mason said, "He happens to have been a man who was killed with a thirty-eight caliber revolver."

"So you thought you could frame something on me?" Chennery asked.

Mason chose his words thoughtfully. "Detectives working on the case reported a car had been parked near Cullens' residence at about the time of his death. The car was described as a red convertible with yellow wire wheels. The license number, as given by the witnesses, may be wrong, in one figure. If it is, it coincides with your license number, and the description of the man who was seen hanging around Cullens' place coincides with your description."

"So you were here, trying to bully something out of my wife?" Chennery asked.

"We asked her questions."

"And intimated I might have killed him?"

"She seemed to think that was what we had in mind," Mason said.

Chennery grinned, a cold, mirthless grin. "All right," he said, "go ahead, frisk me." He elevated his arms so that they were horizontal, his hands outstretched, the thumbs held wide from the palms. Drake searched through the man's pockets, patted him under the arms and said, "He's clean, Perry."

Mason said, "Yes, he'd hardly have been so foolish as to carry the gun around with him. He probably left it at the scene of the murder."

Chennery said, "You boys can't frame anything like that on me."

"You weren't home last night," Mason said, "all night."

Chennery turned to glower at his wife. Mason said, "Don't blame it on her. She hasn't spilled anything. We've had a detective watching the place ever since eleven o'clock last night."

"All right," Chennery said, "I wasn't home last night. So what does that add up to?"

"I don't know," Mason told him. "I want to know where you were."

"You're a lawyer?" Chennery asked. Mason nodded.

"And this other man's a detective," his wife said.

"Out of headquarters?" Chennery said, turning to Drake.

Mason said, "No. A private detective in my employ."

Chennery walked over to the door, held it open and said, "Go ahead, roll your hoops, both of you."

His wife put a pleading hand on his arm. "Listen, Pete," she said, "you can't do that to these men. They're . . ."

He shook her off and said to Mason, "I said, go ahead and roll your hoops."

Mason, for a moment, might not have heard him. He turned, thumbs still hooked in the armholes of his vest, his eyes, narrowed in thought, staring moodily out of the window. Drake said belligerently, "You talk big."

"I'm talking big," Chennery told him, "because I happen to have paid rent on this apartment. This is my home. You haven't any search warrants. Get out!"

"We might have a warrant of arrest," Drake said.

Chennery laughed. "A private detective," he mocked, "with a warrant of arrest. Phooey!"

Abruptly, Mason turned from the window. There was a twinkle about the corners of his eyes. "Come on, Paul," he said, "Chennery has all the aces."

"You mean we're leaving?" Drake asked. Mason nodded.

Chennery stood holding open the door. Wordlessly, Mason and the detective filed past him into the corridor. The door slammed shut behind them. Drake said protestingly, "Hell, Perry, that guy can't push us around. When it comes to a show-down, we're closer to solving the murder of Austin Cullens right now than we'll ever be again. . . ."

Mason linked his arm through the detective's and pulled him toward the elevator. "You forget, Paul," he said, "that *we* don't want to solve the murder."

"What the devil do you mean?" Drake asked.

"If *we* solve the murder," Mason went on smoothly, "Detective Sergeant Holcomb, of the homicide squad, wouldn't get the credit of solving the murder. Therefore, Sergeant Holcomb would be inclined to reject our solution as being a frame-up to get Sarah Breel acquitted. If, on the other hand, Sergeant Holcomb should decide that Pete Chennery should be investigated, he'd naturally . . ."

"My mistake," Drake interrupted. "I'm sorry, Perry. The punch on my jaw probably kept me from thinking as fast as I otherwise would have."

"Does it hurt?" Mason asked.

Drake half turned back toward the apartment. Mason could feel the detective's muscle tense under his coat sleeve. "You're damn right it hurts," he growled.

Mason continued to pull him toward the elevator.

"You can get an aspirin at the drug store," he told him.
"And here's something to bear in mind. We've let
Chennery know he's being shadowed. He won't have
much difficulty in spotting your detective out in front.
His next move will be to take it on the lam and try
ditching that detective. We tip that man off so the ditching won't be too difficult. But, in the meantime, we have
three under-cover detectives rushed out to begin where
this chap leaves off. Do you get me?"

"I get you," Drake said. "It'll be a pleasure to slip
one over on that baby."

"Okay," Mason told him. "You can telephone from
the drug store and then get an aspirin."

"Then what?" Drake asked.

"And then," Mason said with a grin, "you get busy
checking all important gem robberies during the last five
years. If Ione Bedford can't identify those diamonds,
there's a good chance someone else can. Of course, Paul,
I wouldn't want to tell you how to run your business,
but you *might* find some reward money if you checked
up on the activities of one Austin Cullens, deceased."

Drake slowly stroked his sore jaw. "For a detective,"
he said at length, "I *am* dumb."

10

■

Virginia Trent sat up in bed and regarded Mason with
heavy eyes. "Good morning, Mr. Mason," she said thickly.

"How do you feel?" Mason asked.

She made tasting noises with her mouth and said, "I
don't know. The nurse just woke me up."

A nurse, standing by the side of the bed, said, "You
were pretty much unstrung. The doctor gave you a sedative."

"I'll say he did," Virginia Trent said, rubbing her eyes. "I'll bet I look a fright. Give me a mirror and a drink of water."

The nurse brought the water but not the mirror. Virginia Trent drank it petulantly, regarded the heavy flannel nightgown which came high up around her neck and said to the nurse, "That's a nightgown I hardly ever wear. Where did you find it?"

"It was in the bottom of the drawer on the right-hand side. I . . ."

"Well, why didn't you get the ones in the upper drawer on top?"

"You'd had quite a shock," the nurse said. "I was afraid you might get chilled. Your resistance was lowered. The sedative started taking effect in the taxicab."

Virginia Trent said, "I remember now—those officers. They're a bunch of sadists. They love to torture the helpless."

"What did they do?" Mason asked.

"Thundered questions at me and almost drove me crazy," she said. "I guess I had hysterics again."

"You did," the nurse told her.

"Then what happened?"

"Finally a doctor gave you a sedative, and I was detailed to take you home and see that you slept."

"You mean, to see that I didn't try to escape," Virginia Trent said. The nurse was tactfully silent. "Where's my aunt?"

"In the hospital. She had only a very light concussion, and slept most of the night. The doctor didn't let the officers know she was conscious until this morning."

"How is she?"

Mason said, "Don't worry. She's quite able to take care of herself."

"What was all this they told me about finding her bag with the gun which killed Austin Cullens?"

Mason said, "They haven't been able to establish that it's her bag yet."

She yawned prodigiously. "You're going to have to

wait, Mr. Mason, while I wash my face in cold water and clean my teeth."

"All right," Mason told her, "I'm sorry I had to disturb you, but we have work to do."

"About—about—Uncle George—what did they find out?"

"Nothing, so far as I know," Mason said. "If they found out anything, they're keeping it secret."

"Is he—is—that is . . ."

"They had to make a post-mortem on the body," Mason said. "It's at a funeral home now."

"Turn your back," she told him. "I'm getting up."

"I'll do better than that," Mason said, "I'll wait downstairs in the library. Do you feel as though you could talk on an empty stomach?"

"No," she said shortly. "Where's Itsumo?"

"Downstairs," the nurse said.

"All right, I'm going to take a quick tub. Tell him I want tomato juice, with lots of Worcestershire sauce, coffee, scrambled eggs and toast. And you're going to have to wait, Mr. Mason, until I get to feeling halfway decent before I talk about anything."

Mason said, "I'll be downstairs."

"How about joining me with some eggs?"

"No, thanks. I had breakfast long ago."

"Coffee, then."

"I could go a cup of coffee and a cigarette," Mason told her. "I'll be waiting downstairs."

It was a good twenty minutes before she joined him. The Japanese cook served them with swiftly silent efficiency. Mason waited until she had finished eating and was sipping her second cup of coffee after the meal. "Suppose," he said, "you tell me about it."

"About what?"

"About everything."

"I don't know a thing to tell. You know as much as I do."

"How about that gun in the desk—did you know it was there?"

"Good Heavens, yes! I should have. I've shot it enough."

"You have?"

She nodded. "When?" Mason asked.

"Off and on for the last six months. About once a week I go out in the country and practice."

"May I ask why?" Mason inquired.

"Because," she said grimly, "I'm there alone much of the time. There are thousands of dollars worth of jewels in that vault. I certainly don't propose to be stuck up, and stand there like a ninny while some highwayman goes through the vault and cleans Uncle George out."

"Aren't they insured?"

"Some of them are. But it isn't a question of the insurance, Mr. Mason, it's a question of the development of my own character. I want to be self-reliant. . . . If you keep walking with crutches, your legs get weak. I want to stand on my own two feet. . . . I have a boyfriend who . . . well, he likes self-reliant women . . . and he's quite a revolver shot. I want to share in his life. I want to like the things he likes. I want to be his pal. I think a woman who doesn't cultivate the same tastes as the man she's interested in is making a big mistake. Biologically, we know that opposites attract each other, but that's opposite temperaments. After the original attraction has cooled, the basis of companionship has to be a sharing of interests. People can't get along forever, just on the strength of a biological attraction. Companionship between the sexes is comprised of two very distinct stages. First, there's the biological reaction. Then there's the . . ."

Mason said, "I'm talking about revolver shooting. You're talking about matrimony."

"Not matrimony," she said, "just the basic reactions. Matrimony is an outgrowth of . . ."

"Never mind what it is," Mason said. "Let's quit talking about what you're talking about and talk about what I'm trying to talk about." She flushed. "And that," Mason said, "means revolver shooting."

"Well," she said, "there's nothing to add to what I've

told you. For the past six months I've been practicing revolver shooting. And," she said, "I've become quite proficient."

"Your practice was with this thirty-eight caliber?"

"Most of it. I fired some shots from what they call a service revolver, but it had too much recoil."

"Did you," Mason asked, "tell the officers about all this revolver practice?" She nodded. "Then how were you able to convince them you hadn't shot your uncle?"

"Partially," she said, "because of the fact he was killed Saturday afternoon, and, as it happened, I could account for every minute of my time. Tell me, Mr. Mason, are they going to start pounding me with a lot of third-degree stuff again this morning?"

"I don't think so," Mason said.

"What makes you think they won't?"

"Because," Mason told her, "I'm going to be here."

"They won't let you stay," she said.

Mason grinned and said, "It happens that they have nothing to say about it unless they actually arrest you, charge you with murder, and take you to jail. So far, they're not ready to do that. I have a court order permitting me, as your attorney, to confer with you. Of course, the nurse has telephoned the news, and . . . Here they come, now."

A siren sounded, and Virginia Trent pushed back her coffee cup. "I suppose," she said wearily, "I can take it, but . . . well, coming on top of all the other things— and finding Uncle George . . ."

Mason said, "Promise me you won't get nervous. Sit tight and let me do the arguing."

"The officers won't like that," she said.

Before Mason could say anything, there was the sound of steps on the porch of the big house. The nurse beat Itsumo to the front door. She flung it open and said, "They're in the dining room."

Sergeant Holcomb and two plain-clothes detectives marched through the door and into the dining room. "What's the idea?" Sergeant Holcomb demanded of Perry Mason.

"Court order," Mason said, showing him a document.

"I knew I should have kept you in jail," Sergeant Holcomb said to Virginia Trent. "That's what I get for trying to give you a break."

"Don't blame me," she said indignantly. "I was sleeping when Mr. Mason woke me up."

"And, if you'd held her in jail," Mason said, "I'd have had a writ of *habeas corpus,* so it's just as broad as it is thick."

Sergeant Holcomb sat down and motioned the two detectives to chairs. "I suppose," he said to Perry Mason, "you're going to advise her not to answer questions, and stand on her constitutional rights?"

"On the contrary," Mason said, "we're going to do everything we can to assist you."

"Yes, I have a picture of that," Sergeant Holcomb said sarcastically. "You may not know it, but this young woman has admitted to me that she knew the gun was in the drawer, that she's taken it with her into the country on several occasions, and has practiced with it until she's a very fair shot."

"So what?" Mason asked.

"Draw your own conclusions," Holcomb said.

"I suppose," Mason told him, "you've performed a post-mortem?" Holcomb nodded.

"All right," Mason said, "let's go at the thing sensibly. George Trent was killed some time Saturday afternoon."

"How do *you* know?"

Mason said, "I haven't found out just what the autopsy surgeon has to say on the subject, but the body was dressed as it had been dressed on Saturday. There wasn't much of a stubble, the shirt was not particularly soiled. Moreover, the body had been placed in a packing case and lifted to a place of concealment on the top of a pile of packing cases. George Trent was a big man. His niece could no more have placed the body up there than she could have lifted a corner of the office building."

"An accomplice could have done it for her," Sergeant Holcomb said.

Mason nodded. "What's more," Sergeant Holcomb told

him, "don't forget that this man had started out to get drunk. He'd taken his car down and parked it in a zone which is restricted to thirty-minute parking during the daytime. He'd taken out the car keys, put them in an envelope and mailed them to himself at the office. Then he'd gone out to get drunk and gamble."

"Exactly," Mason said, "and something happened to make him return to his office. Now, what was it?"

"I don't know," Sergeant Holcomb admitted. "That's what I want to find out."

"Don't you think you'd get farther if you started investigating from that end before you browbeat Miss Trent simply because she happened to know that a gun was in that drawer and knew how to use it?"

"I'm not browbeating anyone."

"The girl had hysterics last night," Mason said. "You carried her up to headquarters and shot questions at her until she had to be put under the care of a doctor."

"All right, we got a doctor and sent her home when she had hysterics the second time," Holcomb said. "She's all right this morning."

Mason said, "I have reason to believe that the first and only gambling place George Trent went to was The Golden Platter on East Third."

"All right, what of it?"

"Something happened there to make him go back to his office. Don't you think it would be a good plan for you to try and find out what that something was?"

"I'm running my investigation," Sergeant Holcomb said.

"Moreover," Mason went on smoothly, "if you neglect this end of it, and the charge should be made that the officers are deliberately overlooking that angle because it has suited their policy to close their eyes to a gambling establishment running wide open, don't you think . . ."

"Who says there's a gambling establishment there?" Sergeant Holcomb demanded belligerently.

"I do," Mason told him. "Now, what are you going to do about it?"

Sergeant Holcomb thought for a minute and said, "I'm going to make it my business to investigate it."

"All right," Mason said, "and I'm going to make it my business to investigate your investigation. In the meantime, I'm going to account for every single minute of this young woman's time on Saturday afternoon and Saturday evening. . . . You closed the office at noon, Virginia?"

"Yes."

"Where did you go?"

"I went out in the country."

"For a walk?"

"Yes. My boy-friend and I were doing some . . ."

Mason said, "All right, I want to go into that with you in private. I think we'll let Sergeant Holcomb conclude the other angle of his investigation before we . . ."

Holcomb said, "That answer sort of floored you, didn't it, Mason?"

"What's wrong with that answer?" Mason asked.

Holcomb said, "You don't need to be so fast when it comes to covering up, Mason. I know what you're afraid of. Now let *me* tell *you* something. This young woman told us all about that last night. I asked her if she took the gun with her, and she said yes. She and her friend were doing some shooting."

Mason flashed a swift glance of inquiry at Virginia Trent. She nodded and said, "All right, what if I did? We've been doing it for the last six months. He can account for every minute of my time during the afternoon."

"Just who is this boy-friend?" Mason asked.

"Lieutenant Ogilby. He's in my psychology class at night school."

Mason looked at Sergeant Holcomb. Holcomb nodded. "He checks," he said shortly. "They went out about one-thirty. Trent was eating lunch at the counter next to his office building when they left. She arrived back here about six. They'd been together all the time."

Mason said, "Excuse me, I'm going to put in a telephone call. Where's the telephone, Miss Trent?"

"There in the hallway," she told him.

Mason dialed Paul Drake's office, said, "Is Paul in?
. . . All right, let me talk with him. . . . Hello, Paul.
This is Perry Mason. What did your men find out from
the janitor at Trent's office building?"

Drake said, "I have a complete report on that, Perry.
Trent closes his office at noon on Saturday, but there are
lots of offices in that same building which stay open all
Saturday afternoon, so they keep regular elevator service
running until six-thirty Saturday night. After six-thirty,
the elevators all shut down except the one operated by
the janitor. The janitor has an In-and-Out Book that
people have to sign when they ride in the elevator. Now,
that In-and-Out Book shows that Virginia Trent went
up to the office Saturday evening about eight o'clock and
stayed until about nine-ten. Sarah Breel went to the office Sunday morning at ten-thirty, and stayed until twelve-
five. That's all. It doesn't show Trent himself either in
or out. That means Trent must have gone out some time
Saturday afternoon, started to get drunk, and then returned to the office before six-thirty. Up until six-thirty,
he could ride up and down in the elevators without anyone paying any attention to him.

"The janitor went into Trent's office at seven-thirty to
clean up. He was there half an hour. No one else was
there. He saw Virginia Trent leaving the elevator just as
he was leaving the office—so he left the door open for her.
She was alone. Now then, here's something else, Perry.
One of the newspaper boys tells me the autopsy surgeon
has checked up on the time of death pretty accurately.
They've found out where Trent had lunch Saturday, and
when. Their best guess is that he was killed about four-
thirty o'clock Saturday afternoon, very probably not later
than five. The police don't like that, but those are the
facts just the same."

Mason said, "Thanks," hung up and walked back to
the dining room.

"Well, Sergeant," he said, "let's get down to brass tacks.
If you want to put a charge against Miss Trent, go right
ahead."

"I'm not putting any charge against her," Holcomb said. "I'm trying to get facts."

Mason said, "In other words, George Trent was killed not later than five o'clock Saturday afternoon. Miss Trent had that gun in her possession Saturday afternoon, and she has a good alibi."

Sergeant Holcomb leaned toward Perry Mason. "Mason," he said, "you and I have been on the opposite sides of a few cases. Let's not let it keep us from talking sense on *this* case. I don't know what we're going to find out. But I do know that it's a physical impossibility for Virginia Trent to have had *that* gun with her Saturday afternoon. She's mistaken about it, that's all, and if she persists in that mistake, it's going to keep us from getting a conviction when we arrest Trent's murderer. Now, I want this young woman to co-operate, that's all."

Mason grinned at Virginia Trent and said, "Go ahead and co-operate."

"But I don't see what you're getting at," she said. "I . . ."

"Sergeant Holcomb perhaps didn't know as much when he was questioning you last night as he does now," Mason told her. "If he did, he was holding out. Your uncle was killed before seven-thirty."

"But he doesn't need to have been shot with the revolver that was in that desk," she said. "Good Heavens, there are plenty of thirty-eight caliber revolvers . . ."

"No, there aren't," Holcomb said. "Our ballistics department has made micro-photographs of the bullet which killed your uncle and a test bullet fired from that gun. The bullets came from the same gun. Now then, what time did you and Lieutenant Ogilby return?"

"I think we got here at the house at about six o'clock."

"Your friend didn't stay for dinner?"

"No."

Sergeant Holcomb said, "Let's get that Jap in here."

One of the men stepped into the kitchen and brought in the Japanese, who stood squat, poised and inscrutable, his lacquer-black eyes returning Sergeant Holcomb's glowering scrutiny. "What's your name?"

"Itsumo."

"You have another name?"

"Yes, sir. Itsumo Shinahara."

"How long have you been here?"

"Five months three days today."

"Do you remember Saturday night?"

"Very well, sir."

"What time did you have dinner?"

"Thirty minutes behind seven o'clock."

"You mean six-thirty?"

The man grinned. "Yes, sir."

"Who was here at dinner?"

"Miss Virginia and Mrs. Sarah Breel. Mr. George Trent not come."

"You knew he was not coming?"

"No, sir."

"You set a place for him?"

"Yes, sir."

"Do you know what time Miss Trent came in Saturday afternoon?"

"About twenty minutes before dinner time. I look at clock to see about cooking meat."

"What kind of meat?"

"Steak, please."

"How long were they at dinner?"

"You mean how long take to eat dinner?"

"Yes."

"I have Saturday night off," Itsumo said. "I have appointment with friend to study enlargement of films at camera school. Class is eight o'clock. I hurry very quickly, get finished with dishes thirty minutes behind eight o'clock. I telephone my friend and take street car twenty minutes behind eight o'clock. I get to class just short time before class starts, I think perhaps one minute."

"And were Mrs. Breel and Miss Trent here when you left?"

"Miss Virginia leave before I did, perhaps five minutes. Mrs. Sarah Breel is here, please."

Sergeant Holcomb turned to Virginia Trent. "Did you," he asked, "clean the gun after you shot it?"

"Certainly. I cleaned it and oiled it in my room. My uncle showed me how to take care of it."

"And you cleaned and oiled it?"

"Yes."

"And reloaded the gun?"

"Yes."

"And didn't take it to the office until eight o'clock?"

"I think it was almost exactly eight o'clock."

Sergeant Holcomb shook his head and said, "Now, look here, Miss Trent, you're mistaken about that gun. That gun killed your uncle. Your uncle met his death around four-thirty Saturday afternoon. Now then, you couldn't have had that gun with you."

"But I did have it."

Sergeant Holcomb said, "Now wait a minute. You *think* you had it, but you didn't notice it particularly, did you?"

"What do you mean?"

"You didn't check the numbers on the gun?"

She smiled and said, "Of course not."

"You simply took *a* gun out of the desk drawer and put it in your purse, didn't you?"

She nodded. "And all you know is it was a thirty-eight caliber revolver."

"It was the same make," she said, "as the one I'd been shooting. I know that."

"But there's nothing about it which will enable you absolutely to identify it, is there?"

"No," she said slowly, "there isn't."

"Now then, at eight o'clock Saturday night, you returned to the office and put that gun which was in your purse in the drawer, didn't you?"

"Yes."

"Was there any other gun in the drawer at that time?"

"No."

"How were you dressed when you returned that gun to the office?"

"What do you mean?" she asked. "I had on street clothes."

"Were you wearing gloves?"

She frowned for a moment and said, "I was wearing gloves when I came to the office, but I . . . No, I wasn't, either. I wasn't wearing gloves."

"The gun was in your purse?"

"Yes."

"And you took it out and put it in the drawer?"

"Yes."

"Did you handle it at all—that is, did you make any investigation to make certain it was loaded?"

"I opened the cylinder and looked at it to make certain it was loaded, yes. I always do that before I put it in the drawer."

Sergeant Holcomb said triumphantly, "All right, Miss Trent, that proves my point. You didn't have the gun which killed George Trent."

Her silence showed her complete lack of conviction.

"What makes you think she didn't?" Mason asked.

"Because," Holcomb said, "our examination of that gun shows that the last person who handled it had been wearing gloves. Any latent finger-prints which were on it were smudged so they were virtually valueless, and from the manner in which the prints were smudged, our expert figured the gun was last handled by someone with gloves. And it had been handled quite a bit."

Mason flashed a quick glance at Virginia Trent, then turned back to Sergeant Holcomb. "Go ahead, Sergeant, let's hear the rest of it."

Sergeant Holcomb said, "I think you can co-operate with us in this, Mason. You see what happened. Someone removed George Trent's gun and put another one in its place. Some time Monday morning, that person returned George Trent's gun to the drawer and took out the one which had been left there."

"Why do you say Monday morning?" Mason asked.

"Because no one went to the office after six-thirty Saturday night, until eight o'clock Monday morning, with the exception of Miss Trent Saturday evening, and Mrs. Breel Sunday."

"I see," Mason said, "and just what do you want us to do?"

Sergeant Holcomb's tone was almost pleading. "News-paper reporters are going to be talking with this young woman," he said. "I don't want her to say anything about the gun."

Mason turned to Virginia Trent. "Under the advice of your counsel," he said, "you're not to discuss this case with anyone. Do you understand?"

She nodded. Sergeant Holcomb gave Mason his hand. "That," he said, "is damned white of you, Mason."

Mason grinned. "Not at all, Sergeant. It's always a pleasure to co-operate with you."

11

Mason was grinning gleefully as he entered his office. Della Street said, "Why the cat-swallowed-the-canary ex-pression, Chief?"

Mason said, "I was thinking of the logic and beauty of an old bit of philosophy."

"Tell me the philosophy first," she said, "and then I'll tell you whether I agree with you."

"The philosophy," Mason said, "is a quotation having to do with an engineer."

She knitted her brow. "An engineer?" she asked.

Mason, scaling his hat at the hat rack, said, "Uh-huh, and it goes like this: 'For 'tis sport to see the engineer, hoist by his own petard.'"

"Something seems to tell me," she said, "that it's going to get us into trouble."

"On the contrary," Mason told her, "it's going to get us out of trouble. And, by the way, Della, do you know that one of the greatest troubles with police officers is that they lack imagination?"

"Just what in particular are you referring to?" she asked.

"I was thinking," he said, "about the historical background leading up to the identification of bullets by comparison and micro-photography. You know, Della, it's only within the last few years that it's been demonstrated that little marks and blemishes in the barrel of a revolver automatically finger-print a bullet which is discharged from it."

"Sure," she said, "it's only during the last few years that the radio has been perfected. And think of the strides we've made in sales and income taxes, Chief."

He grinned. "Getting serious for the moment, Baggage, where a man is utilizing some scientific invention, you'd think he'd want to know something of the history back of that invention."

"Well," she said, "I hate to distract you from your philosophical contemplation of crime, but it occurs to me that while you're being serious I'd better dissipate your mood of joyous hilarity by telling you the worst."

"What," he asked, "is the worst?"

"One of Drake's detectives is looking for you with blood in his eye."

Mason, still grinning, said, "Did you say blood *in* his eye or *on* his eye, or, perhaps, *around* his eye?"

"How did you know, Chief?"

"More deductive reasoning," he said.

"If the man ever heard you make that crack he'd . . ."

She broke off as Paul Drake knocked his peculiar code sequence on the door. Mason strode over to open it. Drake walked in and said, "Our friend Chennery believes in direct methods, Perry."

"What happened?" Mason asked.

Drake said, "About five minutes after we left Chennery's place, Chennery came out, walked over to the roadster where my operative was sitting and said, 'Your lawyer friend told me I was being shadowed, and you look like the shadow.' "

"Then what?" Mason asked.

"My operative doesn't remember," Drake said, grinning. "He says a building fell on him, but he's probably exaggerating. About ten minutes later, when the extra men I'd telephoned for showed up, they found this bird tied up in the bottom of the car, with adhesive tape pasted over his eyes and lips."

"Chennery?" Mason asked.

"Gone," Drake said. "Slipped through our fingers. But we're tailing his wife, and she'll lead us to him sooner or later."

"She didn't get away?"

"No. Chennery beat up my operative and skipped out. She waited to pack up, and must have left about ten or fifteen minutes after he did. My men showed up just as she was pulling out."

"Where is she now?" Mason asked.

"Out at the Monadnock Hotel, registered as Mrs. Charles Peabody of New Orleans."

"Okay," Mason said. "Sew her up tight. Try and get a dictograph planted in her room. Plant operatives in the adjoining rooms, and keep your eye peeled for *Mister* Charles Peabody."

"That," Drake said with a grin, "has already been done."

Mason said, "You know, Paul, that's a professional trick, taping a man's eyes and mouth."

"I'll say it is," Drake agreed.

"I also noticed that Chennery seemed to know the ropes. As soon as I told him you were a detective, he wanted to know whether you were from headquarters. When he found out you weren't, he started getting tough." Drake nodded. "And," Mason went on, "according to the homicide squad, the light fuse in Austin Cullens' residence blew out because someone unscrewed a lamp globe, slipped a copper penny into the socket, and then screwed the light back. As soon as the lights were turned on, it blew the fuse. That's also a professional trick."

Drake nodded thoughtfully. "You have something there, Perry. Mrs. Breel would never have done that."

Mason said, "A person who would short-circuit a fuse that way would be inclined to use adhesive tape on a man's eyes and lips. There's a certain similarity in the technique, Paul, an efficiency in obtaining maximum results with a minimum effort."

Drake said, "Therefore, I take it, Perry, you want my operative to make a complaint to the police and . . ."

"No," Mason said, "I don't. I'm simply mentioning the point for your own information, Paul—in case you meet up with Mr. Charles Peabody of New Orleans."

"I get you," the detective said. "Here's something else, Perry. Bill Golding is driving a new maroon-colored sedan."

Mason's eyes narrowed. "I'm interested in the adjective, Paul," he said.

"Maroon-colored?" Drake asked. Mason shook his head. Drake said, "I get you, Perry . . . but I doubt if it's that new."

"Find out," Mason told him.

"Okay. Now here's the big thing, Perry. I've identified the Bedford diamonds. Your hunch was one hundred percent right. The stones found in that bag, and being held at police headquarters, were taken in a gem theft in New Orleans six months ago. A bunch of antique jewelry was picked up by professional cracksmen and the insurance companies have been moving heaven and earth, trying to get some trace of them."

"You've notified the insurance company?"

"That's what I wanted to ask you about," Drake said. "The question is, can I go ahead with it? There's a reward of two thousand dollars which we could split and . . ."

"No rewards," Mason said. Then as he saw the detective's face fall, went on, "That is, for me. You take all the rewards. . . . But do you know, Paul, it might not be a bad idea to make a split with Sergeant Holcomb."

"That stuffed shirt!" Drake exclaimed. "Why should I split with him?"

"He might be more willing to co-operate on the other stuff," Mason said.

"What other stuff?"

"I think you'll find plenty of it," Mason told him. "By

the time you go through the stones which Cullens had on consignment with George Trent, and in safety deposit boxes, you might find some more rewards."

"You think Cullens has stuff salted away?" Drake asked.

"I think he was a big fence," Mason told him. "If you collect your two thousand dollars' reward on this, you'll have a fight on your hands. You won't get any other reward. Holcomb will move in and sew everything up. Moreover, he'll claim the stones are in the possession of the police department and . . ."

"I see your point," Drake said. "Is it all right for me to take him into my confidence?"

"First get a definite agreement out of him," Mason said. "Holcomb and I are co-operating on this case."

"You're what!"

Mason grinned. "Co-operating."

"Since when?" Drake asked.

"Since Holcomb asked me to," Mason said.

"Isn't that rather unusual?" Drake inquired.

"That," Mason grinned, "is more than unusual. It's unique."

Drake said, "The district attorney wants to rush that Cullens murder before the grand jury. I've got a complete signed statement from Diggers. . . . This business about the gems being stolen is going to make quite a splash."

"I presume," Mason said, "Sergeant Holcomb will be moving heaven and earth to get Pete Chennery and his wife."

"He would if he knew what we do," Drake said.

"Well," Mason remarked, "Sergeant Holcomb and I are co-operating on the case."

"You mean to tell Sergeant Holcomb all about Mrs. Chennery's story?"

"Oh, I wouldn't go *that* far," Mason said. "After all, the Sergeant is a bit touchy and he might resent having the whole case worked out for him, but Mrs. Ione Bedford went to headquarters with me last night to identify the stones in that bag. She couldn't do it. I told her that

Austin Cullens had been murdered, and she left in something of a hurry. She picked up a taxicab and went directly to Pete Chennery's apartment. You know, if you
dropped a hint to Sergeant Holcomb, he'd probably start
tracing the taxicabs in order to find where Mrs. Bedford went. That would give him pretty much of a line on
the entire situation, and he wouldn't feel he'd received
too *much* help from us."

Drake shook his head and said, "Perry, if you're pulling a fast one, I . . ."

Mason looked hurt. "Good Lord, Paul, be reasonable.
First you jump on me because I'm asking you to do
things which may get the officers down on you, and then
when I give you a chance to do something which will
get you in strong with the homicide squad, you start crab-
bing about it."

Drake said, "I know there's a catch in it somewhere,
but I haven't time to find out where. I'm on my way."

"And, by the way," Mason said, "you might suggest
to Sergeant Holcomb after he's found the Chennery
apartment that it would be a good plan for the two of
you to get some finger-prints out of it. There's just a
chance this man Chennery might have a record. You
know, he seems rather professional."

"I get you," Drake said, starting for the door. "I'm on
my way to see Holcomb."

"And there's one thing I'd like to have you get," Mason said.

"What's that?"

"A photograph of the cylinder of the gun which killed
George Trent."

"You mean the one which killed Cullens, don't you?"
Drake asked. "That's the one which was in Mrs. Breel's
bag."

Mason said sternly, "Don't refer to it as Mrs. Breel's
bag, Paul. It hasn't been identified as hers. No, I mean
the gun which killed George Trent. I'm interested in
that."

"And you want a photograph of the cylinder?"

"Yes," Mason said, "an enlargement if possible. And

I want it just the way it appears now, that is, with the shells in it."

"That should be a cinch," Drake told him, "after the way I'm going to co-operate with the homicide squad."

"On your way," Mason told him. "Start co-operating."

When Drake had left, Mason turned to face Della Street, a smile twitching at the corners of his lips. She studied him thoughtfully for a moment, then said, "You know, if you were a little boy and I were your mother, I'd make a rush for the jam closet . . . and find I'd got there too late. You, Mr. Perry Mason, have been up to mischief. Now, come over here and tell Mamma what it is."

He pushed his hands down deep in his trousers pockets. His eyes twinkled with enjoyment. "I have a surprise for you," he said.

"How much of a surprise?"

"A humdinger of a surprise."

"Tell me."

"Our wallflower," he said, "is a hibiscus in disguise."

"A hibiscus!"

"Well, perhaps an orchid."

"You wouldn't, by any chance, be letting anyone kid you, would you, Chief?"

He shook his head and lowered his voice as though imparting a deep and mysterious secret. "Of course," he said, "I'm no gossip, and I wouldn't say this to anyone but you, and I don't want you to repeat it. Of course, I can't be certain myself because I got it from that snooty old Mrs. Blank, and she's the worst gossip on earth, but her brother-in-law works for a Broadway columnist and his secretary told . . ."

She laughed and said, "Come on, Chief, back to normal, and give me the low-down. My heart's going pitty-pat."

Mason said, "Virginia Trent has a boy-friend."

"Oh-oh," Della Street exclaimed, clapping her right hand over her heart and fanning herself with her left hand. "Air! Give me air! . . . My poor heart! . . . You wouldn't kid a working girl, would you, Chief?"

Mason said, "She went for a walk with him Saturday afternoon, Della—a walk out into the secluded canyons and glades of the hill country back of the city."

"Accompanied, I suppose, by two chaperons and a book on the psychology of courtship," Della Street said.

"No," Mason told her. "But evidently he isn't the ordinary sort of boy-friend. He's an earnest, sober, industrious individual who studies psychology in night school."

"Well," Della Street said, contemplating the problem with an elaborately puckered forehead, "he has possibilities anyway. He didn't take her to the public library, and that's something."

"No," Mason said. "They went out into the wooded pathways—but they do the quaintest things."

"Don't tell me," she said. "Let me guess. . . . They pitch horseshoes . . . no, they study astronomy . . . no. Ah, Wait a minute, I'm getting hot, Chief. It's botany! Or zoology! They go after the flora and fauna with magnifying glasses, and a sober, earnest attitude toward life. If his hand accidentally brushes hers in reaching for a gilded butterfly, he promptly apologizes, and she's so broad-minded she thinks nothing more of it."

"Almost," he told her, "but not quite. The man's a lieutenant in the army, who studies psychology in his spare time, and he and Virginia take these delightful strolls for the purpose of practicing revolver shooting."

Della Street said, "You'd think any man who read the newspapers and realizes that, so far, the legislatures haven't seen fit to put closed seasons on husbands, would know better than to teach a prospective wife how to shoot a revolver."

"You don't need to teach 'em," Mason said. "They never miss. Study the newspaper accounts for yourself."

"Well," she observed, "I see that it's time for me to shed my air of persiflage. Something seems to tell me you are about to get serious, Chief. You didn't bring this up just to give me a thrill over the love-life of a wallflower, did you?"

"No," he said. "The man's name is Ogilby—Lieutenant Ogilby. She met him at night school, where she's been studying psychology. That'll give you a line on him. I want you to find him."

"Then what do I do?"

"Then," he said, "you win his confidence."

"Am I supposed to encourage him to make forward passes," she asked, "or do I imbue him with the idea of gently but firmly taking Virginia Trent by the hand and . . ."

"Not that," Mason said, "but you get him to take you out to the place where he and Virginia were doing their target shooting Saturday afternoon. You get him talking about revolvers . . . and then you ask him to pick up all of the empty shells he can find, and save them."

"All of them?"

"Yes."

"You mean the shells which were ejected from the guns they were shooting?"

"That's right."

"And then what?"

"Simply save them," Mason said, "in some nice, safe place, where Sergeant Holcomb wouldn't be apt to look for them; but, on the other hand, where we can't be accused of tampering with them. I would say it might be well to let Lieutenant Ogilby keep them."

"And if Virginia decides that I'm trying to steal her man and . . ."

"Virginia isn't to know anything about it," Mason said. "You are to impress that on Lieutenant Ogilby."

"Wouldn't it be better," she asked, "to have one of Drake's men get in touch with him? After all, Chief, having me take him in hand and . . ."

"No," Mason interrupted, "it's up to you, Della. I don't want Drake to know anything about it."

"Why?" she asked.

Mason's eyes twinkled. "Drake's co-operating with Sergeant Holcomb."

"I thought you were too," she said.

"I am," Mason told her. "But co-operation is a very elastic term. People have different definitions of it."

"What's Sergeant Holcomb's definition?" she asked.

Mason lit a cigarette. "Oh, Sergeant Holcomb," he said casually, "looks at it about the same way I do."

"I see," she told him, sliding her extended forefinger across her throat, and reached for the telephone.

12

■

Della Street, softly closing the door behind her, said, "Better get your bullet-proof vest out of mothballs, Chief."

"What's the matter?" Mason asked.

"A Mr. and Mrs. Golding are in the outer office, and they're mad."

"Mr. William Golding, who runs the gambling joint known as The Golden Platter?" Mason asked.

"He didn't say what his occupation was, but it seems you've served him with a subpoena to appear as a witness for the defense in the case of People *vs.* Sarah Breel, and he's on the warpath."

"And the woman?" Mason asked.

"She was served as Eva Tannis. And is *she* mad. She says her name is Eva Golding."

"They didn't show you a marriage certificate, did they?" Mason asked.

"No kidding, Chief," she said. "They're going to get tough."

"Fine," Mason said, pushing aside the pile of mail which he had been reading. "Bring them in, Della, and let them get tough."

The woman came through the door first, head high, chin up, eyes flashing. Behind her, Bill Golding walked softly, his face an expressionless mask. Only his eyes, glinting with sullen fires, gave any indication of his feelings. "Sit down," Mason invited. "Close the door, Della."

Golding said, "What's the idea of serving that damned subpoena on us?"

"I want you as witnesses," Mason said.

"On behalf of the *defendant?*"

"That's right."

Golding laughed sarcastically and said, "And I thought you were a *good* lawyer!"

"Opinions differ on the subject," Mason admitted easily.

"You've insulted my wife," Golding went on, his lips tight with rage.

"I'm sorry," Mason said.

"What the devil did you mean by subpoenaing her as Eva Tannis?"

"I understood that was her name."

"Well, it isn't. Her name's Mrs. Golding."

"I'm very sorry, Mrs. Golding," Mason said, "but I wanted the subpoena to be binding, so I wasn't taking any chances."

She regarded him with glittering eyes, the lids slightly narrowed. Her dilated nostrils gave evidence of her emotion. "You're going to regret that, Mr. Perry Mason," she said.

"Regret what?"

"Serving a subpoena on us."

"Oh, I don't think so."

"Well, I do."

Golding said, "Look here, Mason. You know as well as I do that we're running a joint. You bring us into court, and I'm going to be asked about my name, residence, and occupation. Then they're going to ask Eva a lot of things. Those things aren't going to do any of us any good."

"They may do my client some good," Mason said.

"That's what *you* think."

Mason ignored the sarcasm and said, "How about a cigarette, *Mrs.* Golding."

"No . . . thank you."

"You, Golding?"

"No."

Mason took a cigarette and said, "Well, I'll have one. You're driving a new car, aren't you, Golding?"

"What's that got to do with it?"

"Oh, nothing much," Mason said, lighting his cigarette. He shook out the match, exhaled the first deep drag of smoke, and said, "I understand you bought it the day after Cullens was murdered."

"So what?"

"I was interested in the car you traded in," Mason said. "It was in pretty good shape. You'd had it less than six months."

"My God!" the woman exploded. "Do we have to account to a lawyer every time we want to trade in a car?"

Without looking at her, Mason went on evenly, "I became interested in that trade-in, Golding. I had my detectives find out about the car. It was a blue sedan with a crumpled left rear fender. I don't know whether you know it,' but Diggers says that just before Mrs. Breel stepped out from the sidewalk, a car which had been parked at the curb pulled out right ahead of him and swung sharply to the left. It was a blue sedan with a crumpled left rear fender."

Golding and the woman exchanged swift glances. Then Golding said, "That doesn't prove anything. I'll bet a detective agency could turn up a hundred blue sedans with crumpled left rear fenders on twenty-four hours' notice."

"That's possible," Mason admitted readily enough.

"Then why do you want us as witnesses?"

"Oh, I just thought the jury might be interested in hearing about where you went after Cullens left your place."

"That's another thing I don't like," Golding said. "You've been snooping around with my bankers, trying to put the finger on me there."

Mason's eyes became level-lidded as they stared at the gambler. "I don't like that word *snooping*, Golding," he said.

"Well, I said *snooping*."

"I heard you."

The woman said, "Wait a minute, Bill. That isn't going to get you anywhere."

"I'll say it isn't," Mason agreed.

She suddenly got to her feet. "I want to talk with Bill," she said. "Have you an office where we can discuss something?"

"Why not discuss it here?" Mason asked.

She whirled to face him and said, "I'm tempted to."

"Shut up, Eva," Golding warned.

She stared down at Mason and said, "You're asking for it."

"Eva, shut up!"

"Don't be a fool, Bill," she said. "We have to tell him now. He's brought it on himself."

"Tell him nothing," Golding said. "We talk with our lawyer first. Then he talks with Mason."

"As bad as that, eh?" Mason asked.

The woman dropped back in the big overstuffed leather chair and said, "No, Bill, we don't want to see a lawyer. A lawyer would talk, and you can't tell who he'd talk to. We're going to tell Mason, and that's all."

"You're crazy!" Golding said.

She didn't even look at him, but went on steadily, "All right, Mr. Mason. We were out there. We were the ones who were parked in that blue sedan at the curb. We went out about twenty minutes after Cullens left, and . . ."

"Eva! For God's sake, shut up!" Golding said, getting up from his chair and starting toward her.

She turned to face him then. "Get back to your chair," she said, as one might order a dog into a corner. "Sit down. Shut up! You're a hell of a gambler. You don't even know when you hold the losing hand." She turned back to Mason. Her voice had remained low, steady and conversational, and she resumed her story without changing her tone or even glancing at Golding as he hesitated, then slowly stepped back to his chair and sat down. "We couldn't figure what Cullens was making all the squawk about," she said. "It looked like some sort of a frame-up. I didn't like it. We talked it over and decided we weren't going to be pushed around. We went up to

Trent's office building. Trent wasn't there. We telephoned his sister. She wasn't home. Then we decided we'd go out to Cullens' place and put the cards on the table.

"We drove out and parked the car. The house was dark. Bill said, 'There's no one home.' I said, 'We'll go up and ring the bell anyway.' "

"Who was driving?" Mason interrupted to ask.

"I was," she said.

"Go ahead," Mason told her.

"All of a sudden, Bill said, 'Look! There's someone in there with a flashlight.' I took a look. Sure enough, you could see the beam of a flashlight. It wasn't very powerful, or else it was shielded in some way, but you could see the beam moving around across the windows."

"Lower floor or upper floor?" Mason asked.

"Lower floor."

"Go ahead."

"We decided we didn't want any of that, whatever it was," she said, "but we were curious. I kept the motor running, the gear in and the clutch out, so I could get away from there fast. And then we heard two shots."

"Two?" Mason asked.

"Two."

"Coming from the house?"

"Coming from the house," she said.

"And this was after you'd seen the flashlight?"

"Yes."

"Go on," Mason said.

"We saw some more flashlight," she told him, "and then a woman ran out of the house. She came out of the front door and ran toward the street. She was carrying a bag in her hands, and was pushing something down into the bag. I was sitting on the left side of the car at the steering wheel. Bill was on the right, next to the curb. He said, 'That's George Trent's sister,' and that's all I waited for. I shoved in the clutch, and we went away from there."

"You didn't see what happened to the sister?"

"No."

"Where did you go?"

"We put the car in the garage and went back to our place."

"And turned the radio on to police calls?" Mason asked.

"Yes."

"And heard about Cullens being found dead?"

"Yes."

"And notified the police of what you had seen?"

"No."

"Why not?"

"We wanted to keep out of it."

"You haven't told anyone?"

"You're the first living mortal that we've told."

Mason said, "I'm going to think this over."

"Don't be a fool," she told him. "There's nothing to think over. You keep quiet, and we keep quiet."

Mason said, "As a lawyer, it's my duty to advise you that you should communicate what you know to the police."

She got to her feet and said, "All right, you've done your duty."

"You're not going to say anything to them?" Mason asked.

"Not unless we're put on the stand and have to."

"It's going to sound like hell if it comes out for the first time on the witness stand," Mason warned her.

"It'll sound like hell for Sarah Breel," Bill Golding said.

"And for you too," Mason pointed out.

"We can take it if we have to," the woman said. "Sarah Breel can't."

"That," Mason said, "remains to be seen."

Golding laughed unpleasantly. "Quit bluffing," he said, pulling his copy of the subpoena from his pocket. "What do you want me to do with this subpoena?"

Mason met his eyes. "What do *you* think?"

Slowly, deliberately, Golding tore the subpoena in two, nodded to the woman and said, "Come on, Eva."

They walked wordlessly out through the exit door and into the corridor. Mason shoved his hands down deep in his trousers pockets and slumped down in his chair, staring thoughtfully at the top of the desk. Della Street said, "Chief, they're lying. They thought up that whole story so you wouldn't dare to bring their blue sedan into the case. It's just a lie they've made up out of whole cloth to tie your hands."

Mason said moodily, "If it's a lie, Della, it's a damned good one."

"You mean it's going to keep you from putting them on the stand?" Della Street asked.

Mason said, "I'd hardly want to play into the hands of the prosecution by bringing out evidence like that."

"But suppose it's a lie, Chief?"

"Suppose it is," Mason said. "Then what?"

"Then they're just telling that story to protect themselves."

"Protect themselves from what?" Mason inquired.

"Why, from—from—well, having to explain what they were doing out there. Perhaps, from being accused of murder."

"Exactly," Mason said. "In other words they're gambling for big stakes. . . . Get Paul Drake on the line. Let's check up on them and see if we can find out more about what motivation they might have for murder. You see what this means, Della. So far, all of the evidence which connects Sarah Breel with the murder is circumstantial evidence. She was near the scene of the murder; she had the gun in her possession with which the murder was committed; she had some diamonds in her possession which might have been taken from the body. That makes a black case of circumstantial evidence, but it's *only* circumstantial evidence. Now then, along come Golding and Eva Tannis, and put Sarah Breel on the spot at the *exact moment when the murder was being committed.*

"If they're lying, they're doing it to protect themselves from a murder charge. If they're telling the truth . . . well, if they're telling the truth . . ."

"Suppose they are," Della Street asked, "what then?"

Mason frowningly regarded the polished toes of his shoes. "Get Paul Drake on the line," he said.

Della Street called Paul Drake's office, cupped her hand over the mouthpiece, and said, "Drake's out, Chief. Do you want to talk with anyone else?"

"No," Mason said moodily. "Leave word for him to call as soon as he comes in." As Della Street hung up the telephone, Mason got to his feet, pushed his thumbs through the armholes of his vest in a characteristic gesture, and started pacing the floor of the office, his chin sunk in thought. Knuckles sounded on the exit door, and Mason said, "That's Paul Drake now." He strode to the door and jerked it open. Drake, somewhat out of breath, said, "What's all the excitement, Perry?"

"Excitement?" Mason asked, pushing the door shut.

"Yes. About the witnesses."

Mason stared at him for a moment, then exchanged glances with Della Street. "Just what," he asked, "do *you* know about witnesses?"

Drake walked over to his favorite chair, pulled a somewhat crumpled package of cigarettes from his pocket, and said, "Now, listen, Perry. Get this straight. I don't want to butt in on anything you don't want to tell me about. On the other hand, if I'm working on this case, I should know all about it."

"Go ahead," Mason told him.

"Were you going to tell me about those two witnesses who were just here in your office?"

"I don't know," Mason asked. "Why?"

"I should know what I'm up against."

"Just how did you know about the witnesses?" Mason inquired.

Drake said, "I have a radio on my car which I keep tuned in to police calls. I'm not supposed to do it, but, you know, in this racket you have to cut a corner once in a while."

"Well," Mason said impatiently, "what about it?"

"Five or six minutes ago," Drake said, "a hurry-up police call came in for Car 19 to beat it to this office building and pick up two witnesses who were in the of-

fice of Perry Mason, the lawyer. The witnesses were to
be brought to headquarters for questioning. They weren't
to be picked up until after they'd left the office.

"So I figured you had a couple of witnesses who could
dynamite the case, that you'd telephoned Holcomb,
and . . ."

"You figured wrong," Mason interrupted. "Did they
pick up the witnesses?"

"I guess so. I was on my way to the office when the
call came in. When I was a couple of blocks down the
street, a police radio car passed me coming away from
the office building, and there were two people in the back
seat. I couldn't get a good look at them—couldn't see
them clearly enough to get their faces, but I gathered
one of them was a man and the other was a woman."

Della Street said, "Good Lord, Chief. Do you suppose
Golding and . . ."

Mason whirled. "Skip it, Della," he said. She glanced
apprehensively at Paul Drake and became silent.

"Was Golding one of those witnesses?" Drake asked.
"Was it Golding and Eva Tannis, Perry—and why all
the mystery?"

Mason didn't answer the question. Instead he walked
over to the baseboard and started walking slowly along
the edge of the carpet, looking down at the edge of the
baseboard. Paul Drake said, "Good Lord, Perry! You
don't suppose . . ." and was silent.

Mason, without paying any attention to his comment,
continued his inspection. Abruptly, he stooped and
pressed his finger against some white dust on the baseboard. Some particles of that dust adhered to the moist
surface of his forefinger. He tested the consistency by
rubbing thumb and forefinger together and then nodded
to Paul Drake. The detective slid from the chair to cross
the office and stand at Mason's side. Mason pointed toward a framed picture on the wall. Slowly, the two men
raised the picture, and moved it from the curved brass
hangers from which it was suspended. A neat hole had
been drilled through the plaster. In that hole appeared
the ugly, black circle of a microphone. Della Street

stared at it with wide, apprehensive eyes, started to say something, and checked herself. Paul Drake gave a low, almost inaudible whistle.

Mason strode across the office, put a sheet of paper in the typewriter, and tapped out a jerky message with two fingers. Paul Drake and Della Street came to stare over his shoulder as the type bars, pounding against the sheet of paper which had been fed over the roller of the typewriter, tapped out: *"This is unethical as hell. We can make a squawk about it, and that's all. The fat's in the fire now. Holcomb probably doesn't give a damn whether we find out now or whether we don't. The thing has served its purpose. Our only chance now is to throw him off the track; try and back my play. You'll have to ad lib."* Mason pushed back his chair from the typewriter, started pacing the floor of the office, said, "Bill Golding and Eva Tannis were here, Paul. Holcomb must have had them shadowed. I had subpoenas served on them. There must have been a leak somewhere."

"What were they going to testify to?" Drake asked.

Mason said, "Paul, I think they're mixed up in that murder. They're trying to push it over on Mrs. Breel's shoulders."

Drake looked at Mason's face, apparently waiting for some sign or signal. Mason, in pantomime, indicated that Drake was to speak, but the detective seemed slightly uncertain as to what it was Mason wanted him to say.

Della Street, reading Mason's signals, interposed to ask, "What are you going to do about it, Chief?"

Mason flashed her a grateful grin, and by his manner indicated she had interpreted his pantomime correctly. "There's only one thing for me to do," he said. "If they're going to try and convict Sarah Breel on perjured evidence, I'll have to resort to every technicality I can to free her . . . or else I'll have to . . ."

Again Mason made signals. Drake asked tentatively, "Just where will that leave your client, Mason?"

"I don't know," Mason admitted. "It might be better for her to plead guilty, or put in a plea of self-defense.

I don't know. All in all, it's a hell of a responsibility, representing a client who can't tell you anything about what happened and whether she's guilty or innocent. Good Lord, for all I know, she *may* be guilty. I think I'll go talk with her and sound her out about how she feels about pleading guilty. I may be able to get the charge reduced to second-degree murder under the circumstances."

Della Street interposed quickly, "I take it you don't want the officers to have any idea of what you are planning."

"Good Lord, no!" Mason said. "I'd let them think I was getting ready to fight the case, then I'd start trading with them at the last minute. I'd walk right up to trial just as though I intended to fight all the way through. I don't dare to make any overtures now. They'd construe it as a sign of weakness and refuse to give me any sort of a break. . . . The more I think of it, the more I think I'll go down and see Mrs. Breel right now. You folks hold the fort, Della," and Mason, clapping on his hat, shot out of the office, banging the door violently behind him.

When he had left, Della Street said to Paul Drake, "Well, I guess that's all, Mr. Drake. I think if Mr. Mason had wanted you to do anything else, he'd have told you so."

Drake said, "You take it then, Della, that we're to do nothing?"

"Nothing except what the Chief has specifically instructed."

"O.K.," Drake said, "we'll let it go at that." And, with a last apprehensive glance at the dictaphone, he eased himself out into the corridor.

13

Perry Mason entered the hospital room to find Sarah Breel propped up in bed. "Hello," Mason said cheerfully. "How's everything coming?"

"As well as can be expected, I guess," she said with a cheerful smile.

Mason's voice was sympathetic. "I'm minded of the old adage," he said, "that it never rains but it pours. You find yourself with concussion of the brain, a broken leg, a charge of murder hanging over your head, and, on top of that, comes the news of your brother's death."

She said philosophically, "Well, I can either grin and bear it, or bear it without grinning. As far as the murder case is concerned, it's up to you to do the best you can to get me out of it. As far as George is concerned, there's nothing anyone can do. I hope they bring his murderer to justice. Naturally, it's a shock to me. I was fond of him. I'm going to miss him a lot as time goes on; but a person doesn't live to be as old as I am without having had plenty of experience with death, Mr. Mason.

"I try to look at life and death from a broad-minded viewpoint. If you're going to have births, you must have deaths. Life is a stream; death is a part of the scheme of things and it's a necessary part. If babies kept being born, and no one died, the world would become completely overcrowded. If babies weren't born and no one died, it would be a pretty sorry, disillusioned world with no youth and gaiety, no romance, no honeymoons, and no children's laughter. I'm sorry George had to die, but as far as he's concerned, he's dead. As far as I'm concerned, I miss him; but when I grieve about missing him, it isn't being sorry for *him,* it's being sorry for *me.* It's hard to explain, Mr. Mason. It may seem cold-blooded to you. It really isn't. I have a great deal of love and a great deal of affection for George. He's dead. We all have to go sometime."

Mason drew up a chair by the side of the bed and said, "All right, let's talk about you for a while."

"What about me?" she asked.

"About the case against you."

"And what about the case?"

Mason said, "In some ways it doesn't look so good."

Sarah Breel said, "I'm sorry, Mr. Mason, but I can't help you. I haven't the faintest recollection of what happened after noon on the day Austin Cullens was murdered. . . . Don't you want a cigarette, Mr. Mason? I know you smoke, and I don't mind. . . . No, thank you, I won't have one with you. Just light up and smoke. Go ahead, tell me what you have to say. Don't try to break the news gently."

Mason said, "The unfortunate part about not remembering what happened is that you're not in a position to deny anything which anyone *says* happened."

"Just what do you mean by that, Mr. Mason?"

Mason said, "So far, the evidence against you has been circumstantial. Now just suppose, for the sake of argument, that someone showed up who claimed he actually *saw* you in Cullens' house and saw you fire the fatal shot. There's nothing you could do about it. You couldn't deny it."

Her eyelids leveled as she stared steadily at him. "Who says that?" she asked.

"No one," Mason said, and then, after a significant pause, added, "yet."

"What *do* they say?"

Mason said, "A man by the name of Golding and a woman, who is living with him as his wife, had their car parked out in front of Cullens' house the night of the murder. They heard two shots. They saw someone come running out of the front door, pushing something down into a handbag. That something may have been a gun."

"Then what did they do?" she asked.

"They drove away," Mason said, and then added,

"as soon as they recognized the person who was coming toward their car."

"Who was that person?"

Mason, looking her squarely in the eyes, said, "You."

She was silent for several thoughtful seconds. Then when she spoke, her voice indicated only an impersonal interest as though they had been discussing some academic problem. "How soon was it after the shots were fired, before they saw this figure come out on the porch?"

"Almost immediately."

"And they're certain it was me?"

"That's what they say."

"Do you think you can shake their story on cross-examination, Mr. Mason?"

"I don't know," Mason said. "I can't tell whether they're making it up out of whole cloth. There's some possibility that they want to put me in a spot. They know, of course, that you have told the officers you can't remember anything which happened, that your mind is a blank as to the things which took place after noon on the day of the murder. Those two are plenty smart. They're shrewd opportunists who have gone through life taking advantage of every break which had been offered. Naturally, they're smart enough to realize that if you can't remember *anything* about what happened on that day, you can't *deny* anything."

She thought for a moment and then said, "That makes it rather tough, doesn't it?" Mason nodded.

"On me," she said. He nodded again.

"I guess," she told him, "you're going to have to rely on your powers of cross-examination, Mr. Mason . . . . What were they doing out there sitting in a parked car where they could see the door of Cullens' house?"

"They went out to call on Cullens."

"Why didn't they call on him, then?"

"When they drove up to the curb, the house was dark. They were on the point of driving away, thinking no one was home, when they saw the beam of a flashlight playing against the windows. That impressed them as being rather unusual so they sat there in the car watching; and then they heard the shots, and, a few moments later, saw you come out of the door and run down toward the sidewalk. That was all they waited for. They stepped on the gas and drove away."

"That's what they say," she observed.

"That," Mason admitted, "is what they say."

"And that, as you lawyers have it, puts me at the scene of the crime at the time the murder was being committed."

"That's right."

"It also puts *them* at the scene of the crime at the time the murder was being committed."

"Right," Mason said.

"Can you use that in breaking down their story in front of a jury?"

"I don't think so."

"Why not?"

"In the first place," Mason said, "there are two of them, and there's only one of you. In the second place, they can deny that they were in the house, and you can't deny anything. In the third place, the district attorney will be giving them the sanction of his official blessing, which will indicate that he believes their story. In the fourth place, there's no circumstantial evidence involving them, and there's plenty of circumstantial evidence involving you. They found a gun in your bag. They found the diamonds in your bag."

"As I understand it," she said, "when I was picked up, I was lying on the pavement where I'd been knocked by the car. My bag was lying close to me, and I believe it was opened."

"I believe it was," Mason said.

"Have you asked the man who struck me whether he was absolutely certain the gun was *in* the bag or was lying so close to the bag that he thought it had been in the bag and had fallen out when the bag was knocked out of my hand?"

"I haven't asked him that yet," Mason said, "because I haven't had an opportunity to cross-examine him."

"But you will have an opportunity to cross-examine him?"

"Yes, of course."

"And you will ask him that?"

"Yes."

"Suppose he says the gun wasn't actually *in* my bag, but was lying on the street so close to it that he thought that it had been in the bag?"

"That," Mason said, "would be a break for you."

"And you'll remember to ask him particularly about that?"

"Yes."

"And if they can't show that the gun was in my bag," she said, "why then . . ." Her voice trailed away into silence.

"Then, of course," Mason said, "we can probably get *someone* on the jury to believe that the gun had been thrown from the blue sedan which had been parked in front of the house and just happened to be near where your bag struck when it was knocked out of your hand."

"You can't tell," Mrs. Breel said, "but what I might have seen the gun lying there in the street and was running toward it to pick it up when the automobile struck me."

"Could you," Mason asked, "remember that that is what happened?"

"No, I can't remember anything."

"It would help," Mason told her, "if you could remember it about that way."

"I'm sorry. I can't remember a thing."

Mason said, "Okay. It's up to you."

"I'd like to ask you a couple of questions," she said.

"Go ahead," Mason invited.

"As I understand it, one person can kill another in self-defense, and it doesn't constitute any crime. Is that right?"

"That's right."

"And what is meant by self-defense?"

"The fear of death or great bodily harm."

"Any particular circumstances in connection with that?"

"A person must be threatened by someone who seems to have the intention of inflicting death or great bodily harm, and who apparently has the present ability to carry out that threat."

"Then what?"

"The person may shoot in self-defense."

"Let us suppose," she said, "that someone was in Austin Cullens' house. Could that person very well claim that he—or she—had been forced to kill Cullens in self-defense?"

"Not very well."

"Why not?"

"Because," Mason said, "when a person wrongfully and feloniously enters the house of another person, he has forfeited his legal rights. He is then committing a felony. The owner of the premises has the right to defend himself against the intruder. The intruder has no right to defend himself against the owner of the premises."

"How do you know that the persons who entered the premises did so unlawfully?"

"There is," Mason pointed out, "the matter of a device used to short circuit the fuses in the event the lights were turned on. That indicates a felonious breaking-in entry."

"Then if a person had illegally entered the house, that person couldn't have killed Austin Cullens in self-defense?"

"Under certain circumstances, yes," Mason said, "but you could never get a jury to believe those circumstances existed. In the minds of the jury and, save for certain exceptions, within the compass of the law, a man's house is his castle. Within that house, he has the right to do pretty much as he pleases. A person who makes an illegal entry takes his life in his hands. A man has the right to defend his home, his life, and his property. The person who makes an illegal entry is presumed to be the aggressor. Whatever the householder did under those circumstances would be considered as defending himself, not as in the nature of an attack."

"Well," she said, "it's most interesting. I wish I could remember what happened. It might be of some help."

"It *might*," Mason conceded without enthusiasm.

"Did these witnesses say anything about how I acted when I came out of the house?"

"Yes. You paused on the front porch long enough to shove something down in that bag of yours, then you ran down to the curb. They recognized you; that's when they decided to get out of there."

"I was running?"

"Yes."

She sighed and settled back against the pillows. "Well, Mr. Mason," she said, "it's all very complicated. I'm certain I don't envy you your job."

Mason said grimly, "If I lose this case, I've just lost a case; but if you lose this case, you know what it means to you."

"I suppose," she said, "you're trying to break it to me gently that I'd be convicted of first-degree murder."

"Yes."

"And that automatically carries a death sentence with it?"

"Unless the jury recommends life imprisonment," Mason told her.

"Would the jury do that in my case?"

"It's hard to tell. It depends on the evidence. It depends on the jury. It depends on the manner in which the prosecutor presents the case. It's quite possible he could inflame the jury into returning a verdict of first-degree murder without recommendation. On the other hand, the prosecution may not even try to get a death penalty—because of the circumstances. You never can tell." Mason watched her carefully as she digested that bit of information.

"And first-degree murder *with* a recommendation?" she asked.

"Life imprisonment," Mason said.

"All right," she told him. "Do your best. It's all right with me."

"But suppose," Mason told her, "I lose—*we* lose. How are you going to feel then?"

Her smile was almost maternal. "Bless your soul, Mr. Mason," she said, "quit worrying about me. I've lived a full life, and an active life. I've never gained anything by worry. When I was younger, I used to do a lot of worrying. Twenty years ago I decided I was finished with it. I have confidence in you. I know you'll do anything and everything anyone could possibly do. If the jury decides I'm guilty of murder, and that they're going to hang me, why then I'll hang. That's all there is to it . . . and I have an idea I'll walk up the steps of the scaffold without showing any white feather. . . . Now then, Mr. Mason, I've been talking quite a while, and I'm feeling a little drowsy. If there's nothing else you wanted to ask me about, I'll take a nap. . . . I'm sorry about those two witnesses. It complicates the case from your standpoint. I can see that . . . it doesn't look so good for me. . . . However, there's nothing I could say or do that would be of the slightest help, Mr. Mason. I'm afraid it's up to you to do the worrying." She patted a pillow under her head, closed her eyes, and exhaled a long-drawn sigh. An expression of calm tranquillity softened the lines around her face as it settled into repose.

14

Mason unlocked the door which led to his private office. Preceding Paul Drake into the room, he switched on the lights and silently tiptoed over to the picture behind which they had discovered the microphone. He nodded to Paul Drake, and together, each taking a corner of the picture, they lifted it once more away from the wall.

There was no sign of the microphone. A very faint difference in color on the plaster indicated where it had been freshly patched with a quick-drying compound. Mason said, "Well, Paul, that's that."

Drake, staring at the unbroken expanse of plaster, said, "Do you suppose it's somewhere else?"

"No," Mason told him. "They've pulled it out, lock, stock, and barrel."

"Why? Because it served its purpose?"

"No," Mason said, "because they knew we were wise to it."

"How did they know that?"

Mason said, "It's my fault, Paul. I didn't realize it until afterwards."

"Realize what, Perry?"

"You remember that after I discovered the microphone, I went out to the typewriter and typed out a message."

"Yes."

"The sound of that typewriter," Mason said, "sounded plainly over the dictograph. They could tell from the uneven tempo and the ragged touch that I was writing something on the machine. They knew you were in the room, and they knew Della Street was in the room. The only reason I'd have typed anything under those circumstances would have been for the purpose of giving you a silent message."

"And so they pulled the dictograph out?"

"Exactly," Mason said. "They were afraid I'd try to bring them in for contempt of court, or make a squawk which would get public sentiment in my favor."

"You mean that now they'll deny there was ever a dictograph in there?"

"Probably they won't go that far," Mason said, "but they'll certainly deny they knew anything about it or had anything to do with it."

Drake said bitterly, "They talk about the tricks of criminal lawyers, but you know and I know that if we tried to pull the stuff the police pull, we'd be in jail before night."

Mason shrugged his shoulders. "That's neither here nor there, Drake. I had a chance to make a squawk on that dictograph and chase down the wires, find where they led, and do something about it. I passed up that chance. Now, I won't have another one."

"How long do you suppose it has been in, Perry?"

"I don't know."

"And the prosecution knows pretty generally what we've found out and what lines we're working on?"

"Yes."

"What," Drake asked, "are you going to do about it?"

"I'm going to ignore it," Mason told him. "When you can't prove anything, it's foolish to get all worked up over it. . . . Now here's what I want, Paul: I want you to concentrate on this man Diggers. It's becoming exceedingly important to find out about that bag.

"In the first place, I'm not so certain they can identify that bag as having belonged to Sarah Breel. In the second place, I don't think the gun was *in* the bag. The gun was found lying on the pavement where it looked as though it had fallen from the bag, or had been knocked out of Mrs. Breel's hand. I think when Diggers mentioned that the gun was in the bag, he wasn't referring to the fact that he *found* the gun in the bag, but that he assumed it must have . . ."

"I'm afraid you're barking up the wrong tree on that, Perry," Drake told him.

"How so?" Mason asked.

"They've been working on Diggers themselves, and they have him sewed up. Did you see the papers tonight, Perry?"

"You mean the statement of the D.A. that Golding and Eva Tannis have both identified Sarah Breel as having been at the scene of the murder at the time it was committed?"

"Yes."

Mason nodded and said, "That's what I wanted to see you about, Paul. I want you to dig into their records. I want you to uncover everything you can which has been suspected but hasn't been proven. And I want them to know you're doing it. In other words, don't be too secretive about it. Be just a little crude. Let word get back to them of what's happening."

Drake nodded and said, "O.K. You want to frighten them so they'll skip out, Perry. Is that the idea?"

Mason said, "I'd hardly want them to disobey a subpoena which had been served on them. Of course, if they get frightened and pull out of their own accord, that's something else again. Now that their statement has been played up in the newspapers and in interviews issued by the district attorney's office, it's going to look like the devil if they don't show up at the time of trial."

"You mean you'd make them the goats?"

"I'd insinuate they committed the murder, yes," Mason said.

"And planted the gun?"

"Naturally."

"I'm afraid," Drake warned, "you're underestimating the sincerity and ability of this chap Diggers. Personally, I think the D.A. has hypnotized him into thinking a lot of things happened which just didn't happen. You know how it is on something like that. A person runs directly in front of an automobile. The automobile comes to a stop very shortly after the impact. The driver's naturally pretty much excited. I've seen quite a few of them so jittery they couldn't write their own names at the bottom of a traffic ticket. Naturally, a person has a confused recollection of what happened. Usually, if you get the straight of it, it's a series of images which are burnt in on the brain. Later on, as a man tells the story over and over, those images gradually assume sharper details—but those details are usually supplied by some clever lawyer. . . . It's not perjury, it's simply a question of exerting legitimate influence. . . . Incidentally, Perry, I don't think you'll get anywhere arguing with Diggers on the witness stand. He's so absolutely sincere."

Mason said, "The D.A., by the way, is rushing through an indictment, and wants to try Mrs. Breel while public emotion is at its height."

"Why?" Drake asked.

"Publicity for one thing, and for another, he thinks it's a good chance to get a conviction."

"Just what do I do?" Drake asked.

"You," Mason told him, "dig up everything you can. I have my back to the wall. I can't afford to overlook any bet. When I walk into that courtroom, I want to know more about the case than the D.A. does."

"How soon will they come to trial?" Drake asked.

"Perhaps within a week," Mason told him, "as soon as they can get Mrs. Breel into court in a wheel chair."

"I can dig up a lot in a week, Perry."

Mason grinned with his lips. His eyes showed the strain under which he was working. "Get *plenty*," he said, "because I may need it."

15

▪

Larry Sampson, the deputy district attorney who was selected to try the case of the People vs. Sarah Breel, looked across his desk at the somewhat apprehensive features of Harry Diggers. "Now, all I want you to do," Sampson said, "is to tell the truth, the whole truth, and nothing but the truth; but I don't want you to lean over backwards. Do you understand?" Diggers nodded.

"Perry Mason is a clever lawyer. He has all sorts of tricks for breaking people down on cross-examination. You've got to watch out for him." Again Diggers nodded.

"Now, I want you to remember one thing," Larry Sampson went on. "When the district attorney of this county goes into court and asks for a verdict of first-degree murder, the defendant is guilty. The district attorney's office would never ask for a first-degree verdict against a defendant about whose guilt there was the slightest doubt. Unfortunately, murderers are able to secure tricky criminal lawyers to represent them. The percentage of acquittals in this country is a national disgrace. Now, I want you to remember that when you get on the witness stand, you're engaging in a public duty; you cease to be an individual, you become a witness in a murder trial; you become a person who is testifying to certain facts, and it becomes your duty to see that the jury understands those facts, and comprehends them. Now, we have a perfect case against Mrs. Breel. She's committed cold-blooded deliberate murder. We can prove that she committed that murder, and bring her to justice, *if* you keep your head. If you get rattled on cross-examination, we can't do it. Now, let me run over the facts, briefly, as I understand them. You were going along about twenty or twenty-five miles an hour, weren't you?"

"Well, I wasn't looking at the speedometer."

"But," Sampson said, "you were in a twenty-five-mile-an-hour zone. You're a law-abiding citizen, aren't you, Mr. Diggers?"

"Well, yes."

"And you're not a speeder?"

"No."

"Therefore, you would assume that you were keeping within the legal speed limit, isn't that right?"

"Yes, I guess it is."

"All right, remember that," Sampson said. "You don't need to give the process of reasoning by which you arrive at that conclusion. Simply state positively that you were going not faster than twenty-five miles an hour, and stay with that statement. Now then, the defendant stepped out right in front of your headlights, didn't she?"

"Yes, that's right," Diggers said positively.

"And before you could bring your car to a stop, you'd struck her. Is that right?"

"Yes."

"And, as you struck her, she fell to the pavement?"

"I swerved my car, and pretty near missed her," Diggers said. "I couldn't quite make it. The edge of one of the fenders brushed against her, and she went down."

"I understand," Sampson said. "Now, let's pay particular attention to what happened after that. You stopped your car almost instantly, didn't you?"

"Yes, I'd started to stop, of course, before I hit her."

"And you jumped out of your car, and ran around to where she was lying?"

"Yes."

"And she was lying face down on the pavement?"

"Well, sort of on one side—more face down, I guess, than on the side."

"She was carrying this bag when you struck her, wasn't she?"

"Well . . . I guess . . ."

Larry Sampson interrupted positively, "Now that's just the thing I want to warn you against, Mr. Diggers. I know that you're an honest man, I know that you're trying to be fair; I know that whenever you hesitate in answering a question, you're trying to reconstruct in your mind the sequence of events; but, a jury won't understand that. The minute you start hesitating on the witness stand, the jury will say, 'Here's a man who doesn't remember very clearly what happened.' You see, Mr. Diggers, all witnesses that get on the stand know that they're going to be subjected to cross-examination. Therefore, they think things out pretty carefully, so the attorney on the other side can't make fools out of them. Jurors are accustomed to hearing witnesses speak right up. Now, you know whether she was carrying that bag. You don't want Perry Mason to get you out in public and make you look ridiculous, do you?"

"No, I don't, but I . . ."

"And you don't want to appear in the position of being a careless driver?"

"I wasn't careless," Diggers said. "There was nothing any human being could do. She ran out right in front of the headlights and . . ."

"Yes, but you don't want the public to think you didn't see her when she ran out in front of the car, do you?"

"Why, of course not, I saw her. I saw her the minute she stepped off the curb, but it was too late to do anything about it."

"And how far did she run from the curb before she got in front of your car?"

"I don't know, four or five steps, probably."

"And you saw her all of that time?"

"Yes."

"You saw her face, you saw her hands, you saw her feet, didn't you?"

"Well, yes, if you put it that way."

"Now, she must have been carrying that bag in her hand. She certainly didn't stand on the curb and throw it out in the middle of the road, did she?"

"No, of course not."

"Then she *must* have been carrying it in her hand?"

"Yes, I guess that's right."

"Don't guess," Sampson said. "Of course, I know that's just a figure of speech, Mr. Diggers, but you can see what would happen if you got on the witness stand and made a statement like that. Perry Mason would level his forefinger at you, and say, 'Oh, you're guessing, are you?' And then he'd have you on the defensive, and the first thing you knew everybody in the courtroom would be laughing at you."

Diggers fidgeted uneasily, and said, "I don't see why I just can't tell what I saw, and let it go at that."

"You can," Sampson said. "That's exactly what I want you to do, Mr. Diggers. But in justice to you, and in justice to me, and in justice to the people of this State, I want you to be sure to tell what you saw in such a clear-cut, positive manner, that you can't be trapped, on cross-examination, into being made to appear foolish. Now, do you see what I'm driving at?"

Diggers nodded.

"Now then," Sampson went on, "if you saw her hands, you must have seen her bag, because she must have been carrying the bag in her hand. Perhaps you've never thought of it in exactly that way before. Perhaps you haven't reconstructed the scene in all of its details, but after you leave the office I want you to go over the thing in your mind's eye, so that you can see exactly what happened, in just the way it happened. Now, in regard to the contents of that bag—you had the ambulance driver check on the contents, didn't you?"

"I certainly did," Diggers said, "and it's a good thing I did, too; with all those diamonds in the bag, she might have claimed there was a shortage; she might have claimed I not only hit her, but swiped a diamond or two . . ."

"Exactly," Sampson said, "that's just the point I'm going to make in front of the jury, that your action in having the inventory of that bag made, was the action of a careful man, it was the action of a thoughtful man; it was the action of a law-abiding citizen; it was the action of a man who doesn't lose his head in an emergency. It shows that you were cool, that you were calm and collected; that you saw exactly what was taking place, and that your testimony is to be trusted. . . . Now, you found the gun in the bag, didn't you?"

"Well, the gun was just outside the bag, lying on the pavement."

"Not outside of the bag," Sampson said, "the gun could hardly have been *entirely* out of the bag. You must have seen just a part of the gun protruding from the bag. You see, that's one of the things the lawyers will try to trap you on. They'll try to make you swear that these things weren't in the bag when you first saw them. Now, there's a distinction between being in the bag, and being visible through an opening in the bag, and I want you to be careful to remember that. In other words, Mr. Diggers, you haven't anything to fear if you get on the stand and tell the truth, the whole truth, and nothing but the truth; but I want you, in justice to yourself, and in justice to me, to be sure it's the truth you're telling; and I don't want you to guess; and I don't want you to hedge. I don't want you to testify to what happened as though it was a conclusion on your part, but I want you to testify to facts, in a manner which shows they are facts. And above all, I don't want you to let Perry Mason make a fool of you. Remember that when he starts cross-examining you, he may appear to be friendly. He may appear to be just trying to help you get your testimony straight; but regardless of the way he starts out, what he's really doing is trying to trap you; he's trying to get you off guard, trying to lull you into a sense of security, so he can trick you into making some indefinite statement; so he can get you to say, 'I think,' or 'I guess,' or 'It seems to me,' or something of that sort. Now, you're a reasonably intelligent man, Mr. Diggers. Do you think that I can depend on you to hold your own when you get on the witness stand, and not be trapped into telling some lie?"

"I won't lie," Diggers said. "I'm going to tell the truth."

"That's exactly what I want," Sampson told him. "That's your duty to yourself and as a citizen. Now, I want you to go home and keep thinking over and over in your mind what happened until you can see it clearly. I want you to visualize everything which took place, just as though you were looking at a motion picture. Sarah Breel ran out from the curb. You saw her for four or five steps; you saw her hands plainly; you saw the bag in her hand; you saw her run in front of the automobile; you swerved the automobile and put on the brakes; you struck her; you got out and ran around the car; she was lying there, partially on her side, her face down; the bag was lying in front of her where it had been dropped. You looked down at the bag, and the first thing you saw was a gun, partially protruding from the bag; you stopped a passing motorist for help; you summoned an ambulance, and you checked the contents of the bag with the motorist and with the ambulance driver; you found these diamonds when you made that inventory.

"Now, you testify to those facts, and don't let anyone rattle you. And remember, Mr. Diggers, I'm depending on you. The district attorney's office is depending on you.

"Now, I have an appointment, which I'll have to keep, so I'll let you out through this door. The trial comes up day after tomorrow. We're rushing it through. We had the Grand Jury indict Mrs. Breel, so we could dispense with a preliminary examination. We're not going to waste any time. Remember, Mr. Diggers, we're going to depend on you."

And Sampson, with his hand on Diggers' arm, escorted him to the door, pumped his arm up and down effusively, closed the door behind his departing visitor, and rubbed his hands together with a gesture of smug satisfaction.

16

Judge Barnes, taking his place on the bench, looked over the crowded courtroom with judicial gravity, glanced down at the lawyers seated at their tables, and said, "Before starting this case, the Court wishes to say a few words to the gentlemen of the press, who are assembled here. The court realizes that occasionally judges try to enforce a ruling that there will be no picture taking. The result is that some of the more ingenious members of the press manage to smuggle in concealed cameras with high speed lenses, and obtain surreptitious pictures.

"This Court has always felt that the public were entitled to know what goes on in important trials. The Court's objection to photographs has been due to the interruption of proceedings, and the confusion incident to the exploding of flashlights. Therefore, gentlemen, I want it understood that there will be no flashlight pictures taken while Court is. in session, nor are there to be any so-called candid-camera shots taken which will have a tendency to annoy the parties, distract the attention of the witnesses, or counsel. In other words, gentlemen, I am leaving the matter of photographs in your hands, and depending upon your good taste, and your ability to co-operate with the Court. In the event you abuse the privilege, it will be withdrawn.

"Gentlemen, are you ready to begin the trial of the People vs. Sarah Breel?" Counsel for both sides answered that they were ready. Judge Barnes looked down at the white-haired woman who sat in a wheel chair at Perry Mason's side, her right leg encased in a plaster cast, her expression as completely tranquil as was that of the judge himself. "Very well, gentlemen, proceed."

Mason got to his feet, and stood tall and straight, having about him that indefinable something which draws the eyes of spectators like a magnet. "Your Honor," he said, in a resonant voice which seemed not particularly loud, yet filled every corner of the mahogany-paneled courtroom as though he were talking into a microphone, "the defendant in this case wants only a fair trial. She is satisfied the facts will speak for themselves. We offer to stipulate with the district attorney's office that the first twelve persons called to the jury box may be sworn to act as jurors in the case."

"You mean without asking any questions at all of the proposed jurors?" Sampson asked. Mason nodded.

"Suppose they've read about the case? Suppose they have some fixed opinion in it?"

"I don't care," Mason said. "All I want is twelve men and women of intelligence and fairness." He included the jury panel with a sweeping gesture of his arm. "I am satisfied that every one of these people possesses the necessary qualifications. Call twelve names. We'll accept them. We don't care whether they have any prejudices or not."

Larry Sampson scented a trap. One didn't take chances with Perry Mason. Somehow he felt that if he departed from the orderly course of routine trial work, he'd find himself sailing uncharted seas, with dangerous reefs ahead. "No," he said, "I wouldn't care to make that stipulation." Then suddenly realizing that to the ears of the prospective jurors this sounded as though he failed to share Mason's opinion as to their integrity and fairness, he raised his voice and said, "Not that I doubt the intelligence or honesty of any of these men or wom-

en, but I want to find out . . . that is, I mean, I
want to question them."

Mason turned to face the jury impanelment. "Go
ahead and question," he said. "That's your privilege. I
won't ask *any* questions."

Mason sat down, and then, for the first time since
the judge had taken the bench, turned to confer with
Mrs. Breel. "Do you," Mason asked, "feel as though the
evidence might recall what happened to your mind?"

"My mind is a blank," she said, "from Monday noon
until I regained consciousness in the hospital."

The lawyer said, "This is going to be an ordeal. You'll
have to steel yourself to the idea of having the district
attorney's office sketch you as a scheming criminal.
There'll be sarcasm, shouting, a lot of sneering references
to your loss of memory."

She smiled serenely. "I can take it," she said.

The clerk called the names of twelve jurors. Sampson advised the prospective jurors of the nature of the
case. The judge asked a few routine questions, then
turned to the attorneys. "Proceed, gentlemen, with such
questions as you have touching upon the qualifications of
prospective jurors."

Mason, on his feet, scrutinized the jurors as though
searching for something in each face. Then he smiled
and said, "Your Honor, the defendant has no questions
to ask of these jurors. We have no challenges for cause."

Sampson sighed and settled down to an examination
of the jurors, realizing with each question that he had
been forced into a position of seeming to distrust these
men and women. Yet, once having embarked upon such
a policy, he dared not change. And, since the defense
had given him no lead by its questions, he was forced to
plug along, doggedly determined to bring out the facts,
whether they knew the defendant or counsel for the defendant, whether they had read of the facts, or purported facts, in the newspapers, whether they had formed
or expressed any opinion. Once, to his embarrassment,
he disclosed that one of the jurors, having read the
newspapers, had concluded Mrs. Breel was guilty. But

that juror, meeting Perry Mason's disarming smile, promptly asserted that he could and would lay aside such opinion if he was actually sworn to act as a juror, and would try the case solely and impartially upon the evidence introduced.

Sampson knew, of course, that Perry Mason would excuse this juror on a peremptory challenge, and the other members of the panel would understand the exercise of that challenge. But Sampson felt, somehow, as though he were doing Mason's work for him.

Eventually, his examination drew to a close. He passed the jury for cause, and, satisfied that Mason would exert his peremptory on the biased juror, passed for peremptory. Mason said, "Your Honor, I was satisfied with the jury when I first saw them, and I'm still satisfied with them. I pass my peremptory. Swear the jury."

Once more, Sampson experienced a vague feeling of uneasiness. He had expected at least half a day to be consumed in the examination of jurors, but now he found himself swept into the trial after less than an hour, and, somehow, felt that he was on the defensive. However, as he warmed to his opening speech before the jury, he regained his confidence. The mere recital of the facts arrayed against the defendant was sufficient to reassure any prosecutor.

The defendant had been acquainted with the decedent. She had been in the neighborhood—in fact, directly in front of the decedent's house—at approximately the time of the murder. Robbery had been the motive for the murder. The defendant had in her possession the gun with which the murder had been committed. Moreover—and realizing that the prosecution might have some difficulty in actually proving that the handbag was the property of the defendant, Sampson stressed this point particularly —the shoe worn by the defendant had been stained with human blood—the blood of the decedent. The person who had murdered Austin Cullens had stood over the body, taking gems from a chamois-skin belt. In doing this, that person had left the telltale red smears of footprints near the body of the deceased. The jurors would be shown photographs of tracks of footprints in the hall-way. And then they would be shown the left shoe which had been worn by the defendant at the time she was brought to the hospital. That shoe, standing by itself, would be sufficient to warrant a conviction of first-degree murder.

Sampson thanked the jury, and sat down. Mason reserved his opening statement, and Sampson called, as his first witness, an acquaintance who testified briefly, and without objection or cross-examination, that he had known Austin Cullens in his lifetime; that Austin Cullens was dead; that he had seen the body of Austin Cullens at the time of the post-mortem; that the body on which the autopsy surgeon had been working was that of Austin Cullens, who had lived at 9158 St. Rupert Boulevard.

Sampson called the autopsy surgeon, Dr. Carl Frankel. Mason stipulated his qualifications, subject to the right of cross-examination, and Dr. Frankel described the post-mortem, the course of the fatal bullet, and the cause of death. "You may cross-examine," Sampson said.

Mason asked casually, "What time was the post-mortem performed, Doctor?"

"Around three o'clock in the morning."

"You recovered the fatal bullet which had caused the death of Austin Cullens?"

"I did."

"What did you do with it?"

"I gave it to Sergeant Holcomb of the homicide squad, who was standing at my side."

"Let's see," Mason said musingly, "three o'clock in the morning. You had two post-mortems to perform by that time, didn't you, Doctor?"

"I did."

"The other one being that of George Trent, who had also been shot?"

"Yes, sir."

"And you performed both of those post-mortems at the same time?"

"No, sir, I performed the post-mortem on Austin Cullens first, and then the autopsy on George Trent."

"But you performed the post-mortem on George Trent immediately after you had finished with that of Austin Cullens?"

"That's right."

"And Sergeant Holcomb was present at both examinations?"

"Yes, sir."

"Did he leave the room at any time?"

"What's that got to do with it?" Sampson asked.

"Merely trying to get the picture," Mason said affably. "I want to find out what became of the bullets."

"You'll find out when we put Sergeant Holcomb on the stand," Sampson said.

"Well," Mason observed, "I think if the doctor answers this question that will conclude my cross-examination."

"No," Dr. Frankel said, "Sergeant Holcomb did not leave the room. He was present at my side during both of the post-mortems."

"That's all," Mason said.

"Call Harry Diggers," Sampson said.

Diggers took the witness stand. Clearly, almost photographically, he described operating his car on St. Rupert Boulevard. He had just passed Ninety-First Street and was about midway in the block. There had been a blue sedan with a crumpled left rear fender parked at the curb. This sedan had suddenly lurched into motion and swerved sharply to the left. The witness had pulled his car to the right to avoid a collision. At that moment, the defendant had jumped out from the curb, to run directly in front of his headlights. She had flung up her hands as though to ward off the car. The witness had swung his car sharply to the left, but the front end had missed the defendant, and the running board had struck her leg and knocked her down. She was unconscious. He had started to take her to the nearest hospital, but other motorists, who had driven up, advised him to let the ambulance which had been summoned take the responsibility. Diggers had found her bag lying beside her, with a gun protruding from it. He had picked the bag up, and had insisted on having its contents inventoried, at first by bystanders, and then, when he realized the nature of the contents, by the ambulance crew. He read the inventory, and the number of the gun, from his notebook, where he had scribbled them down.

Sampson watched the jury intently. As Diggers read out the numbers, he saw a certain hardness creep into the jurors' eyes. Then their glances strayed from the witness to the defendant. He knew that symptom only too well. Let Mason go ahead and pull his bag of tricks. When jurors lean forward in their chairs to listen to damaging testimony, then, with hard faces, look with steely indifference at the defendant, the verdict is in the bag.

With the conclusion of Diggers' direct examination, the court took its usual midday recess, and Sampson tried hard to keep from swaggering as he walked from the courtroom.

A nurse changed Mrs. Breel's position in the wheel chair so that she would not become cramped. Mrs. Breel smiled at Mason and said, "Well, that wasn't so bad."

"It's going to get worse," Mason warned.

"Then what?" she asked.

"Well," Mason said, "it's always darkest just before dawn."

Virginia Trent came forward, standing tall, thin and austere, her face with its look of grim tension in contrast with Mrs. Breel's carefree smile. "It's a crime," she said, "for them to drag Aunt Sarah into court while she's still suffering from that broken leg."

Mason said, "The district attorney's office wanted to rush her to trial while she was still suffering from a loss of memory."

"Couldn't you have presented a physician's certificate and secured a continuance?" Virginia Trent asked accusingly.

"I could," Mason admitted, "but I had a better idea."

"What?" Virginia Trent asked.

"To go on with the trial before your aunt had recovered her memory."

Mrs. Breel flashed him a swift glance. Virginia Trent said indignantly, "What do you mean by that, Mr. Mason?"

"I just meant that I wanted to try the case while I stood the most chance of getting an acquittal."

"Do you feel certain?" Virginia Trent asked him, her voice harsh with nervousness.

"Well," Mason hedged, "let me put it just the way I explained it to you a few days ago. . . . I'm as certain of getting an acquittal now as I'll ever be. On the other hand, a lapse of time may strengthen the Prosecution's case."

"You've said that two or three times," Mrs. Breel said. "Can you tell us just what you have in mind?"

Mason, shoving papers into his brief case, said, "Suppose you leave the worrying to me."

"I think that's an excellent idea," Mrs. Breel nodded to Virginia Trent.

"Well, I don't," Virginia Trent said. "I think we're both adult, and I think we're entitled to share in the responsibilities."

"Go ahead and worry, then," Mason told her gravely.

Sarah Breel sighed resignedly and said, "Very well, Ginny, since you feel that way about it, I agree with Mr. Mason. We'll let you worry."

Virginia's eyes sparkled dangerously. "You two act as though you were laughing at me all the time," she said. "This isn't any laughing matter. In case you want to know it, Mr. Perry Mason, the general comment around the courtroom has been that you're laying down on the job."

There was something of a twinkle in Mason's eyes. "Don't let that worry you," he said. "You see, I'm mentally lazy. I save all of my energy for fighting where it will do the most good. These lawyers who doggedly contest a case every step of the way use up too much energy. They burn themselves out."

Virginia Trent and the nurse turned Mrs. Breel's

wheel chair around, and Virginia Trent snapped over her shoulder, "Well, you haven't burnt yourself out. If you ask me, you aren't even lukewarm."

Sarah Breel couldn't turn in the wheel chair so she could see Mason's face, but she raised her right hand to wave reassuringly. "Don't mind Ginny," she called. "I always thought she took life too seriously. After all, *I'm* the defendant in this case. Come on, Ginny."

Paul Drake moved forward and whispered to Perry Mason, "Sergeant Holcomb's detectives have found Mrs. Peabody."

"You mean Ione Bedford?" Mason asked.

"Yes."

"What are they doing about it?" Mason asked.

"Nothing," Drake said. "They're keeping her under surveillance, that's all. My men have her sewed up. When these other shadows moved in, they got wise and tipped me off. One of my boys recognized them. They're from Homicide."

"And there's been no sign of Pete Chennery?"

"None. She's sitting tight. . . . And don't think Holcomb is going to do anything to play into your hands, Perry, because he isn't. He has shadows on the job, but that's as far as he'll go."

Mason grinned. "Thanks, Paul. I think this leaves us sitting pretty."

As court reconvened at two o'clock, Mason took up his cross-examination of Diggers. "You say you were going about twenty-five miles an hour, Mr. Diggers?"

"Yes, sir."

"And this defendant stepped out from the curb, directly in front of your headlights?"

"Yes, sir."

"About how long was it after she stepped out from the curb in front of your headlights before you struck her?"

"Not more than one or two seconds, at the most."

"And the defendant threw up her hands just before you struck her?"

"Yes."

"Show the jury just how she did it," Mason said.

The witness held up his hands, palms outward.

"As though trying to push the automobile back?" Mason asked sympathetically.

"That's it exactly."

"You saw both of her hands?"

"Yes."

"Was she wearing gloves?"

"Yes, black gloves."

"You're certain you could see both of her hands plainly?"

"Yes, sir. That is etched on my memory so I'll never forget it."

"You could see the palms of both of her hands?"

"Yes, sir."

"And she was wearing gloves?"

"Yes, sir."

"Which one of her hands could you see the most clearly?"

The witness, feeling that Mason was trying to trap him, grew indignant. "I could see both of them equally well," he said. "She was standing facing me. She had her hands up like this, as though trying to push the automobile away."

Mason appeared to have been defeated. He abandoned that line of cross-examination with the bad grace of one who is retreating hastily in order to save himself from rout. "Now then, after you struck this woman, you stopped your car?"

"Yes, sir. . . . Understand, I'd started to stop the car before I hit her."

"I understand," Mason said. "Where was she lying when you stopped the car?"

"I stopped the car almost at the moment of impact. She was lying right by the right rear wheel."

"You got out of the car on the right side?" Mason asked.

"No, sir," Diggers corrected him, "on the left side. I opened the door nearest the steering wheel."

"Then you walked around the car to where the defendant was lying?"

"Yes, sir."

"Around the front, or around the back?"

"Around the back."

"What did you do?"

"I picked her up and felt for a pulse, then tried to carry her over nearer to the sidewalk. I was just picking her up when some other people came to help me."

"Do you know who these other people were?"

"No," Diggers said, "although I have the names of some of the witnesses who helped me inventory the contents of the bag."

"Oh, yes," Mason said casually. "Now, let's see. You were pretty much excited at the time, weren't you?"

"Well, I was startled, but I didn't lose my head at all."

"And you remember everything which occurred very vividly?"

"Yes, sir, the entire occurrence is etched vividly in my mind."

Mason inquired casually, "Then after you had carried the defendant over to the curb, you first saw this bag lying on the road, is that right?"

Diggers said, "No, sir, that isn't when I *first* saw it. I *first* saw it when the defendant left the curb."

Mason was on his feet, pointing his finger. "I thought," he thundered, "that the defendant raised up her gloved hands in this manner, as though to push back the automobile; that you saw one hand just as clearly as you saw the other. Now, kindly tell the jury how that could have been possible if the defendant had been holding a bag such as this bag which you have identified, at the time?"

Diggers waited patiently until Mason had finished. Then he turned to the jury, just as Sampson had instructed him to do.

"She wasn't holding the bag when she had her hands up, Mr. Mason," he said. "She dropped the bag *just before she put her hands up*, and the bag was lying on the road, right where she had dropped it."

"That bag was lying just about where the blue sedan had been parked, wasn't it?"

"Yes, sir."

"And the blue sedan had been there until just a moment before the defendant stepped out from the curb, is that right?"

"Yes, sir."

"Then, how do *you* know that the bag which you picked up hadn't been dropped by the occupants of the blue sedan?"

"Because," Diggers explained patiently, "I saw the defendant carrying the bag in her hand. The minute I saw her, I saw the bag. If that bag had been dropped by the occupants of that blue sedan, Mr. Mason, the defendant must have dived under the blue sedan, picked up the bag, run back to the sidewalk, and then turned to run out in front of my headlights."

"Now, where was the gun when you *first* saw it—this thirty-eight caliber revolver you have just described to the jury?"

"Practically protruding from the handbag."

"It wasn't lying on the pavement *near* the handbag?"

"No, sir."

Mason sat down. "That is all," he said.

"The witness is excused," Sampson announced, and a note of triumph was apparent in his voice.

Sampson next called one of the ambulance attendants to identify the bag and its contents. Mason offered no cross-examination.

Sampson heaved a sigh of relief. Well, he'd got past that hurdle very nicely. Mason had been forced to surrender the point. He consulted his list of witnesses.

"Call Carl Ernest Hogan," he said, and, with Hogan on the stand, quickly ran through his occupation: ballistics expert for the police force. Once more, Mason stipulated to the qualifications of the witness, subject to the right of cross-examination. And Hogan, testifying with the close-clipped efficiency of an expert who is as much at home on the witness stand as in his own living room, identified the test bullet which had been discharged from the gun found in the bag, identified the bullet which had been handed him by Sergeant Holcomb as the fatal bullet, and then introduced a greatly enlarged microphotograph showing the marks of the rifling on the two bullets. The photograph was offered in evidence, and admitted without objection. The jury needed only to look at it to tell that the two bullets had unquestionably been fired from the same gun. An attempt had been made to trace the ownership of the gun from the numbers. The attempt had been unsuccessful because the records of a merchant, going back over a period of years, had been lost or destroyed. The numbers on the gun, however, had not been tampered with. "Cross-examine," Sampson said triumphantly.

Sampson sat back in his chair, breathing easily while the cross-examination droned on. No, the witness couldn't, of his own knowledge, testify as to the fact that this gun had been found in the bag. It was a gun which had been given him by Sergeant Holcomb of the homicide squad. The witness had, however, checked the numbers, and, as Mr. Mason could observe, the numbers tallied with those which had been written down by Harry Diggers at the time of the accident.

No, the witness couldn't, of his own knowledge, testify that this bullet was the fatal bullet. That bullet, as he understood it, had been taken by the autopsy surgeon from the body of Austin Cullens, given to Sergeant Holcomb, and by Sergeant Holcomb handed to the witness.

Larry Sampson, thinking that perhaps some of the jurors might be misled, took occasion to interpolate a comment to the court. "We're not asking to introduce this fatal bullet in evidence at the present time, Your Honor. It's only been marked for identification. The last link in the chain will be forged by the testimony of Sergeant Holcomb, and then we'll have to have the bullet introduced." Judge Barnes nodded.

Mason said casually, "By the way, Mr. Hogan, you were testing two guns at the same time, were you not?"

"Yes, sir."

"Both thirty-eight caliber revolvers?"

"Yes, sir, but they were of different makes."

"I understand that," Mason said. "I'm simply trying to get the circumstances under which the test was conducted before the jurors. I believe one of the guns was one which had been used in the murder of George Trent, was it not?"

The witness smiled. "I'm sure I can't tell you about that, Mr. Mason," he said. "I know what Sergeant Holcomb *told* me when he handed me the guns. But it is only my province to test guns by firing projectiles from them and comparing them with fatal bullets."

Judge Barnes smiled. Larry Sampson grinned. If Mason thought he could get anywhere cross-examining an expert like Hogan, he had another guess coming. Hogan was deadly as a rattlesnake on cross-examination. Try to crowd him, and he'd strike back in a hurry.

"By the way," Mason said, "do you remember whether you first compared a bullet from the gun which Sergeant Holcomb *told* you had been used in the Trent case, or the one which Sergeant Holcomb *told* you had been found in the bag of the defendant in this case?"

Hogan frowned meditatively and said, "As nearly as I remember, Mr. Mason, I first discharged a test bullet from this gun. Then I discharged a test bullet from the gun which Sergeant Holcomb *told* me had been used in the Trent case."

"And in checking the bullets, what order did you follow?" Mason asked.

"Sergeant Holcomb handed me a bullet which I first compared with a bullet fired from this gun," Hogan said. "I believe I mentioned to Sergeant Holcomb that it wasn't fired from this gun . . ."

"Oh, it *wasn't*," Mason said.

Hogan said acidly, "If you'll permit me to finish my statement, Mr. Mason."

"I wasn't aware that I'd interrupted you," Mason said. "I thought you had finished."

"Well, I hadn't finished," Hogan said. "I was about to remark that I advised Sergeant Holcomb that the bul-

let hadn't been fired from this gun, and Sergeant Holcomb told me of course it hadn't; that the bullet he had
handed me was the one which had been taken from the
body of George Trent. Thereupon, I compared *that* bullet with the test bullet fired from the revolver which
Sergeant Holcomb had *told* me figured in the Trent case,
and found that the bullets were identical. I then compared the bullet which he gave me and which he *told*
me had been taken from the body of Austin Cullens,
and found that it was identical with the test bullet fired
from this gun."

Mason said wearily, "That's all."

"Call William Golding," Sampson said.

Golding came forward to the witness stand and was
sworn. His face was the face of a professional gambler,
cold, expressionless, and observing, completely divorced
from that which was taking place in his mind.

Golding stated his name and address. "Your occupation?" Sampson asked.

"I run a restaurant known as The Golden Platter."

"Are you acquainted with the defendant, Sarah Breel?"
"Yes."

"Were you acquainted with Austin Cullens, the decedent?"

"Yes."

"When did you last see Austin Cullens?"

"On the evening of the day he was murdered."

"Where did you see him?"

"At The Golden Platter—my place of business—at
around seven o'clock in the evening."

"And did you have occasion, later on, on that same
day, to go to the residence of Austin Cullens?"

"I did. About eight o'clock."

"And who was with you, if anyone?"

"Miss Eva Tannis."

"And what did you do?"

"We drove to the ninety-one hundred block on St.
Rupert Boulevard. Miss Tannis was driving the automobile. She parked at the curb in front of Mr. Cullens'
house."

"You could see the house at that time?"

"Yes, of course."

"Were there any lights in the house?"

"Not at that time, no."

"Then what happened?"

"I was just about to get out of the car, when I saw some lights on the windows. My wife—Miss Tannis thought it was a flashlight . . ."

"Never mind what anyone else thought," Sampson said hastily. "Just what did you see yourself, Mr. Golding?"

"I saw a flicker of light on the window. I saw that on two or three occasions; then I heard two shots; then I saw a woman run out of the front door of the house, and run toward my automobile."

"Did you recognize that woman?"

"I did."

"Who was she?"

Amidst a silence in which a pin could have been heard to drop, Golding raised a dramatic forefinger and pointed it at Sarah Breel. "She was the defendant in this case," he said.

"The woman sitting there?" Sampson asked.

"Yes."

"What did she do?"

"She ran toward my automobile. Miss Tannis said that . . ."

"Never mind what anyone else said," Sampson interrupted. "What did you do, if anything?"

"I sat in the car while Miss Tannis drove it away."

"Where was the defendant when you last saw her?"

"About six feet from the curb, running toward the street."

"Running rapidly?"

"Yes."

"You may cross-examine," Sampson said to Perry Mason.

"Why did you and Miss Tannis drive away so hurriedly?" Mason asked.

"Because we didn't want to see Mrs. Breel."

"And you didn't want Mrs. Breel to see you?"

"No."

"Why?"

"Simply because I wanted to see Mr. Cullens without having anyone else present."

"You operate a gambling establishment in connection with your restaurant?" Mason asked.

Sampson was on his feet. "Your Honor," he said, "that is objected to as incompetent, irrelevant, and immaterial. It is improper cross-examination; it is an attempt to discredit the witness in the eyes of the jury by submitting him to . . ."

"The objection is sustained," Judge Barnes interrupted to rule.

Mason smiled, and said, "I'll reframe the question, Your Honor. Mr. Golding, isn't it a fact that earlier in the evening Mr. Cullens had advised you that George Trent had pledged certain diamonds with you to cover a financial loss which he had incurred at the gambling tables in your establishment at The Golden Platter?"

"Your Honor," Sampson said, "I object to this question, and I assign the asking of it as misconduct. I suggest that counsel be admonished by the Court. The Court has already ruled that . . ."

"The Court has ruled nothing of the sort," Judge Barnes said. "The first question might have been considered as an attempt to embarrass the witness by casting reflections upon his character in connection with an extraneous matter. As the present question is worded, it relates entirely to a conversation which took place between Mr. Cullens and this witness on the night of the murder. The witness has already testified that he saw Cullens at that time, and counsel has a right on cross-examination to go into what was said, insofar as it may have any bearing on the present case. The objection is overruled, the witness will answer the question."

Sampson slowly sat down. Golding, with his face calmly expressionless, said, "That is substantially correct, sir."

"And George Trent had lost money over your gambling tables at The Golden Platter?"

"Yes, sir."

"And had pledged certain diamonds as collateral, in order to secure his gambling debt with you?"

"No, sir."

"He hadn't?"

"No, sir, he hadn't."

"Do I understand that you had not received any diamonds whatever from Mr. Trent, pledged as collateral security for gambling losses?"

"No, sir."

"Or for any other losses?"

"No, sir."

"Or to cover any loans?"

"No, sir."

"Or any indebtedness of any sort?"

"No, sir."

"Are you certain that *you* didn't enter the residence of Austin Cullens at St. Rupert Boulevard?"

"Yes, sir."

"You had only parked the car at the curb, and hadn't left the car?"

"That's right."

"Are you certain that the bag, which was found lying on the street about where your car was parked, hadn't been tossed from your car?"

"It had not."

"And the gun, which the witness, Diggers, has testified about, wasn't that in your possession at some time during the evening in question?"

"It was not."

"And you didn't drop it or throw it from your sedan?"

"No, sir."

"Nor did Miss Tannis?"

"No, sir."

"But," Mason said, eyeing him steadily, "you were, by your own admission, on St. Rupert Boulevard, within a few feet of the house in which Austin Cullens resided, on the night of the murder. You were there at a time when you heard two shots fired, which sounds apparently came from the house?"

"Yes, sir."

"And you are unable to give any explanation as to what you were doing there, other than the statement which you have just made to this jury?"

"That's right."

"And your car was a blue sedan with a crumpled rear fender?"

"Yes, sir."

"And you knew that the witness, Diggers, had told the police about seeing such a car parked there at the curb the night of the murder?"

"Yes, sir."

"And you immediately got rid of that car?"

"Yes, sir."

"Why?"

"Because I didn't want to be called as a witness."

"Why not?"

"I wanted to keep out of the whole business. I'm a gambler. I knew that would be brought out somehow. You've done it now. That's going to ruin my business. I'll be closed up."

"Your desire to keep out of it wasn't because you were mixed up in the murder itself?"

"No, sir."

Mason said, "That's all."

"Call Sergeant Holcomb," Sampson said.

Sergeant Holcomb came striding to the witness stand. His manner clearly indicated that he had a sneering contempt for the defendant and her counsel. He was a man who knew what he was going to testify to, and didn't intend to let any attorney confuse him. He was sworn and gave his name, address and occupation to the court reporter. He sat down in the witness chair and crossed his legs, after the manner of one who is thoroughly at his ease, amid familiar surroundings. He glanced at Larry Sampson, and his manner said very plainly, "All right, young man, go ahead."

Sampson started building up his case with Sergeant

Holcomb. The Sergeant testified to finding the body of Austin Cullens, testified to the presence of Perry Mason and Paul Drake, a private detective, at the scene of the crime, to the copper coin in the light socket. One by one, he identified photographs showing the room, the body, the red smears leading from the body to the corridor. Later on, Sampson would use those photographs with telling effect. He'd compare the size and shape of the stains in the corridor with the size and shape of the stains on the sole of Mrs. Breel's left shoe. Right now, he wanted to get the evidence in, and minimize the effect of it as much as possible so that he could crash it home to the jury with dramatic force. And so, the long line of photographs were identified and received in evidence. Then he brought up the fatal bullet.

Sergeant Holcomb identified it. He had been standing by the side of the autopsy surgeon when the bullet had been taken from the body of Austin Cullens. He had received this bullet from the doctor. He had handed this bullet to the witness, Hogan, for the purpose of making tests. He had been present at those tests. The fatal bullet had been fired from the gun which had been taken from Mrs. Breel's handbag.

"Cross-examine," Sampson said to Perry Mason.

"How long have you been attached to the homicide squad, Sergeant Holcomb?" Mason asked.

"Ten years," Holcomb said.

"You've had considerable experience in working up murder cases in that time?"

"Naturally."

"You know what to do when you enter a room where a homicide has been committed?"

"I think I do."

"Do you go through the pockets of the corpse, Sergeant?"

"Not until the coroner gets there. We leave the body just the way it is until the coroner arrives."

"And you did that with the body of Austin Cullens?"

"Yes."

"And then you searched the pockets?"

"We did."

"You found a chamois-skin belt on the corpse?"

"We did."

"Were there some jewels in that belt?"

"There were a few jewels *left* in the belt," Sergeant Holcomb said. "Mrs. Breel had taken the gems from front pockets of the chamois-skin belt and put them in her bag."

"You don't know, of your own knowledge, that Mrs. Breel did that, do you, Sergeant?"

"Well, I have a pretty good idea. . . . As you said, I've been on Homicide for ten years, and I'm not so dumb."

Judge Barnes said, "The Court, of its own motion, will strike out the remarks of the witness as to what Mrs. Breel must have done, as being a conclusion of the witness and not responsive to the question."

"Can you remember what was in the pockets of the corpse?" Mason asked.

"I can by refreshing my recollection from notes I made at the time."

"Do so," Mason said. Sergeant Holcomb produced a memorandum book. "What was in the upper left-hand vest pocket of the corpse?" Mason asked.

"A fountain pen and a pocket comb."

"What was in the left-hand hip pocket?"

"A handkerchief and a pen knife."

"What was in the right-hand hip pocket?"

"Nothing."

"Nothing?"

"That's right. You heard what I said—nothing."

"Nothing at all?"

Sergeant Holcomb said, "I don't know how you can have a nothing, unless it's a nothing at all. When I say nothing, Mr. Mason, I mean nothing."

Mason said, "Let's see, Sergeant, you were present at a post-mortem examination made by Dr. Frankel on the body of Austin Cullens, and immediately following that, you were present at the post-mortem made on the body of George Trent. Is that right?"

"That's right."

"You didn't leave the room where the post-mortem was conducted, from the time Dr. Frankel started to work on the body of Austin Cullens until he finished with the body of George Trent?"

"That's right."

"You received one bullet from Dr. Frankel which had been taken from the body of Austin Cullens?"

"Yes, sir."

"Now, just to keep the records straight, Sergeant, let's refer to the bullet which was taken from the body of Austin Cullens as the Cullens bullet, and the thirty-eight caliber revolver, which the witness Diggers says he found in the handbag of Sarah Breel, the defendant in this case, as the Breel gun. Do you understand that?"

"Yes, sir."

"Now, what did you do with the Cullens bullet?"

"I put it in my left-hand vest pocket."

"Now, a few minutes later you received from Dr. Frankel a bullet which had been taken from the body of George Trent, did you not?"

"Yes, sir."

"Now, for the purpose of keeping the records straight, let's refer to that as the Trent bullet. And, since it is claimed that that bullet was fired from a revolver found in the drawer of a desk in Trent's office, we'll refer to that gun as the Trent gun. Do you understand, Sergeant?"

"Certainly."

"All right. Now what did you do with the Trent bullet?"

"I put that in my right-hand vest pocket."

"Then what did you do?"

"Then I went at once to the ballistics department, where I had Mr. Hogan fire test shells from the gun."

"How did it happen," Mason asked affably, "that you got those bullets confused?"

"That I got *what?*" Sergeant Holcomb roared, half rising from the witness chair. "I didn't confuse any bullets."

"I thought you did," Mason said. "Didn't you hand

Hogan the Trent bullet to check with the Breel revolver?"

"I did no such thing."

"I thought Hogan said you did."

"Well, he didn't," Sergeant Holcomb said, sliding over to the extreme edge of the witness chair, in order to emphasize his remarks, "and," he went on, his face flushed to a brick red, "any insinuation to that effect is a deliberate falsehood. Your . . ."

Sampson jumped to his feet to interrupt hastily, "That's enough, Sergeant, I understand how you feel, but please remember your function here is only that of a witness. Any resentment you may feel for what you consider tactics of obstruction or confusion used by counsel, is to be kept out of the case. You will please be respectful in your answers to Mr. Mason's questions."

Judge Barnes said, impressively, "The witness is a police officer. He is undoubtedly familiar with courtroom procedure. He will answer questions, and refrain from any comments or recriminations."

Sergeant Holcomb's hands were clenched into fists, his eyes glittered dangerously, and his complexion was that of a man who has been holding his breath for several seconds.

"Proceed, Mr. Mason," Judge Barnes said.

Mason inquired casually, "You handed Mr. Hogan the Trent bullet, and asked him to compare that bullet with the test bullet fired from the Breel revolver, didn't you, Sergeant?"

"I did nothing of the sort," Sergeant Holcomb said.

"Just what *did* you do, Sergeant?"

"I took the Trent bullet from my pocket and handed that to Hogan, and told him to compare it. I didn't say with which gun. Hogan compared it with the test bullet from the Breel gun first. Naturally, the bullets didn't match. He told me so, and I said, 'Of course, they don't. That isn't the Cullens bullet, that's the Trent bullet.' So then he compared the Trent bullet with the test bullet from the Trent gun, and they matched. Then I handed Hogan the Cullens bullet, and he compared that with the test bullet from the Breel gun, and *they* matched. Now, those are the facts of the case, and *you can't mix me up on 'em, Perry Mason!*"

Judge Barnes said sternly, "That will do, Sergeant Holcomb."

Mason said, "Isn't it a fact, Sergeant, that *you* confused those bullets? Didn't you first hand Mr. Hogan the Trent bullet under the impression that it was the Cullens bullet?"

"No, sir," Holcomb said, "I told you once, and I'm telling you again, and I'll tell you a thousand times, that I put the Cullens bullet in my left vest pocket, and the Trent bullet in my right vest pocket."

"But when you handed those bullets to the ballistics expert, you first took the bullet from your right waistcoat pocket, did you not?"

"Yes."

"Why?"

"It's natural for a person to do that when he's right-handed," Sergeant Holcomb said.

Mason smiled. "And, by the same token, Sergeant, and following the same line of reasoning, it's natural for a right-handed person to put an object given him first in his right-hand pocket, and an object given him after that in his left-hand pocket, isn't it?"

Sergeant Holcomb's face flared into color again. For a moment he was silent. Then he said, "I'm not talking about what's natural when I tell you where I put those bullets. I know where I put them. I put the Cullens bullet in my left pocket, and the Trent bullet in my right pocket."

"Notwithstanding the fact that you received the Cullens bullet first," Mason said, "and that your natural tendency would be to put that bullet in your right-hand vest pocket, you put that bullet in your *left* vest pocket?"

"Notwithstanding anything, and notwithstanding your attempt to confuse the jury about what I'm . . ."

Judge Barnes pounded on the desk, "Sergeant Holcomb," he said, "just one more violation of the Court's admonition, and you will find yourself fined for contempt. You will answer questions and confine your comments to statements necessary to answer questions. Now, answer Mr. Mason's question."

Sergeant Holcomb said sullenly, "I put the Cullens bullet in my left pocket, and the Trent bullet in my right. I didn't mix them up."

"There's no chance you could have been mistaken?"

"None whatever."

"Not one chance in a million?"

"Not one chance in ten hundred thousand million," Sergeant Holcomb said.

Mason waved his hand in a gesture of dismissal. "That," he said, "is all."

Sampson took occasion to smile at the jury. "Call Eva Tannis," he said.

Eva Tannis took the stand, and answered Sampson's questions in a low well-modulated voice. She gave the impression of being a tigress, with her claws momentarily sheathed as she corroborated the testimony of Bill Golding in every detail.

"Cross-examine," Sampson said, and braced himself to frame indignant objections should Mason seek to insinuate the witness had, at one time or another, posed as Mrs. Golding. But Mason said quietly, "No questions. No cross-examination at all, Miss Tannis, thank you."

The Court thereupon took a brief recess, and Mason, surrounded by newspaper reporters, disclaimed any attempt on his part to confuse Sergeant Holcomb. "I just wanted to establish the facts," he said, "that's all."

At the end of the brief recess, Sampson announced tersely that the prosecution would rest its case.

Mason said, "I desire to make a very brief opening statement to the jury." He arose and walked across the courtroom to stand in front of the mahogany rail which separated the jury box from the courtroom. In a quiet, courteous, almost conversational tone of voice, he said, "Ladies and gentlemen, I am going to ask you to remember that it is not necessary for the defendant to prove herself innocent. She has had neither the time, nor the facilities, to make an investigation which would enable her to establish who actually did murder Austin Cullens.

It is encumbent upon the Prosecution to prove beyond a reasonable doubt that she murdered Austin Cullens. In the event the Prosecution fails to do this, the defendant is entitled to an acquittal.

"Now then, ladies and gentlemen, the entire case of the Prosecution hinges upon the fact that the gun Diggers says he found in Sarah Breel's handbag, and which we have referred to as the Breel gun, is the one which fired the bullet that killed Austin Cullens. We expect to prove to you that it is a physical impossibility that this gun could have killed Cullens. We expect to prove to you that it is a mathematical certainty that this gun *did* kill George Trent. And, in the same manner, ladies and gentlemen, we expect to prove to you that the Trent gun killed Austin Cullens."

Mason turned from the startled faces of the jurors to glance at Larry Sampson. "Will you, Mr. Sampson," he asked, "stipulate that George Trent was murdered on the Saturday afternoon in question some time between the hours of two o'clock in the afternoon and seven-thirty o'clock in the evening; that the best evidence available by your autopsy surgeon is that he met his death at approximately the hour of five o'clock?"

Sampson hesitated, and was aware that the eyes of the jurors were on him. He knew that he shouldn't hestitate. His manner should be that of striving to be fair, of asking only for justice. And yet, he sensed a trap. There was a peculiar sickening feeling in the pit of his stomach. After all, Sergeant Holcomb might . . .

"Because," Mason went on smoothly, "in the event you do not so stipulate, I will call your own witnesses, one by one, as my witnesses and prove absolutely that George Trent was shot by a thirty-eight caliber revolver at approximately the hour of five o'clock in the afternoon.

Once more Sampson hesitated. There seemed to be a ringing in his ears, as a confused medley of thoughts crowded his mind, demanding his attention. Suppose Mason should be right . . . But he couldn't be right. . . . But could he confuse the issues . . . Did he dare to stipulate . . . Suppose he didn't stipulate . . . My

God, this hesitation was the worst possible trial strategy! It looked as though he had something to conceal. Well, for God's sake, make up your mind. . . . But did he dare stipulate . . . "I am waiting for my answer," Mason said.

Larry Sampson took a deep breath. "I will so stipulate," he said. "But you understand, Mr. Mason, I am not stipulating anything whatever about these bullets or these guns. The Prosecution stands absolutely on the testimony of Sergeant Holcomb."

"I so understand," Mason said courteously. "My first witness will be Lieutenant Ogilby."

Lieutenant Ogilby advanced to the stand with military bearing. He testified that he was a Lieutenant in the United States Army; that, as such, he was interested in revolver shooting; that he was friendly with Virginia Trent, a niece of George Trent; that they occasionally took walks in the country; that he had taught her revolver shooting; that his service revolver was too heavy for her, but that her uncle possessed a light thirty-eight caliber revolver, shooting a shell known generally as a thirty-eight short, which suited Miss Trent's hand. That, under his guidance, she had become an expert shot. That on the Saturday afternoon when George Trent had been murdered, he had called for Virginia Trent in his automobile. That she had taken the gun from the upper right-hand drawer of the desk in George Trent's office. That at the time, Trent had been out to lunch. That the witness saw Trent eating lunch at a lunch counter near the building where he had his offices. That the witness and Virginia Trent had gone out into the hills and had fired some fifty shots at targets. That he had returned the witness to her home at approximately six o'clock in the evening.

Mason turned to Sampson and said courteously, "Now if the Prosecutor's office will kindly produce the gun which was found in the drawer of George Trent's desk, and the gun with which it is claimed George Trent was killed, I will ask the witness to identify that gun."

Sampson said, "It will take a few minutes."

"Very well," Mason said, 'the Court will perhaps, take a brief recess."

The Court took its recess. Newspaper reporters crowded around Mason, asking questions. Spectators, feeling that courtroom history was being made, refused to leave their seats. The jurors glanced at Mrs. Breel as they filed out. Their glances no longer contained hostility. There was curiosity, interest, and, here and there, a glance of sympathy. Perry Mason continued to sit at his counsel table. There was about him nothing of the swagger of one who is putting across a tricky play. He had, instead, only the attitude of a disinterested expert who is trying to assist intelligent jurors in discharging their duties.

Mrs. Breel indicated by a beckoning forefinger that she wished to talk with Perry Mason. He moved his chair over to her side. "Do you," she asked, "know what you're doing?"

"I think so," Mason said. "I'd hoped, of course, I could keep them from definitely establishing that it was your handbag. Now, I'm having to fall back on my second line of defense."

"Well," she said, weighing the issues as judicially as though her own fate had not been involved, "it seems to me that you're getting out of the frying pan and into the fire."

"Well," Mason observed, smiling, "that at least will be a change of scenery."

She thought for a moment, then said, "Do you know, Mr. Mason, I believe that if I concentrated real hard, I could get some glimmerings of memory about what took place . . ."

"Don't concentrate, then," Mason said.

"Why? Don't you want me to remember?"

"I don't think it will be necessary."

"Do you think it would hurt anything?"

"I'm sure I don't know," Mason told her. "So far, I'm proceeding simply according to logic. But when we check up on events, it's sometimes startling to find how illogical events actually are."

"Well," she told him, "you know your own business best, but I don't think there's a single person on that jury who believes that the man from the homicide squad got those bullets mixed up. He's too positive, and he's had too much experience."

"Yes," Mason said simply.

"Now, what do you mean by that?" she asked.

Mason grinned. "That he's *too* positive," he said, "and that he's had *too* much experience."

Sarah Breel laughed. "Promise me," she said, "that you'll be careful."

Mason patted her hand. "Leave the worrying to me," he told her. "I believe that was the bargain, wasn't it?"

"No," she said with a smile, "Virginia took over the worrying concession."

"That's right," Mason admitted, "perhaps she's worrying now. Who knows?"

Sarah Breel flashed him a swift glance of pointed interrogation. But Mason, apparently intending his last remark merely as a pleasantry, moved back to the counsel table and started arranging his papers.

Court reconvened at the end of five minutes, and Carl Ernest Hogan, the ballistics expert, stepped forward and said, "Let the record show that, purely for the purpose of evidence in this case, I submit for inspection a certain revolver numbered R, nine-three-six-two. And the record can also show that I'm not going to let that gun out of my possession."

"That's quite fair," Mason said. "I understand that this weapon is being held as evidence in connection with the homicide of George Trent."

"That's right," Carl Ernest Hogan said.

"Lieutenant Ogilby, I am going to ask you if you have ever seen this gun before?"

"I have."

"Is that the gun which Virginia Trent had with her on the Saturday afternoon in question?"

Lieutenant Ogilby snapped open the cylinder, spun it swiftly and said, "It is."

"Is that the gun which was fired by her at that time?"

"Yes, sir."

Mason said to Sampson, "You may cross-examine."

Sampson jumped to his feet, as though fairly tearing into the witness. "You say that is the *same* gun," he thundered, "and yet you have given it only a casual inspection. You haven't even looked at the number on the gun."

"No, sir," Lieutenant Ogilby said. "I didn't make my identification from the number on the gun."

"The company which manufactures this revolver makes thousands of absolutely identical revolvers, made by machinery, and alike in every respect, save only that, for the purposes of identification, each one of those revolvers is given a number by the manufacturer. Isn't that right?"

"Yes, sir."

"Then how can you presume to recognize this gun and differentiate it from the thousands of other identical guns which have been made, unless you look at the only positive mark of identification, to wit, the number stamped on the gun by the manufacturer?"

Lieutenant Ogilby smiled. "You'll pardon me, Mr. Sampson," he said, "but I happen to know firearms. It's a hobby of mine. While you are correct in your statement that these firearms are absolutely identical when they're manufactured, just as automobiles are identical when they leave the factory, before guns have been in use very long, they take on certain individualities. For instance, on this gun, the front sight was a little high. Miss Trent shot low with it. I tried to get her to take a coarse sight, but she couldn't understand doing that, so I filed the sight down myself. The file marks are quite visible on this sight. Moreover, in order to absolutely check so there could be no question of doubt, I went out to the place where we had done our target shooting, at the request of Mr. Mason, and picked up the empty shells which had been ejected from the gun when I reloaded it."

"What have the empty shells got to do with it?" Sampson asked sneeringly.

"Simply this," Lieutenant Ogilby said. "Before the

science of ballistics learned that bullets fired from a gun
could be identified by marks made by the rifling, the
only method of determining whether a shell had been
fired from a given gun was to center the firing pin on
the percussion cap. Firing pins, theoretically, strike in
the center of the percussion cap. Actually, they do no
such thing. Furthermore, in the course of use, each firing pin develops little peculiarities of its own. There is
not only the position of the indentation made by the
firing pin on the percussion cap, but there are also little
irregularities in that impression which are distinctive. I
satisfied myself that each one of those shells had been
fired from this same gun."

"You didn't have the gun to compare those shells
with," Sampson said.

"No, but I had a photograph of the cylinder of this
gun which was furnished me by a newspaper, and which
I have every reason to believe was authentic. But just
a minute, Mr. Sampson, if you wish, I'll make that check
right here and now."

He produced a discharged shell from his pocket, took
the gun from Hogan, opened it and said to Hogan,
"You're an expert. You can see for yourself."

Hogan leaned forward, and Sampson said, "I object
to that form of examination. Let the witness answer the
question so the jury can get it."

Mason grinned and said, "He's your own expert. Take
him away if you don't want him there."

Hogan stepped back, looked at Sampson, and nodded
almost imperceptibly.

"Just step up to the jury," Mason said to Lieutenant
Ogilby, "and show them the marks made by the firing
pin on the discharged shell which is in the cylinder of the
weapon, and the discharged shell which you hold in
your hand and which you picked up where you had
been engaging in target practice."

Lieutenant Ogilby stepped over to the jury rail. The
jurors crowded forward. The lieutenant pointed out the
points of similarity made by the mark of the firing pin.

Sampson engaged in a brief whispered conversation with Hogan, the firearms expert of the homicide squad, and then said lamely, "That's all. There are no further questions on cross-examination."

His head was in a whirl. Facts shot through his mind in a confused procession. He tried to arrest them long enough to follow his ideas to their logical conclusion, but the confusion was too great. He felt as though he had been standing at the local station in a subway, watching express trains thundering past, and trying ineffectively to stop them. He was aware that people were looking at him, aware that Judge Barnes was frowning in puzzled concentration; that Mason was smiling; that the jurors were staring. He felt mental vertigo amounting almost to nausea. There was a dry taste in his mouth.

He heard Mason saying, "Now, if the Court please, having demonstrated that George Trent could *not* have been killed with the so-called Trent gun, he *must* have been killed by the Cullens gun, since it is established beyond question that there are only two guns, the Trent gun and the Cullens gun, and only two fatal bullets, the Trent bullet and the Cullens bullet. The bullet taken from Trent's body matched the test bullet fired from *one* of the guns in the possession of the ballistics department. Since that couldn't have been the bullet fired from the Trent gun, it *must* have been the bullet fired from the Breel gun.

"Now then, your Honor, in view of the circumstances, I now ask that the jury be permitted to go to the house of Austin Cullens for the purpose of viewing the premises."

Sampson's only instinct was to fight. He jumped to his feet and said, "For what purpose, your Honor? Surely, nothing can be gained by having the jurors make such an inspection."

"What is there there you *don't* want them to see?" Mason asked.

"Nothing," Sampson said lamely.

"Then why not let them go?"

Judge Barnes took a hand. "Just a moment, Mr. Mason," he said, "you will please refrain from arguing with counsel, and address yourself to the Court. Just what reason have you for asking that the jurors go to these premises?"

"Simply this," Mason said; "the gun, which the witness Diggers says was found in the Breel handbag, actually came from the hip pocket of Austin Cullens. You will note, from Sergeant Holcomb's testimony, that there was nothing whatever in the right-hand hip pocket of Austin Cullens' trousers. The reason there was nothing there is that Cullens was in the habit of carrying a gun there. In that pocket, he carried a gun which killed George Trent. That is the gun which the witness Diggers claims was found in the handbag of the defendant in this case. Now then, your Honor, note the significant portion of the testimony given by the witnesses, Golding and Tannis. They, both of them, state there were *two* shots. The testimony of the autopsy surgeon is that there was only *one* bullet found in the body of Austin Cullens. There has been no explanation of what gun fired the other shot. Under the circumstances, the defendant feels that the jury should be given an opportunity to view the premises for themselves, and, if they desire, make some investigation to find out if there's another bullet . . ."

Judge Barnes shook his head. "I don't think that it's a fair interpretation of the privilege of viewing premises to make the jurors witnesses to the discovery of some fact which may have a vital bearing on the case. However, the Court will appoint a disinterested investigator to make such a search if Counsel so desires, and that investigator can be accompanied by Counsel for both sides, and report to the Court in the morning."

"That is quite satisfactory to me," Mason said, "and, in order to show that my desire is only to establish pertinent facts, I will suggest that the Court appoint Carl Ernest Hogan, the ballistics expert of the police department, to make this investigation forthwith in the presence of Mr. Sampson from the district attorney's office, and myself as the representative of Sarah Breel."

Judge Barnes nodded. "It is so ordered," he said, "and Court will adjourn until tomorrow morning at ten o'clock."

An uproar gripped the courtroom.

17

■

All the way out to Cullens' residence, Larry Sampson maintained a thoughtful silence. Gradually, he commenced to pick up the loose threads of various ideas which had been flitting through his head and weave them into a comprehensive pattern. Hogan also was silent, the careful silence of one who is afraid to say anything lest he say too much. Perry Mason, on the other hand, was filled with conversation, but his conversation had nothing to do with the case of the People *vs*. Sarah Breel. Instead, he told stories, discussed politics, and, in general, kept up such a constant flow of words that the others were interrupted in their attempts to center their minds on the problem which had assumed a position of such importance.

Behind the official car containing the lawyers and the man appointed by the Court to make the official inspection, there came a police car and three automobiles filled with newspaper reporters and photographers. Sampson turned uneasily in the seat to frown at the glaring headlights which poured in through the back window. "Look here," he said, "we don't want all of this bunch in there tramping around."

"Why not?" Mason asked.

"They might interfere with our finding evidence. And besides, the Court said that only the three of us were to go in."

"Oh, no," Mason said affably, "the Court remarked that Hogan was to be the Court's disinterested viewer.

We were permitted to accompany him to see fair play. Nothing was said about the others."

"Well, I don't want them in there."

"All right," Mason said, laughing, "you take the responsibility of keeping them out—you know how the newspaper reporters will feel about that."

"Why don't *you* keep them out?" Sampson asked. "You know, I'm holding a political office. I can't very well antagonize the press."

"I'd just as soon have them in," Mason said.

And so it was that as Hogan entered the room where the body of Austin Cullens had been found, newspaper reporters crowded in the hallway. Photographers snapped pictures as flash bulbs exploded, and those photographs, subsequently published in the morning papers, showed Perry Mason smiling, affable, good-natured, while the deputy district attorney's expression showed only too plainly the worry which was gnawing away the last underpinning of his self-possession.

Hogan went about his business with calm efficiency. "The body," he said, "as I understand it, was lying about here. Now, it's your contention, Mason, that this bullet had been fired by Cullens from a gun which he took from his pocket. Therefore, Cullens must have been facing in approximately this direction when he was killed. The bullet might be anywhere from the level of the floor to a point, say, six feet from the floor level. . . . I see no evidence of any such bullet."

"Well, let's keep looking," Mason said. "I feel the gun must have been discharged about as I pointed out. It's the only logical explanation which accounts for the facts. However, it's certain the bullet hole isn't where it could be readily detected or it would have been seen. . . . What's this in the chair?"

Hogan dropped to his knees to inspect an opening between the arm of a leather-upholstered chair and the seat cover. On the under side of the seat was a peculiar rip, the edges stained with black.

"That," Hogan said, "*might* be something."

"Pull the seat out and take a look," Mason said.

Hogan pulled out the seat. Back of it, and in such a position that it had been concealed by the seat cushion, was a small, round hole. Hogan looked at the back of the chair. There was no hole in the back of the chair.

"If that's a bullet," Mason said cheerfully, "and it looks like a bullet, it's still in the chair. Suppose we find out."

Hogan said, "I think we'd better have some photographs of this before we go any farther."

Newspaper photographers were only too willing to oblige. They pushed forward and shot a dozen pictures.

Hogan opened a sharp-bladed knife, took a pair of long-nosed pliers from his pocket and said, "Here we go."

He cut back the upholstery of the chair, pulled out some hair stuffing. A bullet was embedded in the oak frame of the chair. "How about it," Hogan asked Sampson, "do I dig this bullet out?"

"Better photograph it first," Mason suggested, "and then dig it out. That's what we want. We want to see the rifling marks."

Once more, there was a succession of flashes as newspaper photographers took pictures. Reporters disappeared down the corridor to rush flashes to their papers. Hogan calmly set about digging out the bullet, taking care not to touch the lead with the point of his knife. The oak was hard. The cutting was slow. But, eventually, Hogan twisted the point of his knife in behind the bullet and worked it out. "There's going to be no question that *this* bullet was substituted," he said taking an envelope from his pocket. "I'm going to seal this envelope and have both of you men write your names across the flap. The bullet will be on the inside."

Mason pulled out his fountain pen. "Fair enough," he said. Mason and Sampson wrote their names across the flap of the envelope, which was sealed and put in Hogan's pocket. "If you don't mind," Mason told him, "I'm going to follow this bullet to its ultimate destination—at least until we've made micro-photographs."

"Come on," Hogan invited. "I understand that I'm

appointed on this phase of the case as a disinterested expert. Let's go."

They went to Hogan's office. Hogan said, "I fired two or three test bullets from that Breel gun, Mason. There's no objection to using any one of those, is there?"

"None whatever," Mason said.

Hogan placed the bullets side by side in a specially constructed holder which enabled them to be rotated slowly. He pushed the holder under the lenses of a double-barreled microscope, focused the eyepiece, and slowly started rotating the bullets. Mason, watching the man's hand as it slowly turned the screw, saw it pause, turn the screw back for a fraction of a turn, then come to rest. Hogan stared intently through the eyepiece of the microscope. Slowly, he straightened and turned to Sampson. "All right, Sampson," he said. "These bullets are from the same gun."

A veritable battery of cameras clicked as Hogan made the announcement. "I presume," Hogan said, "we'll want micro-photographs, but they're a mere formality. The bullets are the same. You can see for yourself."

Mason grinned and said, "Thanks. I'll take your word for it, and I'll trust you to see that the bullets aren't substituted or switched in any way, Hogan. I'm headed back for my office. I have some work to do."

Sampson said savagely, "I don't care what legal hocus-pocus you use on those guns, you can't get away from the blood on her shoe."

"I'm not trying to," Mason told him, and left.

At his office, Paul Drake and Della Street were waiting.

"Well?" Della Street asked.

Mason nodded cheerfully and said, "No one had noticed the bullet because it went through a crack in the upholstery of a chair and lodged down below the seat level in the back."

Della Street said, "Look here, Chief, do you know just what you're getting into?"

"What?" Mason asked, raising his eyebrows.

"You're getting Sarah Breel out of a murder case by getting Virginia Trent in it right up to her eyebrows."

"Oh, sure," Mason said cheerfully. "After all, you know, *someone* had to kill him."

"But, Chief, Virginia Trent's also your client," Della Street objected.

"Sure," Mason laughed, "and they're not trying her yet."

"No, but they're going to be if you keep on."

"Well," Mason said, "I'll keep on. Let's go eat. I'm famished."

18

■

As court convened, there was not a vacant seat anywhere in the room. People were standing along the walls in back of the chairs. There was an atmosphere of tense, hushed expectancy. Only those jurors who had been too conscientious even to glance at the headlines or at photographs published in the newspapers were in any doubt as to what had occurred. Judge Barnes, taking his position on the bench and listening to the bailiff call court to order, glanced at Perry Mason with eyes which held a glint of puzzled admiration. Larry Sampson, his mouth a thin line of grim determination, sat doggedly at his desk. His case was crashing about his ears. But he still had a few cards with which he hoped to trump Mason's aces. "I'm going to ask Mr. Hogan to take the stand," Mason said.

Hogan took the witness stand and testified to what he had found. He produced the bullet that had been found embedded in the chair, as well as photographs. "And, in your opinion," Mason asked, "this bullet was fired from the weapon which the prosecution introduced

as an exhibit in this case and which has been referred
to as the Breel gun?"

"There's not the slightest doubt of it," Hogan said.

"Now then," Mason went on, "at the time this gun
was found in the bag of the defendant, only *one* shell
had been fired, is that right?"

"I can't answer that," Hogan said. "I know that when
the weapon was turned over to me for examination, only
one shell had been fired."

"Thank you," Mason said. "That's all."

"No cross-examination," Sampson announced.

"Call Paul Drake to the stand," Mason said. Paul
Drake came forward, was sworn, and took the witness
stand. He seemed somewhat ill at ease. "You're a private detective," Mason asked, "and, as such, have been
employed by me?"

"Yes."

"Did you have occasion to shadow a woman who
was known as Ione Bedford and who purported to be
the owner of certain jewelry which Austin Cullens had
left with George Trent?" Mason asked.

"Objected to as incompetent, irrelevant and immaterial," Sampson sputtered. "It doesn't connect up with
the present case in any way."

"I expect to connect it up," Mason said.

"I don't see just what you have in mind," Judge
Barnes remarked.

Mason said, "If the Court please, this is rather an unusual case. Ordinarily, it is incumbent upon the Prosecution to prove the defendant guilty beyond all reasonable
doubt. It is not incumbent upon the defendant to prove
himself or herself innocent. However, in this case, since
the Prosecution has really proved how the murder could
not have happened, the Defense is going to show how
the murder *could* have been perpetrated."

"And you expect to connect this evidence up?" Judge
Barnes asked dubiously.

Mason said, "I do, Your Honor."

"I'll permit it," Judge Barnes said, "at least for the
present. But it will be subject to a motion on the part

of the Prosecution to strike out in the event it isn't connected in a way which the Court deems pertinent and relevant."

"That is quite satisfactory," Mason said. "Answer the question, Mr. Drake."

Drake said, "Yes."

"You shadowed this woman?"

"Yes."

"From where?"

"From police headquarters."

"Where she had been taken and where she had failed to identify the stones in this bag as being her property?"

Sampson, on his feet, shouted, "Your Honor, I object. That question is leading and suggestive, it calls for hearsay testimony, it's incompetent, irrelevant, and immaterial, it doesn't make any difference what . . ."

"The objection is sustained as to what she had done or failed to do," Judge Barnes ruled. "The witness may state where and when he followed her."

Drake said, "We followed her from police headquarters. I don't know what she'd been doing there."

"And where did you follow her to?" Mason asked.

"To the Milpas Apartments on Canyon Drive, to apartment three-fourteen."

"And did you investigate to see how she was known in that place, or under what name she was going?"

"I did."

"And what name was it?"

"Objected to as incompetent, irrelevant, and immaterial," Sampson said. "Also, it's hearsay. It makes no difference what name she was going under."

"Sustained," Judge Barnes ruled.

Mason frowned, as though in annoyance. Mason said, "I'll try and get at it this way, Mr. Drake. Was there a person living in that apartment house known as Pete Chennery?"

"Yes, sir."

"In what apartment did he live?"

"In apartment three-fourteen," Drake said, before Sampson could object.

Sampson said, "Your Honor, I object to this. I move to strike out the answer until I have an opportunity to interpose an objection. I object on the ground that it is incompetent, irrelevant and immaterial, that it has nothing whatever to do with the present case."

"I think the objection is well taken," Judge Barnes said, "unless you can show some theory on which it would be admissible."

Mason said irritably, "If the district attorney's office will keep from throwing legal monkey wrenches into the machinery, I expect to show that Pete Chennery murdered Austin Cullens. I expect to show it by proof which . . ."

"That will do, Mr. Mason," Judge Barnes interrupted. "You have no call to refer to Counsel as throwing legal monkey wrenches into the machinery. Counsel has interposed objections which, so far, the Court has deemed to be well taken. The Court has asked you only to explain why you consider this evidence relevant."

"I will connect it up," Mason said. "I will connect it up by proving that this defendant couldn't have killed Austin Cullens because Pete Chennery did."

Judge Barnes said, "This is a very unusual procedure."

"It's a very unusual case," Mason said.

"For the moment, I will overrule the objection," Judge Barnes said, "but will strike out so much of the answer as relating to the apartment where Pete Chennery lived. There is no evidence connecting Pete Chennery with Ione Bedford."

"There is no evidence," Mason said, "because the Prosecution won't allow us to introduce that evidence."

"The Prosecution has nothing to do with it," Judge Barnes said. "It is the Court which is controlling the order of proof. You will proceed, Mr. Mason, and confine your remarks to the Court."

"Very well," Mason said. "I will ask you, Mr. Drake, whether or not you took, or caused to be taken under your supervision, photographs of latent finger-prints in the house in which Austin Cullens lived."

"I did."

"I will ask you whether you secured photographs of the finger-prints of Pete Chennery."

Drake said, "I entered the apartment where he had been living. I developed latent finger-prints. I found there the finger-prints of a man which I assume were those of Pete Chennery because they were the only finger-prints which I found in any number in the apartment occupied by Pete Chennery."

"Who was with you when you took these prints, Mr. Drake?"

"Sergeant Holcomb."

"From those finger-prints, did you ascertain whether Pete Chennery had a criminal record?" Mason asked.

"I object to that," Sampson said, "as incompetent, irrelevant, and immaterial on the further ground that no proper foundation has been laid, and as assuming a fact not in evidence. The witness himself has admitted that he doesn't *know* that the finger-prints were those of Pete Chennery."

Mason glanced up inquiringly at Judge Barnes.

Judge Barnes said, "The objection is sustained. After all, the question before the Court in this case is whether this defendant killed Austin Cullens. Within reasonable limitations, any evidence tending to prove that Cullens met his death at the hands of some other person is, of course, proper, but there must be limits to that, and the evidence must be adduced in proper form."

"Of course, Your Honor," Mason pointed out urbanely, "I am but a private practicing attorney. This man is a private detective. We, neither of us, have available the facilities which are at the command of the district attorney's office for making complete investigations."

"I fully understand that," Judge Barnes said, "but that is something which doesn't concern this Court. This Court is only concerned with having evidence pertinent, proper, and admissible. What this witness may have assumed to be the case isn't binding on the Prosecution."

Mason said, "Well, perhaps I can get at it in another way. I'll withdraw this witness temporarily and ask that Sergeant Holcomb be called as a witness for the Defense."

Sergeant Holcomb came belligerently forward, his manner all too plainly indicating that he certainly didn't intend to be of any assistance to the Defense.

"I will ask you," Mason said, "if you have located the owner of the jewelry which was found in the bag which it is claimed belonged to the defendant in this case."

"Objected to," Sampson said, "as incompetent, irrelevant and immaterial. It makes no difference who owned the jewelry."

"But," Mason said, "I thought it was the contention of the Prosecution that this jewelry had been taken from a chamois-skin belt found on the body of the decedent."

"There is no such contention," Sampson said. "The photograph of the body shows the position of the chamois-skin belt and its condition, but beyond a necessary inference, we have made no claim that . . ."

"I think the necessary inference is there," Judge Barnes ruled. "The witness sought to make that inference even more pointed. I'm going to permit this question to be answered. Have you ascertained the owner of that jewelry, Sergeant Holcomb?"

"We have," Sergeant Holcomb said sullenly.

"That jewelry had been stolen?" Mason asked.

"Yes."

"From someone in New Orleans?"

"That's right."

"And an insurance company had offered a reward for the recovery of it?"

"Yes," Sergeant Holcomb said shortly.

"And you, as one of the discoverers, have claimed a part of that reward?"

"Yes."

"How much of the reward?"

"Objected to as incompetent, irrelevant and immaterial," Sampson said. "It doesn't go to show the interest or bias of the witness—in this case in the least."

"Sustained," Judge Barnes ruled.

Once more, Mason appeared nettled. "When you ex-amined the premises, Sergeant," he said, "immediately following the discovery of Mr. Cullens' body, you found that a fuse had been blown out."

"That's right."

"And did you ascertain what had caused the blowing out of that fuse?"

"Yes. An electric light globe had been unscrewed from one of the sockets. A copper penny had been inserted in the socket, and then the globe had been screwed back in. As soon as the electric switch was turned on, the fuse blew out."

"Now then," Mason asked, "did you test that copper penny for latent finger-prints?"

"Objected to as incompetent, irrelevant and imma-terial," Sampson said.

Judge Barnes frowned, then looked down at Sampson. "Is it," he asked, "the position of the Prosecutor's office that the defendant is not to have the advantage of any evidence uncovered by the police which may have in-dicated the crime was committed by some other person?"

Sampson said, "If the Court please, it's the position of the Prosecutor's office that we don't want the issues clouded. There is absolutely no evidence in the case as it now stands tending to show that any person other than the defendant entered that house."

"But, as I understand it," Judge Barnes said, "it was your position at the time of your opening statement that robbery had been a motive and . . ."

"Sometimes," Sampson said, "if the Court will par-don the interruption, a prosecutor deems it necessary to change his trial tactics in order to meet varying condi-tions which develop during the trial."

"I understand that," Judge Barnes said, "but this evi-dence is clearly proper. It would have even been proper on cross-examination. This witness is now called by the Defense. The objection will be overruled. Did you de-velop latent finger-prints on that coin, Sergeant Hol-comb?"

Sergeant Holcomb said, "Yes."

"Did you," Mason asked, "take finger-prints of the defendant in this case?"

"Yes."

"Did you compare the finger-prints of the defendant with the finger-prints on that copper coin?"

Sergeant Holcomb said, "She was wearing gloves. She wouldn't have left any finger-prints."

"I'm not asking that," Mason said. "I'm asking if you compared the two finger-prints."

"Yes."

"Were they the same?"

"No."

"Now then, if the Court please," Mason said, "I would like to have Sergeant Holcomb produce photographs of the finger-prints which were developed on that penny, and give the witness, Drake, an opportunity to demonstrate that these were the finger-prints of Pete Chennery, a man with a known criminal record."

"I object to that. I object to the statement. I object to the procedure, and I object to the manner in which this offer is made before the jury," Sampson said. "It is an attempt to cloud the issues. The Court has already ruled that the witness, Drake, has no means of knowing whether the finger-prints which he took are those of Pete Chennery."

"Do I understand that the Prosecution wishes to keep the Defense from showing the identity of the person who placed that copper coin in the light socket?" Judge Barnes asked.

"I fail to see where it has anything to do with the present case," Sampson said. "It's simply going to cloud the issues. Let us suppose that some person *did* enter the dwelling for the purpose of robbery at some time prior to the murder. That has nothing to do with this case."

"No," Judge Barnes said ominously, "but suppose that person entered the dwelling *at the time of the murder?*"

"In that event," Sampson said, "it makes no difference who that person was. There is already evidence before this Court showing that the finger-prints on the copper coin were not the finger-prints of the defendant. That's all that the defendant is entitled to show. . . . That is, Your Honor, I don't want to appear in a position of blocking any legitimate proof, but from a technical standpoint, the defendant is only entitled to prove that she did not participate in the commission of a robbery or in short-circuiting those lights. Having once established that fact, the identity of the person who did tamper with the lights becomes absolutely incompetent, irrelevant and immaterial, unless it is shown that such person was acting in a conspiracy with the defendant. And the Prosecution makes no claim that such is the case."

Mason threw up his hands. "All right. If the Prosecution doesn't want the jury to know who killed Austin Cullens, *I'm* not going to waste my time trying to do *their* work. The question is withdrawn. The witness is excused."

Sampson said, "That's unfair. You're just trying to razzle-dazzle the jury."

Mason shouted, "You're the one who's . . ."

Judge Barnes banged with his gavel. "Gentlemen," he said, "we will have order in the court. There will be no more such remarks. Mr. Mason, your remark was improper and uncalled for. Mr. Sampson, your accusation as to Mr. Mason's purpose in asking questions was entirely out of order. The Court would administer a more stern admonition to you, Mr. Sampson, were it not for the fact that Mr. Mason's remark which called forth your statement, was so obviously improper. The fact remains, gentlemen, that we are going to have no more personalities injected in the case. This is the Court's last warning."

Mason sat back and said resignedly, "All right. That's the defendant's case."

"You mean you quit?" Sampson asked.

Mason glanced up at the Court and said, "Since I must address my remarks to Your Honor, may I suggest to the Court that the Court advise Counsel for the Prosecution that when the defendant announces, 'That's the defendant's case,' it is improprer for the Prosecution to seek to capitalize on that by addressing remarks to Counsel. As a matter of fact, I believe the jurors will understand that the Defense has made every effort to solve this case, and that the only reason the Defense has not solved it is . . ."

"Careful, Mr. Mason," Judge Barnes frowned.

Mason finished with a smile. " '*Only too obvious,*' were the words I was going to use, Your Honor."

Judge Barnes said, "Do you wish to argue the case, gentlemen?"

Sampson did, and his argument sought to go just as far as a district attorney dared to go in commenting on the failure of a defendant to deny the charges which had been made against her. He brought forward the defendant's shoe, which had been introduced in evidence, pointed to the tell-tale stain on the sole, and challenged counsel to explain how that stain got on the shoe if it did not indicate the guilt of the defendant. "Standing, as it does," Sampson thundered, "unchallenged, undenied and uncontradicted."

He cited the attempt of the defendant to bring in some mythical criminal, who must have entered the house and, by implication, killed Austin Cullens, and, above all, excoriated Mason for his attempt to becloud the issues by confusing Sergeant Holcomb and mixing up the bullets.

When he had finished, Mason approached the rail, to stand in front of the jurors with a smile. "Ladies and gentlemen," he said, "the Court will instruct you that in order to warrant a conviction on circumstantial evidence, the circumstances must not only be consistent with the guilt of the defendant, but inconsistent with every other reasonable hypothesis. In the event there is any reasonable hypothesis, other than that of guilt, on which the circumstantial evidence can be explained, then it becomes your duty to acquit the defendant.

"This is a case in which the Prosecution relies on circumstantial evidence. As far as the gun is concerned, that evidence has proven a boomerang. The evidence proves conclusively that the gun found in the defendant's handbag—and I will admit to you, ladies and gentlemen, that it *is* the defendant's handbag, not that she has told me so, because her mind is a blank as to what transpired, but because I think it's a fair inference from the evidence that it *was* her handbag—that gun did *not* kill Austin Cullens. But that gun *did* kill George Trent. There are only two bullets in the case. If the bullet from the Breel gun didn't kill Cullens, then it must have killed George Trent. Now then, on the evening Cullens was killed, there was only one shot fired from this gun. That one shot was fired by Austin Cullens at someone who was in the room with him. That shot lodged in the back of a chair. Cullens carried that revolver in his right hip pocket—which was the reason the coroner's examination disclosed nothing in that pocket.

"Now then, gentlemen, what more reasonable than to suppose that Mrs. Breel guessed that her brother was dead, and strongly suspected that Austin Cullens had killed him. Austin Cullens had every reason to want George Trent out of the way. There is every reasonable inference to indicate that George Trent had uncovered evidence which, when communicated to the police, would convict Cullens of a series of gem robberies. Therefore, Cullens killed Trent. In order to cover up that killing, he did various and sundry things, such as pretending that Trent had pawned gems with a gambling house. And to bolster up that claim, Cullens even went to the gambling house and put on an act, trying to establish a false motive for Trent's death.

"It is very evident, gentlemen, that, as in the case of Cullens, Trent couldn't have been killed with the gun that the Prosecution claims was used in that murder. Therefore, it becomes equally evident that he *must have been killed with the other gun,* since there are only two guns and only two fatal bullets, one fatal bullet fired from each gun. It's very evident that Sergeant Holcomb naturally assumed that the gun in Mrs. Breel's handbag had killed Austin Cullens, and that the gun in Trent's office had killed Trent. He took from his right-hand vest pocket the bullet which the autopsy surgeon had handed him as having killed Cullens, and handed it to the witness, Hogan. Hogan checked it with the guns and advised Sergeant Holcomb that that bullet had been fired by the gun found in Trent's office.

"What happened?" There was a moment of tense silence, while Mason waited for the point he had made to soak in. "You have seen the character of Sergeant Holcomb," he said. "He exhibited that character very plainly on the witness stand. He *thought* that he had confused the bullets; that he had inadvertently transposed the bullets in his pockets, when he had in reality done nothing of the sort. In order to cover up what he fancied was his mistake, he immediately handed the other bullet to Hogan with the statement that that bullet had been the one which killed Cullens.

"It is a little thing, ladies and gentlemen, but it is one of the important little things which become increasingly vital in a case. It is an index to the character of Sergeant Holcomb. Doubtless, he would never have sought to frame this defendant had he thought that she was innocent. But, having thought he'd make a mistake, he tried to cover that mistake, and carried his subterfuge so far as to go on the witness stand and testify to what is a manifest impossibility. Regardless of what the deputy district attorney may tell you, and in spite of Sergeant Holcomb's testimony, it's a physical impossibility for the bullet which killed Austin Cullens to have been fired from the Breel gun. On the other hand, it's a physical impossibility for George Trent to have been killed by the Trent gun.

"Now then, ladies and gentlemen, *if* I had been permitted to pursue my proof, I believe I could have demonstrated to you who did murder Austin Cullens. However, since I wasn't permitted to follow that proof to its logical conclusion, I will take the facts *as they now stand,* and give you a reasonable hypothesis which will explain away every fact in this case. And not only is that hypothesis consistent with the innocence of the defendant, but the innocence of this defendant is the only hypothesis under which the facts can now be explained.

"Something happened on the afternoon of Cullens' death which convinced Sarah Breel that Cullens was responsible for her brother's disappearance, possibly his death. She went to his house to get evidence. Someone had been there before her. Who was that someone? That was someone who was a dead shot with a revolver, someone who went there for some undisclosed purpose, someone who had access to the revolver with which it now appears the murder *must* have been committed.

"Austin Cullens saw that person. He knew what that person wanted. He was overcome by the consciousness of his own guilt. He suddenly whipped his revolver from his right hip pocket and fired. The shot missed. But that person had also prepared against just such a contingency. That person was armed. That person fired, and that person did not miss.

"Some time later, Mrs. Breel went to the house. She found the door open. She found the lights out. Remember, ladies and gentlemen, no flashlight was found in her bag. She had to grope her way through the darkness. She did not know that the body of Austin Cullens was lying on the floor. Stumbling her way along the dark room, she suddenly touched something with her left foot.

"There was only one way in which she could investigate, and that was by a sense of touch. The room was dark. She had no flashlight in her bag. She had no matches in her bag. She bent down, exploring with the tips of her gloved fingers. She touched something hard. She picked it up. It was a revolver. And then she touched a body. Panic-stricken, she wished to call the police. She mechanically, automatically and unconsciously shoved the revolver into her bag and fled from the house, screaming for police. There was no one to hear her screams. She dashed out into the boulevard, and found herself suddenly confronted by a pair of headlights. In her terror, she had forgotten to look before she jumped out into the street.

"That, ladies and gentlemen, since I have been precluded from making any other explanation, is the explanation which I think you will be forced to adopt from a consideration of the circumstantial evidence in this case.

"You have sworn to act fairly and impartially. I made no effort to pack this jury with persons who would be favorable to the defendant's side of the case, because I knew I didn't have to. All I wanted was people who would be fair. Why, one of your number even mentioned that he had formed an opinion as to the guilt of the defendant, but said he could set aside such an opinion when he entered upon the trial of the case. I had the right to challenge him with a peremptory charge and remove him from the jury. I did not do it. Why? Because I felt that he would be fair, because I knew that he was intelligent. And because all on earth that the defendant in this case wanted was fairness and intelligence. Is that the attitude of a lawyer defending a guilty client? Is that the attitude of one who seeks to 'razzle-dazzle' a jury?

"Ladies and gentlemen, you have sworn to follow the law in this case. When you hear the instructions of the judge, you will realize that this means that you have taken a solemn oath that if the facts of this case can be explained on any reasonable hypothesis other than that of guilt, you will acquit the defendant. Ladies and gentlemen, I leave you to your solemn duty."

Mason turned and walked back to his seat. Sampson, his face livid, struggling hard to control his voice, leaped up. "Just one word in rebuttal, ladies and gentlemen. Let me challenge Counsel to carry his own argument to its logical conclusion. . . . Who was that person who was such an expert revolver shot? Who was that person, who, by his own evidence had access to the revolver with which he now claims Austin Cullens was murdered—could it have been Virginia Trent, the niece of the woman who is on trial! It must have been! I challenge him to deny it!"

Mason, on his feet, drawled, "Your Honor, I dislike to interrupt the deputy district attorney, but do I now

understand the deputy district attorney is contending that
Virginia Trent murdered Austin Cullens?"

"According to your own reasoning, it's as plain as the
nose on your face," Sampson roared.

"Well," Mason asked, "can you find any flaw in that
reasoning? If so, please point it out to the jury." The
color drained out of Sampson's face. His jaw sagged open
in surprise. Mason turned to Judge Barnes. "I was going
to suggest, Your Honor, that if it is the contention of
the Prosecution that the evidence now shows Virginia
Trent murdered Austin Cullens, that this jury must be
advised to acquit the defendant in this case. But if the
deputy district attorney really wants to know who killed
Austin Cullens, I suggest he talk with Paul Drake . . ."

"That will do, Mr. Mason," Judge Barnes said. "That
statement is improper. You will be seated. The Court
will not entertain any motion for a directed verdict, but
will let the jury speak for itself—that is, unless it is now
the contention of the Prosecution that Virginia Trent committed the crime."

Sampson hesitated, gulped, then said abruptly, "No,
I was only showing how absurd Mason's argument was."

One of the jurors fixed Sampson with a suspicious eye.
"What's absurd about it?" he asked.

"It's just a smoke-screen," Sampson asserted, "behind which he's trying to hide his client."

"But what's wrong with that theory?" the juror insisted.

Sampson said, "Everything. However, I—I have com-
pleted my argument. You have evidence that—that Cullens was killed with the gun found in Mrs. Breel's
handbag. Other evidence introduced merely confuses the
issues. I trust you ladies and gentlemen won't be misled. I thank you." He walked back to his seat at the
counsel table.

Mrs. Breel tried anxiously to catch Mason's eyes, but
the lawyer kept his own gaze averted. Judge Barnes
instructed the jurors as to the law, swore the bailiff to
conduct them to a safe place for their deliberations. And

then, as the jurors left the Court, announced that Court would take a recess pending a receipt of the verdict.

Sarah Breel beckoned Perry Mason over to her. "You should never have done that," she said.

"What?" Mason asked.

"Dragged Virginia into it."

Mason grinned and said, "On the contrary, I dragged her out of it. You heard Sampson say it was absurd to think she could have murdered Cullens."

"Where is she? I want to see her."

Mason said, "My secretary took her for a ride in the country. I thought some fresh air would do her some good. I persuaded her that it would be to her advantage not to be present at the conclusion of the case."

Sarah Breel sighed. "Well, while we're waiting for the jury to bring in its verdict, since you've admitted that was my bag, suppose you see if I can have the knitting out of it. I might just as well keep working on that sweater for Ginny while I'm waiting to see what the jury does."

Mason patted her hand. "I think you'd better try crossword puzzles. It might be safer."

"Will we have long to wait?" she asked.

"My guess," Mason said, "is ten minutes."

Events proved that Mason missed his guess by exactly twenty minutes. It took the jury half an hour to come filing into court with its verdict. Judge Barnes said, "Have you agreed upon a verdict, ladies and gentlemen?"

"We have," one of the men answered.

The clerk took the folded document and handed it to Judge Barnes, who scrutinized it for a moment, then passed it back. "Read your verdict," he said.

The foreman read the verdict. "We, the jury, impaneled to try the above entitled case, find Sarah Breel not guilty of the crime charged in the indictment. The jury suggests to the district attorney's office that it forthwith arrest Virginia Trent and try to prosecute her more intelligently than it has the defendant in this case."

The corners of Mason's mouth were twitching. "I take it it may be stipulated that in entering the verdict, only the portion which finds the defendant not guilty is to be entered in the records."

"So stipulated," Sampson said sullenly.

Judge Barnes waited until the verdict had been entered, and then regarded the jury thoughtfully. "Ladies and gentlemen," he said, "in discharging you, the Court wishes to compliment you upon the manner in which you have performed your duty. This has been one of the most astounding cases this Court has ever witnessed. Right at present, the Court is frank to state that it doesn't know whether the evidence points, as the jury apparently believes, to the fact that Virginia Trent fired the shot which killed Austin Cullens, or whether this Court has witnessed one of the most astounding pieces of legal legerdemain which has ever been perpetrated in a courtroom. Subsequent events will doubtless prove which is correct. The defendant is discharged from custody and court is adjourned."

19

Mason drove his car through the arched gateway which bore the sign THE GABLES HOTEL. the rural hotel loomed as a huge dark pile against the sky, with, here and there, the lighted oblong of a window marking human tenancy. Mason parked his car, gave his bag and suitcase to a sleepy-eyed bellboy who emerged from the lighted interior of the lobby, crossed to the desk and said to the clerk, "My name's Mason. I believe you have a room reserved for me, Mr. P. Mason?"

"Oh, yes, Mr. Mason. Your room's all ready. Do you wish to go up now?"

"Yes."

Mason followed the bellboy up a wide flight of stairs, down a long corridor, and into a typical country hotel

bedroom. He tipped the bellboy, removed his coat and
vest, washed his hands and face, locked the corridor door,
put on his coat and vest again, and, entering the bath-
room, stood with his ear against the door which led to
the connecting room. He could hear the sound of low,
steady sobbing. Mason tapped on the door. After a moment, Della Street's voice said, "Who is it?"

"Mason," he told her. She opened the door.

Virginia Trent, her eyes red and swollen from crying,
her hair looking like unbraided rope, looked up at him
from the bed; then grabbed at a kimona, which partially
covered her. "Where did *you* come from?" she asked.

Mason crossed the room to sit down on the edge of
the bed. "I came from court," he said, "just as soon as
I could get away."

Virginia Trent pushed the damp, stringy hair back
from her forehead, sat up on the bed, wadded a tear-
soaked pillow into a ball and pushed it behind her. "I'm
going back," she said. Mason shook his head. "Yes, I
am. I'm going back and face it. I tried to all day, and
Della Street wouldn't let me. Is that why you had her
take me out here?" Mason nodded. "Well, I'm going
back. I'm going to tell them . . ."

"Tell them what?" Mason asked.

"Tell them everything."

Mason said, "Tell me first, Virgie."

She said, "Aunt Sarah is covering up for me. She hasn't
lost her memory any more than I have. I don't care
what you say, Mr. Mason. I don't care what she says.
I know that Aunt Sarah is in danger. There's a good
chance the jury will convict her. The newspapers seem
to think the case against her is dead open and shut,
and . . ."

Mason said, gently, "The jury has just acquitted your
aunt of murder, Virginia. They found her not guilty."

"*Not* guilty?"

"Yes."

"How . . . how did that happen?"

Mason said, "I think the jury got a pretty good idea
of what actually happened."

"What do you mean by that?"

"Suppose," Mason said, gently, "you tell me exactly what *did* happen, Virgie."

In a voice which broke occasionally, under the hysterical reflex of sobs, she said, "I'm going to tell you the whole truth, Mr. Mason. Austin Cullens telephoned and asked me to get Aunt Sarah and be at a certain street corner at a designated time. He said he'd drive by and pick us up. He did. He said he thought we should make a determined effort to find Uncle George. He said the three of us could split up, and each of us could take a certain district and cover the gambling clubs in that district. He said he'd give us a list of the places where Uncle George went. He picked us up in his car, all right, and drove us out to his house, in order to get the list of the places we were to go to."

"You had a gun with you?" Mason asked.

"Yes. I knew I was going to be in some questionable places, unescorted. I had a gun and a flashlight in my handbag."

"Go ahead, what happened?"

"Mr. Cullens drove us out to his house. He put the car in the garage and started for the house. I saw a light flash in one of the windows, and he yelled out that someone was in the house. He had a gun in his hip pocket. He drew it and made a run for the door. I didn't want to follow him in, but Aunt Sarah said, 'Come along, Virgie,' and started to follow. Naturally, I took the gun out of my purse. You know how it is when you're good at something, you get to rely on it. I'd become a pretty good shot, and . . ."

"Yes, I know," Mason interrupted. "Go ahead and tell me what happened."

"There was some man in the front room of the house. I had just a confused glimpse of him. Mr. Cullens started to turn on the lights, and the fuse blew out and everything went dark. The man ran right past me and out of the back door."

"Then what happened?" Mason asked.

"I took the flashlight out of my bag, and gave it to Mr. Cullens."

"And you were still holding the gun in your hand?"

"Yes."

"And then what happened?"

"Mr. Cullens said that he'd been robbed of a lot of jewels, and my aunt asked him why he kept jewels in the house that way, and all of a sudden he said to her, 'By God, I believe that wasn't a thief at all, but a detective you've had on my trail,' and she said, 'Why Aussie? Is it because you know those gems of yours had been stolen?' and he said, 'So that's it, is it?' and she said, 'Aussie, I'll promise you that if you'll tell me where George is, and he's safe, we won't do anything at all; but if you don't I'll tell the police that . . .' That was as far as she got. Aussie screamed out something about not being taken alive and flung up his gun and shot right square at Aunty."

"And what did you do?" Mason asked.

"Whatever I did," she said, "was just an unconscious reflex. Honestly, I have no recollection of pulling the trigger. The first thing I knew, Mr. Cullens was lying on the floor, and my aunt was just as cool as a cucumber. She said, 'Virgie, we have to keep our heads on this. I'm afraid something awful has happened to George, and we're going to have to make Aussie talk.' She said, 'We'll have to telephone for an ambulance and get him to the hospital, but before we do that I think he has some evidence on him we're going to have to get,' and she bent over him and opened his vest and shirt and found a chamois-skin belt with some gems in it. She took the gems out and picked up the gun which he'd dropped and put it in her bag, and said to me, 'Find a telephone, Virgie, and telephone for the police,' and then while I was still groping around trying to find a telephone, she called to me and said, 'Wait a minute, Virgie, he's dead.'"

"Then what happened?" Mason asked. Virginia Trent shook her head as though trying to dislodge a memory, and dove into the protection of the pillow. Mason put his hand on her shaking shoulders. "Now, wait a minute, Virgie, you're all upset. Snap out of it. Tell me what happened."

After a few moments, she turned her head so that her mouth was clear of the pillow, and said sobbingly, "Aunt Sarah said she thought the stones that he had on him were stolen. That if they were, we'd be all right. That if they weren't, we were going to be in an awful jam; that no one knew anything about our having been there, and that evidently a burglar had been in the house, and the best thing for us to do was to clear out and say nothing to anyone. She told me to take the back door, and she'd take the front. . . . And then . . . well, you know the rest."

"And you'd gone up to your uncle's office and put the gun back in the drawer just before I came in, Virgie?"

"Yes."

"And you had no idea your uncle's body was up there?"

"Good Lord, no. Coming on top of everything else, it almost floored me. I thought I'd go crazy that night."

"So then what?"

"Then," she said, "you know just as much as I do. Aunt Sarah never would admit to me that she remembered anything that happened. She kept saying that her mind was a blank, and seemed perfectly cheerful about it, and said I wasn't to worry, but was to leave everything to you. She wouldn't even let me talk to her about anything that happened. She said her mind was a blank and she wanted it that way."

"Perhaps her mind *is* a blank," Mason said.

"I don't think so. I think she's just trying to protect me."

"But you don't *know?*"

"No."

Mason glanced at Della Street. "Virgie," he said, "I'm going to tell you something. I want you to remember it. If your Aunt Sarah's mind is a blank, that's one thing. If it isn't a blank, and she's trying to cover up for you, that's something else. As far as you're concerned, it doesn't make a particle of difference. You shot in self-defense. There's no question but Austin Cullens intended to kill both you and your aunt. He'd killed your Uncle George, when your uncle had found out that the Bedford diamonds were stolen gems. Probably your uncle sent for Cullens. Cullens came up to the office; they had a showdown. When he saw he was trapped, and your uncle started to call the police, Cullens jerked the gun out of his hip pocket and killed your uncle. He concealed the body in a packing case, removed all evidences of the crime, went home, reloaded his gun, and, because he knew of your uncle's habits, mailed in the keys to the car.

"Now then, I didn't know what had happened, but I had my suspicions. I felt certain that Pete Chennery's wife had confessed to her husband everything which had taken place with Austin Cullens, and her husband, Pete Chennery, a gem thief, saw an opportunity to make a good haul; so he had his wife continue to string Cullens along. He was engaged in going through the house when Cullens drove up.

"Now, I felt certain that Cullens had killed your Uncle George. At first, I didn't know how I could definitely prove it. I couldn't tell whether your aunt really had lost her memory, or whether she was trying to protect someone. I felt that if she was trying to protect someone, that you would be that someone. I realized that circumstantial evidence pointed at Pete Chennery as the burglar who had entered Austin Cullens' house. I thought perhaps I could use him as a red herring to drag across the trail, so that I could get your aunt acquitted, because I felt certain the evidence would show the bullets had been mixed up. Then when Sergeant Holcomb got on the witness stand and tried to cover up his mistake by testifying so positively in regard to the bullets, I realized that I had a perfect opportunity to let him unwittingly serve the real ends of justice.

"Frankly, Virgie, I don't know just what would have happened if the Prosecution had sensed the truth and made a fair investigation. They'd have arrested you charged you with murder, and you'd have had to plead self-defense. Under the circumstances, it wouldn't have sounded so good. When a man is killed in his own house, it's rather difficult to establish self-defense."

She sobbed and said, "I know it."

"But," Mason went on, "Sergeant Holcomb thought he must have made a mistake and handed the ballistics expert the wrong bullet. In many ways, you can't blame him. It was a perfectly natural conclusion for him to reach, and a police officer could hardly be expected to be so conscientious that he'd allow a murderer to escape, simply because he'd inadvertently confused bullets which had been handed him by an autopsy surgeon.

"But Sergeant Holcomb's testimony on the witness stand was so belligerent, and so positive, that I saw my big opportunity to fix it so you could never be prosecuted."

"Why can't I be prosecuted?" she asked.

"Because," he said, "the State can never prosecute you for the murder of Austin Cullens, unless they show that Cullens was killed with the gun which you must have placed in the desk drawer in your uncle's office. The only way they can do that is to trace the bullets from the body of Cullens. And the only way they can do that is to put Sergeant Holcomb on the stand, and Sergeant Holcomb has testified so positively and so belligerently, that he can never back up on that testimony now—not without submitting himself to a prosecution for perjury, as well as a storm of public ridicule. They'll never do that."

"Then they won't do anything with me?" she asked.

"Not if you keep your mouth shut," he told her. "I don't want you to ever tell anyone anything about what happened."

"I didn't want Aunty to stand up there and take it," she said. "I wanted to come in and confess. I . . ."

"I knew you would," Mason said, patting her shoulder, "but I thought your aunt was quite capable of carrying on. Now, buck up, Virgie, I want you to be as good a campaigner as she was. I've had you held virtually a prisoner out here. That's all over with. You can go back now, telephone or . . ."

"How . . . how did she take it?" Virginia Trent asked.

Mason grinned. "Right in her stride. She shot her wheel chair out in front of the jury right after the verdict, thanked them, and then, as cool as a cucumber, reached up on the clerk's desk, took the knitting out of her bag, and started right on knitting your sweater."

Virginia Trent grinned wistfully. "She would," she said. "And, if the verdict had been the other way, she'd have done the same thing."

"Yes," Mason observed, thoughtfully, "I believe she would."

"Now then," Mason announced, turning to Della Street, "I'm starved. I dashed out here just as soon as I could get away from the courtroom and ditch the people who were hanging around trying to interview me, shake my hand, and take photographs for the newspapers. The question is, *when* do we eat, *where* do we eat, and *what* do we eat?"

Della Street said, "We eat in the little restaurant across the street, because the hotel dining room is closed. The probabilities are we'll eat hamburger sandwiches, and we're going to have them just as soon as Virginia Trent can take a shower, splash some cold water on her eyes, and realize that there's nothing to cry about any longer."

Virginia Trent said, "That would take me too long, I'm afraid. . . . Anyway, I'm not hungry. . . . You folks go ahead and eat. . . . I—I want to telephone someone'"

Della Street said, "I've been wrestling with this disciple of black despair all afternoon, Chief. Give me fifteen minutes to freshen up. Can you do that?"

"Fine," he told her, "I'll meet you in the lobby."

20

■

Mason slipped his arm around Della Street's waist as they walked down the driveway toward the main highway, where the headlights of automobiles streamed past. Just beyond the highway a bright red electric sign bore the legend, "Hot Dogs."

"Have a hard day?" Mason asked.

"Pretty much. She went all to pieces when she broke."

"I was afraid she was going to."

"Did you know you were going to get Sarah Breel acquitted?"

"I felt pretty certain of it. I knew it was a cinch unless Sergeant Holcomb broke down and told the truth on cross-examination."

"And you didn't think he'd do that?"

"No. When you come right down to it, you can't blame him. Almost anyone would have done the same thing under similar circumstances. Particularly, anyone who regarded attorneys for the defense as natural enemies."

"Will they try to arrest Virginia Trent now, Chief?"

"I don't think so," he said. "I injected Pete Chennery into the case so that the police will grab him as an alibi. They'll claim Chennery was the one who did the shooting; that he must have deliberately entered George Trent's office, secured possession of the gun, killed Cullens, stolen a bunch of gems, returned the gun, and skipped out."

"Then what'll happen when they catch Chennery?" she asked.

"They won't catch him," Mason said, with a grin. "Chennery reads the newspapers, and he knows the ropes. You see, Della, it's one of those cases where a lawyer has to remember that the ultimate goal of every good attorney is to see that justice is done. There are times when methods must be subordinated to results."

"You mean when you have to fight the devil with fire?"

"Not exactly. Of course Sergeant Holcomb *was* distorting the facts—not to deliberately distort them, but under the mistaken impression that he was keeping them straight. I had to take that into consideration."

They walked in silence for a bit, then Mason asked, "How about Virgie? Is she going to snap out of it?"

"I think so; she put in a long distance call for her boyfriend."

"One of those disinterested, academic conversations," he asked, "about the ballistics of pistol bullets, and . . ."

She interrupted him with a laugh, and said, "You'd be surprised about Virginia."

"You mean she was mushy over the telephone?" Mason asked incredulously.

"Well, she was pretty sugar-coated, and just before she hung up, she . . ."

"She what?" Mason asked.

Della Street laughed. "I couldn't *tell* you," she said, "it would be betraying a sacred confidence."

"Could you," Mason inquired, "*show* me?"

She paused long enough to make certain there was no one else on the driveway. "Well," she conceded, with a throaty laugh, "I might. Bend over so I can reach. . . ."